RANSOM

In his third Scobie Malone novel Jon Cleary has written an even more gripping and convincing book than *The High Commissioner* and *Helga's Web*. The newly married Malones are on a delayed honeymoon trip that culminates in a visit to New York. Lisa Malone gets toothache, makes an appointment with a dentist – and vanishes.

It was her misfortune to share a lift with the wife of the Mayor of New York, for whom a political kidnapping had been arranged. Within minutes the Mayor hears the price of the two women's lives. Five anarchists awaiting trial on an assassination charge in The Tombs prison are to be put on a plane to Cuba by noon next day – or else.

For Malone, the professional detective, it is a new experience to be the victim of a crime. Even more unfamiliar and alarming is the sense of helplessness instead of being in charge. Yet a sympathetic Negro police officer stretches the rules, and allows him to follow up the few threads that perhaps lead out of the labyrinth. Not only the urban guerillas are involved. The Mafia too, it seems, knows something. Or may do. The baffling, tantalizing nature of the crime is conveyed with all the imaginative power that makes Cleary such a superb storyteller.

The New York underworld, the grim squalor of The Tombs at night, the smart, rich, supercharged life of a Mayor who is widely tipped for the White House, the Silent Majority who want a quiet life but know that they are trapped between old prejudices and new hatreds, all the explosive features of present-day America make a background worthy of the excitement and tension that builds up to a brilliant climax.

Books by Jon Cleary

RANSOM

Jon Cleary

COLLINS
8 Grafton Street, London W1

William Collins Sons and Co Ltd
London · Glasgow · Sydney · Auckland
Toronto · Johannesburg

01694347

ISBN 0 00 221694 9

First published 1973
This reprint 1986

Made and Printed in Great Britain by
William Collins Sons and Co Ltd, Glasgow

to Nick Scoppetta
for his considerable help

Chapter One

"Law and order," said Scobie Malone. "There's something wrong with the system when that becomes an election issue."

The newscaster on the television screen paused and looked straight at Malone as if he had heard him. He seemed to sigh, then he said, "More election news right after this message." He disappeared from the screen and a girl in a four hundred-dollar peignoir floated on to take his place. She stood in the middle of a bathroom that could have been a set left over from a Busby Berkeley film, just an ordinary American working girl, looked straight at Malone and asked him if, as a woman, he would like to smell like roses where it counted. Malone, untroubled by vaginal odours, a short back-and-sides holdout against long-haired unisex, stood up and switched off the television set.

"I'm here in America and I just don't believe a word of what I see or hear. I think I'll ask for our money back on this part of the trip – "

"East 69th Street," said Lisa. "Would that be far up-town?"

We've arrived at it, thought Malone with amused resignation. We have reached the stage of being an old married couple. Eight weeks, and already we're not listening to each other, just like my mum and dad after thirty-eight years.

"Why don't you go down to the desk and ask them to recommend a dentist? They'd know one around here."

"I make it a point never to ask hotel desks to recommend anything. Everyone who works in the front of a hotel has a vested interest – himself. If he recommends anything, it's because he's getting a kickback."

"I don't know that I'll ever learn to live with your mean Dutch suspicion."

7

"That's good, coming from a mug copper."

"You're starting to sound like a real Aussie," he said with approval. "I wondered how long it would take. Now if I can just get you off wine and French cooking on to beer and sausage rolls – "

He kissed the back of her neck as she leaned over the yellow pages of the Manhattan telephone directory. Lisa had lost a filling last night and this morning at breakfast she had discovered that a nerve in the tooth had been exposed; she was now trying to find a dentist who could give her a temporary filling without delay. So far she had tried four dentists, all of whom had told her they could fit her in for an appointment next Monday week. New York was either short of dentists or there was an epidemic of tooth decay in the city.

"East 69th Street would be a long way uptown from here."

"I'll go to Boston or Philadelphia if a dentist there says he can see me this morning. Anyhow, I have to go to the Holland Society and that's on 58th Street, so it won't be much farther. Dr Willey. I'll try him."

She picked up the phone and Malone walked to the window and looked out. He and Lisa had been travelling for eight weeks and each time he looked out of a hotel window he was still surprised not to be looking out on the familiar. None of the world's cities was really unfamiliar any more: the television screen was everyone's window. But pictures, whether from television or films or magazines, never gave you the *feel* of a city; and he was a man very conscious of the feel of his environment, a policeman who felt the grit in the air, the tension in a crowd, the sad or sometimes menacing loneliness in a deserted street. The world rubbed against him like a constant nagging wind, and sometimes he marvelled that he had not succumbed to the erosion of it, that he could occasionally smile at what he saw and felt. His humour had become dry but he was not drought-stricken.

He had not yet got the feel of New York, but it was working on him. The sky had a peculiarly grey colour to it, the blue-grey of bruising; that, he guessed, might be the fore-runner of the hurricane that was coming up the East Coast; the weather forecast was that the storm would swing east and miss the city. From the window he looked over towards the East River, saw the tall red, white and blue smokestacks of Con Edison, like patriotic phallic symbols: the Americans dressed up everything. Leaning forward and craning his neck, he saw a gull planing down past the windowed cliffs of the New York University Medical Center; on the ground white-coated interns moved from building to building, their coats flapping open like the clipped wings of larger birds. An ambulance, its siren the magnified cry of pain of the patient inside it, came up First Avenue and swung into the Center. Even the wail of the siren sounded unfamiliar to him, a cry in another language; yet he understood pain well enough, knew he would recognize it anywhere in the whole suffering world. But Christ, he thought, as he had thought each time he had looked out of every window that had presented itself since they had left Sydney, what a tight blind little world I lived in. It had been just that realization that had prompted him to blow five thousand dollars on this honeymoon trip round the world, and every step of the way had proved to himself that he had been right.

"You've gone mental," Lisa had said when he had suggested it. "I've heard of this happening when people un-expectedly come into money – "

"Look, that twelve thousand dollars was a windfall. I've been buying lottery tickets for twenty years and I've never even won a fiver before. It was just a weekly habit – like washing my car or having a beer with the boys. I never even thought about what I'd do if I won a major prize – "

"I'm learning about you. I've been telling myself there was something of a dreamer buried in you – "

"There is," he had admitted, pleased she had discovered it. The girls he had known in the past had never credited him with much imagination, never having bothered to

9

search for it; perhaps they had too easily accepted the Australian male at his own face value of professing not to be interested in anything that could not be backed, imbibed or bedded. "But I never dreamed about lottery prizes – "

"What did you dream about?" She had a woman's habit of not allowing a discussion to go in a straight line: I'll walk out on her, he thought, after twenty years or so of this.

"Meeting someone like you. Now shut up. Look, I've made the down payment on our house and I've got enough money to furnish it – I had all that when I proposed to you."

"I remember. You had your bank statement in one hand while you had the other up my skirt."

"I was just seeing what your credit was – "

She had hit him at that, then kissed him. "You want to check my credit again?"

He pushed her away. "Lay off – and please *shut up*. Well, now I've been made Inspector – "

That, like the lottery win, had been totally unexpected. The promotion had come several years ahead of schedule and over the heads of a dozen more senior men, all of whom had, like true Public Service believers in the dogma of seniority, promptly but unsuccessfully protested. It had been a month of windfalls and with his inborn Celtic pessimism, with which he fought a continual battle, he had wondered if his luck was proving too good, if sooner or later he would be expected to pay for it all in some dreadful way. Like losing Lisa. When he had gone home to tell his mother of both pieces of good fortune she had rushed at him and half-drowned him in holy water, warding off the Devil before the latter could demand payment.

"All right," Lisa said patiently, seeing now that this was something he had thought through fully before mentioning it to her, "so we have security. But we could invest that twelve thousand dollars and who knows what it would be worth in, say, another ten or fifteen years. Especially if we put it in land or property. *Then* we could take a trip and still have quite a bit left over to educate our children – "

"Do me a favour. Don't start our marriage by being a thrifty wife – "

"I thought that was what you wanted me to be. You're the man who counts out the fare right down to five cents when you're paying a taxi-driver."

"That's different."

"Yes, there is a difference between five cents and five thousand dollars. I've heard of husbands like you – they drive their wives crazy, then ask for a divorce on the grounds of the wife being mentally unbalanced. You add up the household bills every week, complain if the wife has bought fillet steak instead of hamburger, then go out and buy a new car to replace one that's only two years old. But go on, don't let me interrupt you."

"What have you been doing?" But Malone kissed her, raised his hand and gently brushed back the lock of blonde hair that had fallen down over her forehead. She was much too beautiful for him and he would never fail to marvel at his luck in having won her: she was the biggest, most incredible windfall that would ever happen to him. "Look. You and I have nothing in common except that we love each other. Right?"

She kissed him in return. "Right. Isn't that enough?"

"No, it isn't. And once you're over your starry-eyed condition about me you'll realize it. Look at my background. Born and raised in Erskineville, a slum that even the rest of Sydney seems to have forgotten. I left school at sixteen and the only time I've been to university was to arrest a lecturer for exposing himself – "

"I thought students were broad-minded about that sort of thing."

"These were economic students – I gather they don't like being distracted by the humanities. Shut *up*. I've been a cop for seventeen years and the only time I've been out of Australia was when I came to London on police business and met you."

"Darling, I'm not marrying your background – "

11

"You *are*, that's just it. And I'm marrying yours. What other cop in Sydney, even a Detective-Inspector, has got a wife who was born in Holland, educated in Switzerland – "

"That was only for a year at finishing school – "

Malone wearily raised his eyebrows. "*Only*. Even the Police Commissioner's wife didn't go to finishing school – some of us reckon he found her in a reform school. But that's not all – you know Europe better than you know Australia. You worked for our High Commissioner in London, you have forgotten more about the diplomatic life than I'll ever know – "

"Darling, I don't know what you're worrying about. You're intelligent, you know what's going on in the world – there'll always be something for us to talk about – "

Malone shook his head. "Sooner or later you'll be looking for someone to talk to about the things *you* know – " He shook his head again. "We'll invest five thousand dollars in *that*. I think the dividends when we're old and fed up with each other will be worth it. I'm a great believer in shared memories."

"Whom else have you shared memories with?"

"No one. That's how I *know*."

Lisa's arguments against the suggestion had been more a matter of form than anything else; she was excited by the prospect of the trip, but already she knew that in their life together she would often have to play the role of devil's advocate to tone down Malone's Irish fecklessness. He knew his weakness and he kept a tight hold on it, but she knew there would be times when she would have to take over the reins. The argument now had been good practice, though she felt a hypocrite going against the grain of her own overwhelming desire to take off that minute for the other side of the world, for the Europe that she would not have left had not her parents been sent out to Australia in the course of her father's job. In her view there were only two good things about Australia: sunshine and Scobie.

But Malone knew nothing of what had gone on in Lisa's

mind during their discussion and all through the trip he had been complimenting himself on his good sense in suggesting it. They had visited Bangkok, Hong Kong, Athens, Rome; they had wandered back and forth across Europe, visited Lisa's relatives in Holland, seen summer fade in France and watched autumn come in in Britain; now it was early November, they were in New York on their way home, and in another two weeks he would be back at work. He had had three months' leave due him and he had been glad of it, but now he was becoming bored with travelling and filling in his days with sightseeing. He had crossed the Atlantic in a chockablock-full jumbo jet and wondered why he had not been labelled as livestock instead of a passenger. He had grown tired of hotel and restaurant food and longed for one of his mother's steak-and-kidney pies, a bottle of Cawarra claret and pawpaw and ice-cream to follow. He had seen enough museums and art galleries to last him for several years, and he was looking forward to getting back to flipping over the Wanted posters and looking through the artefacts gathered from criminals who were going on their own extended leaves, five to ten at Bathurst Jail.

Once a copper, always a copper. Con Malone, his old man, had been right. Con, who chewed his prejudices as if they were his cud, had no time for policemen and in his own mind he had never lived down the disgrace of his son, his only child, having become one. Malone wondered how his father would have voted on the law and order issue in this New York mayoral election.

He glanced down at the copy of *The New York Times* lying on the chair beside the window. The Mayor's face smiled up at him: Michael Forte, all teeth and sparkling eyes, looking ready to burst into *O Sole Mio*; yesterday Malone had bought the Sunday edition of *The Daily News*, which supported the Mayor's opponent, and seen that it called Forte the Harvard Gondolier. Politics in America seemed more interesting, if only because the newspapers could be more libellous. But he had had enough of politics in his own work back in Sydney and he knew he would never be comfortable as a cop here in New York, where, he had heard, politics was an essential part of the system, to be defended as much as law and order.

He looked at the other headlines: the late-season hurricane was working its way up from the Carolinas, a family of four had been murdered in Spanish Harlem, people were dying by the thousands from a famine in Bengal, war was imminent on a dozen fronts. He turned over the newspaper, feeling callous and selfish: he wanted nothing of the world's troubles while he was still on his honeymoon.

Lisa hung up the phone. "His nurse says he's fully booked, but if I can get up there by nine-forty-five she thinks he might be able to fit me in." She looked at her watch. "I'll have to hurry."

"What are you going to the Holland Society for?" They still had not yet got into the habit of confiding fully in each other. That would come in time, he mused without resentment. Then, of course, there would be the completion of the circle when they would return to keeping their confidences to themselves. Being a policeman made you cynical about the long-term prospects of a marriage. Then he cursed himself for his treasonable thought and, as compensation, moved towards Lisa and kissed her again.

"You're love-sick this morning, aren't you? But don't stop. I can give you two minutes."

"Not long enough. I'd feel like the bloke who was double-parked outside the brothel and didn't want to get ticketed."

She kissed him back; they were like a couple of teenagers in love for the first time. "I'm going to the Holland Society because Mother wants me to find out how far the Pretorious family has spread throughout the world. She's a snob, you know that, and I think she'd like to discover that it was actually a Pretorious who founded New Amsterdam. After I've been there I'll do some shopping for presents to take home. I'll meet you back here for an early lunch, then we'll do that boat trip round Manhattan."

"Don't go mad. This city is only for millionaires."

"I didn't tell you, but I brought some of my own money with me."

Again the tiny secret. How long would it take before they had no secrets from each other? Probably never: he knew only too well that no one, not even the simple-minded saint, ever fully told the truth about himself. "I'm supposed to be the bread-winner."

"Don't let's go into that again." In Sydney she worked for a public relations firm and till he had been promoted had earned more than he did. "I'm going back to work as soon as we arrive home."

"I'll get you pregnant and put an end to your working."

"What makes you think being pregnant isn't work?" She kissed him again. "You men have it so easy. A couple of minutes' exercise for you and nine months' hard labour for us."

A few minutes later Malone, still at the window, watched Lisa as she crossed the street and hailed a cab on the corner of First Avenue. This hotel in the East Thirties had been highly recommended by the travel agent in Sydney, but Malone now suspected the travel agent was another of those who had a vested interest. The hotel was clean and comfortable and comparatively inexpensive, once Malone had raised his sights from what Lisa called his Salvation Army hostel complex; she had pointed out, with what *he* called her heavy Dutch sarcasm, that just because jails provided free accommodation, hotels did not have to operate on the same principle. Still, he thought the rooms in this hotel had been designed for skinny dwarfs, the windows could not be opened and the central heating was at an unchangeable level that was better for breeding orchids than for warming guests. Added to that it was in an area through which Malone, even had he been here in New York by himself, would not have liked to walk at night. Down below, on the other side of the street, he could see two men, drunks or junkies, lolling on the steps of a shabby tenement; farther up the street a gang of long-haired youths were blocking the sidewalk, making passers-by step into the gutter to walk round them. The cop in him bristled; then he relaxed. Stay out of it, Malone. Your business is ten thousand miles away and you'll be back there soon enough.

He went into the tiled closet that was called a bathroom, took off his robe and began to shave. The man in the mirror, twisting and turning his face under the electric shaver, was no stranger, but sometimes he wondered how much he knew of himself. The face was not handsome, but the features had enough symmetry about them to stop it short of being plain or ugly; the chin was strong and the eyes had enough humour left in them to persuade even the meanest villain that maybe this wasn't the worst pig in the world. The body was long and broad-shouldered and the legs also were long; so far none of the six feet and one hundred and eighty-five pounds of Malone had begun to turn to fat; there was still a resemblance to the fast bowler he had been ten years ago when he had played for his State at cricket. But lately he had begun to look at other, slightly older men as he had never looked at them before, searching for warning signs: the slowing walk, the thickening gut, the solidifying prejudices. The stranger round the corner of next year and the next and the next, the man you never met till they finally closed your eyes and you saw him there on the inside of your lids.

He finished shaving, showered, then dressed, putting on the clothes Lisa had laid out for him. He had no interest in clothes, but he was good-humouredly allowing himself to be groomed by Lisa, just so long as she appreciated that a cop was never meant to be a fashionplate, that the best detective was the one nobody could ever remember meeting. She had him in a grey suit today, with a blue button-down shirt and a dark blue tie that at first glance he thought was patterned with foetuses but which, when he looked closer, he was relieved to find were sea-horses. When he was dressed he didn't look at himself again in the mirror: whatever failings he had, and he knew he had as many as the next man, vanity was not one of them. If Lisa thought he would look all right in this outfit today, that was good enough for him. From now on she was the only one he really wanted to please.

He left the room, went out of the hotel, walked several blocks across town and caught the subway down to Police Headquarters, to make the courtesy call that Police Commissioner Venneker back in Sydney had asked him to make. He was glad he did not belong to the New York Police Department, not with their crime figures. The longer he was away from Sydney the more he appreciated it. So far that was something he had kept from Lisa.

2

The phone rang in the office on the tenth floor of Cornwall Gardens on East 69th Street. Polly Nussbaum took the carton of sugar out of the filing cabinet and moved across to her desk. She had been promising herself for years to have the cabinet moved in back of her desk, but somehow she had never gotten around to it: Procrastinating Polly, her mother had always called her. But now her feet were about to force her into it; even the few short steps across the office were killing her. Maybe she should have gone to work for a chiropodist instead of a dentist. Never any trouble with the teeth – "You're my best advertisement," Dr Willey was always telling her. But the feet! . . .

"Dr Willey's office."

"This is Mrs Michael Forte's private secretary." The woman's voice was soft and pleasant.

Polly Nussbaum always admired nice voices, but at forty-nine she had left it too late to do anything about her own. In a Jewish apartment overcrowded with her quarrelling parents and her five loud-mouthed brothers and sisters, who got to speak like Claudette Colbert? Claudette Who? You're dated, Polly, you live your life in the Late Late Show. "Yeah – yes?"

"I am just double-checking Mrs Forte's appointment for ten o'clock this morning."

"Yes, we are expecting her at ten."

"Thank you. Mrs Forte will be on time."

Polly Nussbaum hung up, sat back in her chair and eased her shoes off under the desk. She poured sugar into the cup of coffee she had made for herself and prepared to enjoy the only five minutes of leisure she would have from now till one o'clock. Dr Willey did not get in till nine-fifteen and the first patient was due at nine-thirty. She hoped she had done the right thing by trying to fit in that (she checked her book) Mrs Malone. Mrs Malone would never know it, but it had been *her* voice that had got her the appointment.

Come to think of it, Mrs Forte had a nice voice too. But underneath it all, she suspected, Mrs Forte was holding back a screech just like Momma's. I wouldn't want to work for her, not even if some day she ends up as the President's wife. She would be a bitch to work for, always making sure you never forgot the tiniest thing. That was probably why she had had her secretary check twice in the past week on this morning's appointment.

Polly spread out *The Daily News* on her desk, began to leaf slowly through it. Hurricanes, famine, murder, drugs: she didn't know why she bothered to waste her money each morning. Misery even at ten cents was too expensive. Then she stopped. Michael Forte, handsome in that nice Italian way that always reminded her of Marcello Mastroianni, smiled up at her, inviting her vote. Okay, Mr Forte, you got my vote, especially if you can bring law and order back to this town. Your wife I can do without; but she's your pain, not mine. I got rid of my pain, Irving Nussbaum, ten years ago. May God never send him back.

She pulled on her shoes, got up, went into the small washroom and washed her cup, came back into the office and stood for a moment at the window, looking down at the ants in the street. Poor schlemels, even at this height none of you look happy. Toothache, aching feet, ache in the heart. When did I last see a smile on the face of someone my age on the street?

Who'd want to be Mayor, trying to straighten out such a town?

3

"I have to be at Dr Willey's at ten," said Sylvia Forte.

"What?" said her husband abstractedly.

He was a handsome man of just above middle height, with a broad, dark face in which bone and flesh would for the next ten years be fighting a battle; if the bone won he would remain handsome till he was an old man. He had a quick nervous energy to him, exemplified by his wide smile; though some people, mostly those who voted against him, thought the smile was prompted by St Voter's Dance, the politicians' endemic, and was not a natural characteristic. Which showed how little he was understood by almost half of the city's population.

He stood at the window gazing out at the East River that was dull as dirty pewter under the grey November sky. The trees in the grounds of Gracie Mansion, the official residence of the Mayor of New York City, had no shine to them in the dull light; the fall foliage was the colour of stained leather and bad wine, a dismal frame for what might be the eve of his dethronement. He looked up at the sky, hoping that Hurricane Myrtle would swing away east before it reached New York: not only would it strip the trees of their leaves and perhaps even their branches, it would also strip the polling booths of voters. New Yorkers did not think enough of their politicians to go out into wind and rain to register their approval or disapproval of them.

Despite the dull light he could see up beyond the Triborough Bridge to the northern tip of Astoria on Long

Island; on such days he imagined he could see clear into the past, the family history that he had never experienced. Old Michele Forte, his grandfather, had settled over there in Astoria when he had arrived in America from Lerici in Italy in 1895, getting off the ship with a wife, three small children, forty dollars, a strong back and a driving ambition that had almost consumed him like a cancer. The family construction business had begun there and the Triborough was one of the monuments to it: M. Forte and Sons had been one of the contractors on the bridge. Michael knew that Sam, his father, the last surviving son of old Michele, never looked back at Astoria, but maybe that was understandable. America was full of first-generation sons trying to escape from their background. But then Sam Forte had never run for political office, had never had to convince the voters that, though rich, he was as good and humble as they were.

"I hope you listen to your ward bosses more than you do to me," said Sylvia.

Michael smiled at her, his husband's smile, not his politician's. "Sorry. I'll be able to give you my undivided attention after tomorrow – I hope. What are you doing this morning?"

She sighed, a little impatiently. "I'm going to Dr Willey's at ten, I'm blessing children or something at St Mary's School at eleven – " She was not a Catholic, but there had never been any religious arguments between them and they felt secure enough to make small jokes about each other's faith. "I'll remind the nuns to vote for you."

"They'll vote for me anyway. I donated all the rosary beads for the last First Communion class."

She shook her head in mock wonder. "It's just like dealing with the Indians – you're buying Manhattan again. What order do you think Mother Teresa and the nuns belong to – the Algonquins or the Delawares?"

"I've never seen the Pope as Sitting Bull, but it's a thought."

"Then I'm due at a luncheon at the Colony Club – " She used the word *luncheon* instead of *lunch*, but then she would not have been a member of the Colony Club had she done otherwise. She would also have not been a member had she been only Michael Forte's wife and no more; but being the daughter of Henry and Clara Veerkamp was another matter. It might take Michael to get her into the White House, but the Veerkamp name had got her admitted to everything that counted in the State of New York.

"Why there? They're not the sort who'll vote for me."

"They may – perhaps I can persuade them to. According to Scotty Reston this morning – " she tapped the copy of *The New York Times* that lay on the breakfast table – "you'll need every vote you can get tomorrow."

He looked at her admiringly; and with some sympathy that he hoped she would not detect. She was the perfect political wife: beautiful, with that red-gold hair that was a sensation on colour television, hard-working, always polite to the right people, never wasting her time on the wrong ones: if I don't make it tomorrow, he thought, she is the one who is going to be disappointed. She and Old Sam.

As if one cue, Nathan, the black butler, came to the door of the small dining-room where the Fortes usually breakfasted. "Mr Samuel is here, sir."

Michael smiled to himself at his father's punctilious formality. Ever since Michael could remember, his life had been run by his father, but once he had reached political office, first as a Congressman in Washington and then as Mayor here in New York, his father had always had himself announced when he called. Preparing for bigger things, Michael thought with slightly sour amusement: Sam would never expect to enter the White House without being announced. To Sylvia and Old Sam, Gracie Mansion was just a wayside stop on the road to the ultimate destination.

Sylvia got up from the table, moving with the graceful fluidity of a woman who had never been awkward even as a child and which had been improved by ballet lessons and the watchful eye of a vigilant mother. She went forward to kiss her father-in-law as he came in the door. There was warm affection between the two of them; they were related by ambition as well as by marriage. Michael, standing off, had to admit they made a fine-looking pair: the lovely red-haired woman and the stiff-backed, white-haired old man. A pity that these days Americans would not vote a June-December couple into the White House. They had accepted the marriage of the middle-aged Cleveland and his 21-year-old bride, but that had been almost ninety years ago, when Americans had been less respectful of the office of President.

"You're breakfasting late. Sorry if I'm too early – " Samuel Forte had not quite managed to eliminate the roughness of his early years from his voice. He had gone to work for his father at eighteen and it had been ten years before he had been able to escape from the shouting above the job noises and the yelling at the immigrant construction workers in the dialect that they understood. He had a town house in the East Sixties, an estate an hour out of town that overlooked the Hudson and a small mansion at Palm Beach in Florida; but Astoria was still there on his tongue. You may never look back at the past, Michael thought, but you'll always hear the echoes of it.

"No, we're finished. We had a late night and we're going to be late again tonight. We gave ourselves the luxury of an extra hour in bed this morning."

They had made love that morning, she stifling her cries against the possibility of being overheard by the servants. They had always enjoyed each other in bed, but the demands of public life too often tired them out; and the privacy of their bedroom was always subject to the urgent phone call or the knock on the door by Nathan or one of the other servants to say there was an unexpected visitor downstairs. Michael sometimes wondered if hernia, as well as a heart-attack, was a health hazard with those in power.

Sylvia brought her father-in-law to the table and poured him a cup of coffee. The old man sat down, carefully arranging the creases in his trousers, and looked up at his son. "The day after tomorrow you may not need to get up at all. I've been talking to Ed Horan – he says things are going against us up in the Bronx. He thinks you have been too complacent, Michael."

Michael held in his temper; it was too early in the day to start expending his energy that way. "Ed Horan is an uneducated horse's ass. He wouldn't know the meaning of complacency."

"The word was mine. Ed actually said you had left it too late to get off your butt and take your finger out. Excuse me, Sylvia."

"Think nothing of it. I gather the Duke of Edinburgh uses the same expression." Sylvia looked at her husband. Lately she had noticed that after they had made love she often became impatient with him, almost as if he had left her unsatisfied; she sometimes wondered if other couples went through this post-coital reaction, as if hurt had to be added to love. "It seems rather apt, don't you think?"

"No, I don't." Michael kept his voice down, though he was tempted to shout at them both. "It's easy for Horan to sit up there in the Bronx telling me what I should have done. When anyone criticizes him, he can brush it aside – he's not running for office, never has." He paused, looking at his father; but Sam Forte, impervious to barbs from his son, was carefully measuring sugar into his coffee. "When Tom Kirkbride came out with his campaign for law and order, what was I supposed to do? Tell Des Hungerford that the police force had to go out and double its daily quota? Already we're arresting more law-breakers than we have room for – the bail bondsmen are making more money than they've ever made in their lives before. *They* will vote for me," he said bitterly. "One of them told me so last week."

He turned away from them and went back to the window. A uniformed patrolman stood leaning against a tree in the grounds, idly watching a squirrel as it shopped among the

23

leaves for its winter larder. Out on the river a Fire Department tender, all fresh red and white paint, moved up towards Hell Gate, fastidiously skirting a garbage scow as the latter came downstream heading for the open Bay. Who will they vote for tomorrow, the fire tender crew and the cop? He recognized the squirrel and felt surer of its vote. At least when he went out into the grounds occasionally and fed it, it didn't put one paw behind its back and cross its toes.

"I've done everything I can," he said, still gazing out the window. "From now on it's a question of luck."

"Luck should never come into an election. It suggests a poor campaign or a poor candidate."

He turned round slowly and faced his father. "And what do you reckon you've had of those two?"

Sam Forte tasted his coffee, nodded approvingly at Sylvia. "Excellent coffee – but then it always is. How do you do it?"

"Never trust to luck," said Sylvia. "I make it myself and time the percolation exactly."

"One second for every granule," said Michael, "sucked dry like a voter. But you haven't answered my question."

Sam Forte took his time, as he always had with his son. When his boy had been born he had taken the long view: it took years, decades, to put a man into the White House, especially when you decided, when he was one day old, that that was his destination.

"You have been a good candidate, Michael. You have been a good mayor too, even though you have had a lot of critics. But the Holy Spirit himself couldn't make a success of running New York."

"And, no reflection on you, I never had the Holy Spirit's family behind me. But you don't think I've run a good campaign this time?"

"No." Sam Forte finished his coffee, wiped his mouth deliberately with the napkin Sylvia gave him; she knew his fastidiousness, as if he were afraid of finding himself flecked with some grit from the past. "You let Kirkbride get away too soon with his claim that he can bring back law and order if he is elected. You should have hit him right at the start."

"How?"

"By giving him the same argument you've given me. Ask him where the money is coming from for more police, for more prisons – "

"Do you really think people listen to that sort of argument? When they're scared to walk down the street after dark, scared to open their front door for fear they're going to be mugged, do you really think they're going to listen to logical argument?"

"It would have been worth a try – "

"Jesus!" Michael gestured in exasperation. "Look, I *believe* in law and order – I believe in it so much, as a – a way of life, if you like, that I find it hard to accept it as an election issue. But how do I convince the ordinary guy in the street that I'm even more concerned than he is, because it's *my* responsibility? He's a Monday morning quarterback when it comes to politics, knows all the answers – but when the issues get right down to the street he lives on, he's a knuckle-head, he knows nothing and he doesn't want to know. He just expects miracles and he votes you out if you don't produce them."

"You could have made some sort of gesture – "

"A gesture at a miracle? I'd need the Holy Spirit for that one." He looked out the window again. A bald-headed jogger in a track-suit went past on the path outside the mansion grounds, head bobbing up and down as if it had come loose on his neck; he had the despairing look of a man tempted to catch the first cab he saw back home, someone who saw no logic at all in what he was doing. "When we had the British Prime Minister to dinner here last year, I remember something he told me – if you wanted to stay in politics and enjoy it, always remain in Opposition. That way no one can ever blame you for anything, but you always get marks for trying."

"That may work in the House of Commons. But there's no Opposition in the White House. Nor even in City Hall," Sam added as an afterthought.

"Don't curl your lip. There are a lot of people who think City Hall is more than just a bus station. Tom Kirkbride is one."

"Tom Kirkbride has no ambition. Not *real* ambition."

Not like you, thought Michael. He heard the clatter of the Police Department helicopter as it went over the house and down to the wharf below. Once a week he rode downtown by helicopter, one week going down the East Side, the next down the West, like an old-time king surveying his domain: he sometimes wondered if the P.D. pilot had the same thought. He had been doing it every Monday for four years and he still got the same thrill: the tall buildings seeming to shuffle into ranks as he swept by them, the giant spiders' webs of the suspension bridges glinting in the morning sun, the million mirrors of the windows reflecting the helicopter as it went by: when you stood off from it New York was still the most exciting city he had ever seen. From the helicopter you never saw the maggots that were already at work in the body that was not yet a corpse.

"It's time I was leaving."

"I'll stay and have a little talk with Sylvia. We haven't seen much of each other this past month."

"You can drive me down to my dentist," said Sylvia. "We can talk in your car."

"How will you get to St Mary's?" Michael asked; he was forever worried for her, though he knew in his heart she was stronger than he was. "I don't want you riding around in some crummy cab, with the hackie recognizing you and telling you what's wrong with me."

"Lester can pick me up at ten-thirty." She kissed him, loving him but still wondering why lately she had begun to lose patience with him. "Don't worry, darling. I shan't expose myself to any strangers."

"Sometimes I wonder if it's all worth it," he said, and

his father and his wife glanced sharply at him. "There's some safety in anonymity."

"It's a little late for that," said Sam Forte.

"Yes," said Michael. "You saw to that."

4

Abel Simmons, cruising slowly down Second Avenue like a driver who knew exactly what pace you had to maintain to catch the traffic lights all the way downtown, glanced at his watch. Nine-forty: time to move. He stepped on the gas pedal as he came to East 70th, then had to brake sharply as a green-and-white police car, badly in need of a wash, pulled out from the kerb right in front of him. He cursed; and cursed again when he saw the lights go red at the corner. He halted behind the police car, bouncing his hands impatiently on the steering wheel of the delivery truck. He was going to miss the lights at East 69th and if he did that it could blow the whole show. He could feel the sweat beginning to break on him and his legs began to tremble. Carole was going to be down there in the garage waiting for him, the Forte woman on her hands, the garage jockey wondering what the hell was going on, and all because a couple of pigs didn't follow their own rules about pulling out into moving traffic. It would serve them right if he took the gun out of his pocket and shot both the bastards in the back of the head.

The light turned green and instinctively his hand touched the horn button. The two cops turned round in their seats and for a moment he thought the guy beside the driver was going to get out and come back to him; he took his hand off the wheel, put it in his pocket and clutched the gun; then he smiled and waved the other hand in an apologetic gesture. Neither of the cops smiled back, just stared at him a moment longer, then they faced forward again and the driver un-hurriedly set the police car going. Abel, resisting the temptation to speed up past them, fell in behind; he didn't want them following him, for Christ's sake. He could see the light still green at 69th, but he hadn't noticed when it had changed and he could not guess when it would turn red. The police car cruised slowly on, the driver and his partner lolling negligently in their seats, and Abel, trembling so much now he could feel his headache coming on again, tried to memorize the number of the car. When this job was over he'd come back here and kill those two pigs.

Then they were at 69th Street. The police car swung slightly to the right and Abel felt his stomach empty, then tighten; but the police car straightened up and went on down Second Avenue, and he swung the delivery truck on to 69th just as the lights turned. He wanted to stop, sit there for a minute or two and regain his cool. But there wasn't time . . .

Up the street Carole Cox was already turning into the steps that led up into the small garden fronting the building known as Cornwall Gardens. She was dressed in a plain grey suit, wore dark wrapround glasses and a short curly wig that was much darker than her own straight brown hair; she hoped she looked like a thousand other working girls in New York City, felt sure that she did. Over the past four years she had come to accept anonymity, something she had once thought impossible for her: till she had met Roy in her last year at college and fallen so deeply in love with him, she had wanted recognition, to be an actress, a writer, *someone*. But even after today she would still be anonymous: that was part of the perfection of the plan.

She paused at the top of the steps, looked down the street and saw Abel driving up in the delivery truck. He had come by here twenty-five minutes ago and she hoped no one had seen them speaking to each other when he had pulled into the kerb across the street; they had exchanged no more than half a dozen words, but it had been necessary to confirm that Sylvia Forte's appointment with her dentist was still scheduled for ten o'clock. Maybe a signal would have been enough, but there was always the chance that a signal could be misunderstood. And nothing must be left to chance in this operation.

She saw Abel drive up past her, carefully not looking at her, then swing out of sight down the curving ramp that went under the garden to the basement garage. She hoped Abel had no trouble with what he had to do down there; she felt her palms in her brown kid gloves starting to sweat. She checked her watch: nine-forty-five. She moved on to a side path, watchful that she did not brush her stockings against the scruffy bushes bordering the path. God, how New Yorkers grabbed at their piece of greenery like people prizing shards of a bygone age. A hundred feet by twenty of patchy lawn, an ornamental pool that appeared to be filled with sludge oil, and several clumps of shrubs that looked as if they were hosed daily with acid: Walden Pond-on-69th. She glanced up at the tall building above her: how many tenants there ever looked down here hoping for a reflection of Thoreau? Probably none; but she felt no pity for them. She checked her watch again, feeling impatience taking hold of her like a chill. Nine-forty-seven. Would Sylvia Forte be early, right on time, or late for her appointment? Then the answer came up the street, the big black Lincoln Continental pulling into the kerb below her. The door opened and Sylvia Forte, red-gold hair so easily recognizable, got out of it . . .

A faded and dented yellow cab lurched in behind the Lincoln and Lisa Malone got out of it. She shoved two dollars at the driver and moved quickly to the steps that led up to Cornwall Gardens. As she did so she heard the red-haired, elegantly-dressed woman who had just got out of the big black car turn back and say, "I'm early, but I don't think Dr Willey will mind."

But *I* will, thought Lisa, seeing her own appointment suddenly disappearing; and she hurried up the steps. Out of the corner of her eye she saw the white-haired old man lean forward in the rear seat of the black car and say something; the woman smiled, blew a kiss from the tips of her gloved fingers and followed Lisa up the steps. As they crossed the small strip of garden Lisa saw the dark-haired girl standing to one side, looking down the street as if waiting for someone who had promised to meet her here and was late. Lisa hoped the girl was not another of Dr Willey's patients who had turned up early for an appointment. Her hollow tooth began to ache again – with impatience, she guessed.

She went into the lobby, crossed to the elevator and entered it. There was no time to check what floor Dr Willey was on: the red-haired woman was already in the elevator with her, pressing the button for the tenth floor: that must be where Dr Willey had his surgery. The two woman stood side by side at the rear of the elevator, Lisa looking at the other woman out of the corner of her eye, the women seemingly oblivious of Lisa. They were both dressed in brown wool suits; but Lisa guessed her own had cost less than half of what the red-haired woman must have paid for hers. Then there was the clack-clack-clack of high heels across the terrazzo floor of the lobby and the girl Lisa had seen waiting outside came quickly into the elevator. She stood in front of the control panel, pressed the master button, then a second button, waited till the doors closed, then turned round and faced Lisa and the red-haired woman. In her gloved hand was a small revolver.

"I am sorry, Mrs Forte, but you will have to see your dentist another day."

Lisa felt the elevator going down beneath her: at first she wasn't sure that the feeling was not just an emotional one. Then the elevator bumped gently to a stop, the doors opened and Lisa, looking past the girl, saw they were in a basement garage that seemed full of cars. A grey delivery truck, its rear doors open, was backed up almost against the elevator exit. A young blond man in coveralls, wearing the same sort of wrapround dark glasses as the girl, stood by the open doors of the truck.

The girl jerked the gun at the red-haired woman. "Please don't make any trouble, Mrs Forte, or you'll get hurt. Get into the truck."

"Jesus!" The young man sounded worried. "Who's the other one?"

The girl shook her head, then seemed to look at Lisa for the first time. "I don't know who you are, but you're out of luck. You'll have to come with us – "

"Jesus, we don't want *her*!"

"Shut up!" The gun shook for a moment in the girl's hand; Lisa flinched, waiting for an involuntary squeezing of the trigger. "I know we don't want her. But we're stuck with her. What the hell else do we do with her?"

"Jesus, I don't know – " Despite the dark mask of the glasses, worry and indecision showed in the thin face of the young man.

Then there was the sound of a car coming down the ramp. The young man swung round, looking on the verge of panic. "I put the chain across the top of the down ramp! The bastard's coming down the other side!"

The girl jerked the gun at Lisa and the red-haired woman. "Into the truck – quick!"

So far the red-haired woman had not moved. Now she looked at Lisa and, her voice only faintly showing signs of strain, said, "I'm sorry. I think we had better do what they say."

Lisa could not believe what she was involved in, yet there was no mistaking the blunt truth of the gun in the girl's hand. She had been engaged to a policeman for six months and married to him for eight weeks: she knew that crime was more than just an abstract headline in one's daily newspaper. But hearing Scobie talk of it, seeing the occasional mental scar that came to the surface in him, was far different from *this*. "I'm staying here! I don't want any part of it – !"

The young man cursed savagely, stepped into the elevator, grabbed her and shoved her out towards the truck. She struggled violently, but he was too strong for her; she felt a blow across the back of her neck, everything was suddenly blurred and next moment she was flung headlong into the back of the truck. When she rolled over on her back, her gaze clearing, she saw the red-haired woman being pushed into the truck and the girl scrambling in after her. The doors were slammed shut and a moment later she heard the young man jump up into the front of the truck. She heard the other car come down the ramp into the garage, then its horn was tooted twice. The engine of the truck was already running; then the truck jumped forward, the sound of the suddenly revved-up engine roaring in the low-roofed confines of the garage. She tried to sit up, but the girl, sitting on the floor of the truck beside the red-haired woman, leaned across and poked the gun into Lisa's bosom.

"Lie still! If you move, I'll shoot you!"

Lisa lay back, sliding to one side on the slippery metal floor as the truck, engine roaring, swung round the newly-arrived car parked outside the attendant's office and went up the ramp out of the garage. She could see the red-haired woman flattened against the other side of the truck, her face suddenly wide open in her first expression of fear. The girl waved the gun at both women, her mouth snarling word-lessly, then she crawled forward to the partition that separated the back of the truck from the driver's seat. She hammered on the partition with her hand.

"Abel – slow down! We don't want to be pulled in for speeding!"

Up front Abel Simmons eased up off the gas pedal, feeling the effort in his calf muscle as if he were trying to lift a weight with his foot. He opened his hands, letting the strain run out of them; his fingers felt as if he had been hanging by them from a cliff-edge. His head was aching, as it always did when he was worried. His face was streaming with sweat and his dark glasses were beginning to fog up. But he couldn't take them off yet, not till he was out of 69th and had turned up Third Avenue. They had worked out the route a dozen times, taking the longer way, always putting a corner behind them and moving with the traffic instead of going right across town. All he had to do was not panic.

Everything had been going so well until the blonde bitch had unexpectedly appeared in the picture. There had been no trouble with the garage jockey. He had been lounging in a chair in the tiny office as Abel had pulled up the truck, swung down and entered the office. He had looked up, both hands holding a comic book in his lap, the transistor radio behind him playing a number from *No, No, Nanette*; he had said nothing as Abel had come at him with the butt end of the gun, just opened his eyes wide in a visual parody of the banal words of the song being sung behind him. Maybe the guy had been slow-witted; Abel had felt sorry for him as he had fallen backwards. His chair had tipped over right in front of the toilet where Abel meant to hide him. Abel had come in here two weeks ago on the pretext of looking for a job; two minutes in the tiny office had been enough for him to remember its lay-out. This morning it had taken him less than a minute to gag the guy with the tape he had brought with him, tape his hands behind him, then shove him into the toilet and lock the door.

The music had stopped and a disc jockey, a licensed con man, was burbling a message: "Does that pluck at the old memory strings, you older gals? If you want your own taste of nostalgia, why not try Sara Lee's Cherry Pies – "

Abel had switched off the radio, run back up the ramp and put the chain across the entrance, hanging the *Garage Full* sign on it. Two minutes later he had had the truck waiting outside the elevator, back doors open, engine running, everything ready just for Carole and the Forte dame to put in an appearance. Then the elevator doors had opened and there were Carole and the Forte dame and the blonde bitch besides. Then to top it all there had been the guy who took no notice of signs, who drove down an Up ramp – Jesus, what if they had met him halfway up the ramp!

The sweat broke more profusely on him, blinding him this time as it ran down into his eyes. He caught the green

33

light at the corner, barely seeing it through his fogged-up glasses, swung right up Third and at once whipped off the glasses. He rubbed them quickly on his thigh, then put them back on; they were still smeared but at least he could see through them. He saw the light still green at 70th and he speeded up, caught it and turned right again. At the end of the block, at Second Avenue, the light was red: it stared at him like an hemorrhaged eye. He took a handkerchief out of his pocket, wiped his glasses clean, mopped his face and put the glasses back on. Then he willed his cool to come back, telling himself the worst was now over. Even if the guy who had driven down into the garage found the attendant in the toilet, they wouldn't know what else had happened. It could be hours before anyone learned there had been a kidnapping.

The light turned green and he moved the truck on, driving at a good speed but not fast enough to catch the notice of any prowling pig. He saw the police car he had seen before and for a moment his foot lifted off the pedal; but the police car was parked at the kerb, the driver was missing and his partner was reading a newspaper; he drove on, laughing to himself at them. Just below East 60th he turned sharply left, heading for the Queensboro Bridge. Once on the bridge he speeded up a little, the tyres whirring on the metal surface beneath the truck. He came down on to Queens Boulevard and almost at once had to slow down again. The women shoppers were just making their appearance, cruising their cars down the boulevard as if they were pushing trolleys down the alleys in a supermarket: *Hold it a minute, Josie . . . No, it don't matter, I thought I seen something . . . Look, there's a parking space! . . . No, you missed it . . .* Abel cursed them: goddam women were all alike. All but the lovely one in the back of the truck. Carole: the greatest thing that had ever happened to him in his whole screwed-up life.

In the back of the truck Carole sat with her back braced against the partition that separated her from Abel. Mrs Forte and the blonde sat on either side of the truck, facing each other, and she watched them carefully, wondering which one of them was going to speak first. Neither of the women had said a word since they had been bundled into the truck; maybe, she mused, they had both been so scared they had been struck dumb. She herself had been scared when Abel had grabbed the blonde girl; God knows what he had intended doing, but it had looked as if he were going to kill her. She would have to watch him carefully too: he seemed to lose his head too quickly when things got panicky.

Sylvia Forte smoothed back her hair, then looked at her trembling hand and cupped it in the other hand. She looked across at Lisa. "Perhaps we had better introduce ourselves. I am Sylvia Forte."

"Lisa Malone." Lisa smoothed back her own hair, looked down at the holes in the knees of her stockings. She reached out for her handbag, but Carole grabbed it and also took Sylvia's. "There's nothing in there but what any woman carries."

Carole smiled, nodded at the gun in her hand. "Today I was carrying *this* in mine. You can fix your face when we get where we're going."

"Where are you taking us? And why?"

Carole just shook her head, but Sylvia said, "We're somewhere on Long Island – I heard us come over the Queensboro Bridge."

"Very smart, Mrs Forte," said Carole. "You must be a great help to your husband if you are always so observant."

Lisa suddenly tightened her gaze on the woman opposite her. "Are you Mrs *Michael* Forte? The Mayor's wife?"

"I'm surprised you recognize me. You're not American, are you?" But Sylvia was pleased: one never really knew how much interest the rest of the world took in Americans, especially American wives.

"No, Dutch." Then Lisa corrected herself: she would have to get used to the idea: "Or Dutch-Australian, I suppose. My husband is an Australian and that's where I live. I still can't believe this is happening – " She glanced at the gun in Carole's hand. "I don't think it would happen back home."

"You're not going to get hurt," said Carole. "If Mrs Forte's husband listens to reason you will be released within thirty-six hours."

"Thirty-six hours?" Sylvia looked at her watch, pondered for a while, then looked up. "You're waiting till tomorrow, Election Day? Is this a political kidnapping, then?"

"Very smart again, Mrs Forte." Carole looked at Lisa. "You're not part of the politics, Mrs – Malone? You're just unfortunate. You might say you're one of the poor non-voters caught in the cross-fire. It happens too often in this country." Beneath the wrapround dark glasses the wide sensitive mouth suddenly thinned with bitterness. "But Mrs Forte's husband and men like him never know it and never care. But he'll know *now*."

Chapter Two

Malone stuck the stamps on the postcards and put the cards
into his pocket; he would post them when he and Lisa went
out to lunch. They were not large cards but it had taken him
half an hour to compose the messages on the backs of the
three of them. His police reports had never been noted for
their literary quality; their only virtue had been their
brevity. Something like that had been good enough for Russ
Clements, his sidekick in Y Division back home (though now
he came to think of it he and Russ were no longer partners:
Inspectors did not have sidekicks, only subordinates and
superiors); but the cards to his parents and to Lisa's had
needed more thought. Jan and Elisabeth Pretorious were
sophisticated, educated people: her father, a lover of Proust,
would not be satisfied with *Having a wonderful time, wish you
were here*. Malone had never read a line of Proust, but he
gathered he was a French poof and he did not think he and
Marcel would think along the same lines; he was not himself
an uneducated reader, but Paris of long ago was not his
territory. Con and Brigid, his own parents, though uneducated, had the Irish respect for garrulity: they might not
look for fine words but they wanted a lot of them. He had
been sweating out these messages everywhere they stopped
off and he was glad these cards were the last he would have
to send. The telephone was sometimes a bloody nuisance,
but it had its advantages. He was the same thing to all men
on the phone.

He looked at his watch: what the hell was keeping Lisa?
She was the most punctual woman he had ever met and
though she had set no time to meet him back here at the
hotel, she had mentioned an early lunch which, for a hungry
man like himself, was any time after eleven-thirty. It was

now 12.20 and she had been gone three hours. He began to worry, thinking of what Captain Jefferson had told him that morning of the increasing number of attacks on women in broad daylight.

"Sometimes I think this city is like Vietnam – we can never win. Last year we had 912 murders – this year up to the end of last month we've had 924 and we got two months to go. I'm not boasting – I'm ashamed to be quoting the figures to you. But maybe it's the same all over, eh? I mean the figures going up. Maybe we been fighting the wrong enemy, the Communists and such. Maybe the criminals, the villains as the British call 'em, are gonna take over the free world."

Captain Jefferson had been the officer who had greeted Malone at Police Headquarters and taken him on the conducted tour. He was a middle-aged Negro and Malone had at once recognized him for what he was, a desk detective who had grown fat in his chair and cynical in his lazy routine; there were one or two like him at Police Headquarters back home, their only difference from him the colour of their skin. He was a man of only medium height but must have weighed more than Malone; the latter guessed that if Jefferson had to take a physical he would fail it. He had been friendly enough, but Malone, as sensitive as litmus paper when it came to reception of himself, guessed that Jefferson was a professional greeter: the smile on the plump-cheeked black face was part of his police equipment, like the gold shield that he carried in his pocket. Malone wondered how long he had been in this job, how many other unwelcome visitors he had escorted around Head-quarters.

Malone had been surprised when he had approached Police Headquarters. He had not known what to expect, but he had not, for instance, expected New York to accommodate its law enforcement headquarters in circumstances that compared so unfavourably with those in London, a much older and less affluent city. The New York accommodation did not look any better than what was afforded back in Sydney, only larger. The surroundings looked as if they had been designed to bleed out any optimism any rookie policeman might have nurtured that he was contributing to a Brave New World. Shops and loft buildings, shabby and decrepit enough to have been shipped over wholesale from the back streets of eighteenth-century London, were thrown up against the brown cliffs of the police building; Malone wondered if it was a licensed area for cut-price gin-mills and whorehouses where the trainees in the Vice Squad could learn their trade, till he noticed policemen and policewomen coming and going in and out of the buildings; the tenements were annexes of Headquarters itself. On the green-domed tower on top of Headquarters the clock had stopped at 7.15 (on what morning or night of what day of what year? Had crime finally brought time to a standstill?) and the front of the main building was veiled by scaffolding (was the building being demolished or just patched up?). Inside the building he had a feeling of *déja vu*: the citizens of the world, with a few exceptions, usually those in a police state, expected their police to work in an environment designed to give them no more encouragement than the villains they were expected to catch. Drab walls that matched the morning complexion of an old whore; light that filtered down like the illumination from a tax budget that had blown its fuse several levels higher; floors that magnified the sound of every footfall, as if soft-footed cops were all right out on the beat but suspect in their own headquarters. Home sweet bloody home, Malone thought: I should have brought some ceremonial gifts, a few bones, from the tribe Down Under.

"You saw the construction work going on outside?" said Jefferson. "That'll be the first renovations we've had here in God knows how long, and we got a bunch of anarchists to thank for it."

Malone then remembered an item he had read in the newspapers before he had left Sydney: only the worst aspects of any country were news in another country. "That was where they planted the bomb?"

"Right there. Blew out three rooms and killed two of our guys and injured another six. But we got the jerks who did it – they're down in The Tombs waiting trial. We got them in only two days."

"Good going."

"It didn't satisfy everybody. Some people wanted to know why it took us so long. Others wanted to know why we could act so fast and efficiently when it was a coupla cops who were killed, but took our time when ordinary citizens were murdered. You can't win."

"Do you expect to?" asked Malone.

"We have a force of just 30,000 men," said Jefferson, reciting figures with the slightly defensive air of a man who had too often been exposed to criticism by outsiders, "and if we doubled it, then we might, and I repeat *might*, just begin to start controlling this town again. How many you got in Sydney, Inspector?"

Malone had left Sydney two days after his promotion had been gazetted: he was just a little slow in replying to being addressed as Inspector. "Eh? Oh, just over seven thousand, I think. But that covers the whole State. We have State police forces in Australia, not city."

"Seven thousand for how many people?"

"About four and a half, maybe five million." Malone had never been good at statistics. It never meant anything to him that the crime rate had risen 10 or 15 or 20 per cent in a year, that there was one man in prison for every 422 or 844 walking around outside, 50 per cent of whom might be just as larcenous as the man locked up. When crime became just a statistical problem, he would give up. Involvement, with both criminals and their victims, was his strength and his weakness, but it was what kept him in his job. You could never become involved with percentages.

"We got about twelve million – two million here on Manhattan alone, eleven miles long by two miles at its widest point – and Christ knows how many come in every day to work. Three, four, maybe even another five million." He sounded tired, as if suddenly he realized the futility of fighting statistics. Then he smiled, as if he also realized he was letting the side down in front of a stranger. "But we survive. Us cops, I mean."

"Where would they be if we didn't?" Malone grinned in reply. He knew Jefferson would know whom he meant by *they*: the outsiders, the taxpayers who expected miracles, who hated cops but always came demanding help and sympathy when things went wrong with them personally.

Jefferson's smile widened, became personal and not official: he recognized a member of the club. "We should swap reminiscences, Inspector. Maybe we could have lunch – ?"

Then a young uniformed policeman came hurrying down the long corridor where they stood. At once Malone, an expert at reading expressions, knew that something unusually serious had occurred: cops, even young ones, did not normally look as agitated as this one. Jefferson, another expert, saw the policeman coming and moved towards him: young Fairfax looked as if he had come to announce the outbreak of World War Three.

"Captain, you're wanted in the Commissioner's office at once. The Mayor's wife has just been kidnapped!"

Jefferson looked quizzically at the young policeman, then shook his head. "I was gonna say you must be joking – Okay, Tim, I'll go along right now. Will you show Inspector Malone the way out?" He came back to Malone. "You heard that? I been in the force thirty-three years and I can still be surprised. Jesus!" He shook his big round head again; for the first time Malone saw the flecks of grey in the dark crinkly hair. "Looks like we might not get together again, Inspector. But you understand – "

He held out his hand and Malone shook it. "I'll read the papers and see how you make out. Good luck. I'm just glad I'm not in your shoes."

"It's not my pigeon, but when something like this happens – the Mayor's wife – Jesus!" He shook his head yet again. He reminded Malone of a bush cop who had just realized what a jungle a city could be; but Jefferson was too old and bitterly experienced for that image to be true. "Everybody's gonna be called in on this. If you were thinking of robbing a bank or something, now's the time."

He waved a plump hand, then went off down the corridor, walking quickly and with that surprisingly light step that some heavyweight men have, as if it was all they had been able to reclaim from the long gone spring of their youth. Or perhaps, Malone thought, it's just the thought of getting away from his desk for a while.

"Have the kidnappers made any demands?" he asked Fairfax.

"I couldn't say, sir. I'm afraid at my rank we're always the last to know."

"Too true," said Malone. "I never knew a thing till I got to sergeant. But ignorance is bliss. It just doesn't pay as well."

"Too true, sir," said Fairfax, but his smile showed he meant no offence by echoing Malone.

So Malone had come back to the hotel, the policeman in him wanting to stay at Headquarters and watch another force in action during an emergency such as this, the ordinary man in him wanting to be gone from it and glad that he did not live in this city of extraordinary violence. He stood up and walked to the window, looked out on the street below. Two black women, big and round as barrels, were rolling along on the other side of the street; they passed a white derelict sprawled on the steps of a condemned tenement, said something to each other and looked the other way; Malone didn't need to be able to see their faces, their contempt was outlined in the straightening of their round bodies. A young white woman with two small children came down the street and passed the derelict; neither she nor the children gave him a glance: he was part of the scene to them, one with the garbage in the gutter, the scraps of newspaper blowing along the sidewalk. Malone all at once felt a deep sadness for the two million people who lived here on Manhattan. They were walking about in their own graveyard.

The phone rang and he picked it up, wondering where Lisa was calling from. Had she discovered that a Pretorious *had* founded New Amsterdam, was she now being feted at the Holland Society and she wanted him to join her? What had a Malone founded? Come to think of it, what had *any* Irishman founded? "Sir, there is a Captain Jefferson downstairs here. May I send him up?"

Malone put down the phone, puzzled and beginning to be worried. Why would a captain of detectives, in the middle of an emergency, come all the way uptown to call on him at the hotel? Why hadn't he just phoned?

He had the door open before Jefferson knocked on it. "What's the matter? Has my wife been hurt or something?"

Jefferson's plump face creased in puzzlement. "How did you know?"

"Know what? Christ, I don't know anything! But you haven't come all the way up here for that lunch – "

"No." Jefferson's voice was a rumble of despair. "I wish that *was* the reason – "

"Come in." Malone closed the door. Jefferson had not yet told him anything, but he knew that for the first time in his life a cop had come to *him* with bad news; he could not remember the number of times he had knocked on strangers' doors and with a feeling of utter helplessness watched their faces crumble and their eyes go opaque as he had delivered the bad news he had been burdened with. He leaned back on the door for support he might need and said, "What has happened to my wife?"

"The kidnappers took her with them when they took the Mayor's wife."

Malone did need the door: he felt his legs go weak. One part of his mind, the professional part, wondered if his eyes went blank: for a moment he could not see Jefferson or anything else in the room. Then he blinked, blurted out, "I don't believe it! Why the hell would they want to take her – ?"

"They said it was an accident." Jefferson told Malone all the police so far knew, that the kidnapping appeared to have taken place somewhere in the Cornwall Gardens building where Mrs Forte's dentist had his office, that a young blond man in dark glasses had slugged the garage attendant, that the kidnapped women must have been in a grey delivery truck that had been driven at speed out of the garage as another man had driven down into it. "Accidents like this do happen. You're a cop – you know that – "

"Did the kidnappers phone or what?"

"Some woman called the Mayor, told him they had his wife and another woman named Malone, an Australian. I didn't know about your wife when I got to the Commissioner's office – I didn't know about her till the Commissioner went down to City Hall to see the Mayor, then called me back. I was going to call you from Headquarters, then I thought it better – " He made a vague gesture.

"Thanks. I'm glad you didn't phone – I'd have thought it was someone trying a sick joke." He moved across and sat down on the bed. "How's the Mayor taking it?"

"I don't know – I haven't seen him. But a coupla kidnappings we've had in the past, while he's been Mayor, he's really ridden us. He's so uptight about law and order, there are some cops wonder if he knows what we're up against."

"What do the kidnappers want? Money for my wife as well?"

"I don't know what sort of demands they're making. If they're socking the Mayor, you can bet the price is gonna be high – he's a very rich man. Maybe they'll include your wife in the price."

"Don't talk like that!" Then Malone looked up. "Sorry, it just made my wife sound like some sort of commodity."

"I don't know if you've had any experience with kidnappers – "

"Once. The only time we've had a kidnapping in my State in my time."

"I've been on three of them and I know the history of most of the big ones here in this country. As far as kidnappers are concerned, their victims are a commodity and nothing else. That's brutal, I know, but you're a cop and sympathetic bullshit isn't gonna be any comfort to you. Not when you come to think about it."

Malone nodded, looked out the window from where he sat. The buildings uptown glimmered dully like stacked mesas of pure quartz; behind all those windows how many other people had just been shocked into numbness? An ambulance's siren wailed down in the street: pain never stopped: dying, like living, was a daily occurrence. He looked up at Jefferson again, almost unable to ask the question: "Do you think my wife – and the Mayor's wife – are still alive?"

The answer seemed to sicken Jefferson as much as the question. "We can't tell. You know the statistics – no, maybe you don't. Most times the kidnappers panic – Jesus, why am I talking to you like this!" His face screwed up in pain and he dropped his chin on his chest. He stood in silence for a few moments till he had regained his composure. Through the thin wall there came the sound of a television set in the next room: a studio audience laughed their heads off and a band struck up a pell-mell tune: someone had just won a prize for making a fool of himself. Jefferson raised his head and listened to the laughter as if puzzled, then looked back at Malone. "It's not gonna be easy for you, Malone. It's never easy for anyone in these circumstances, but it's gonna be harder for you. You're a cop and you're not gonna believe any of the crap we usually dole out under the heading of 'hope for the best'. I'd like to say the chances are your wife is okay and unharmed, but we just plain don't know."

"What's happening then? What are you doing?"

"I can't tell you till I go back down to Headquarters.

You're welcome to come down there with me – it'll be better than sitting here on your butt doing nothing – "

Malone was already on his feet. They went out of the hotel, the desk clerk looking inquisitively after them as they went through the lobby, and got into the police car drawn up at the kerb. Malone noticed that the car was badly dented and scratched, and when he got into the back seat with Jefferson he felt the cracked and torn vinyl beneath him. The New York City Police Department did not pamper its captains of detectives with luxury transport; but then he'd noticed that all the police cars he'd seen here were shabbier than those back home. And we think we are hard done by with our Holdens and Falcons. Jaguars and Rovers in Britain, Porsches and Mercedes in Germany, Fiats and Alfa-Romeos in Italy: maybe a country needed to be ruined by war to get the best of everything, even for its police.

"Crummy, eh?" said Jefferson, seeing Malone moving away from a split in the upholstery.

But Malone had already forgotten what he had noticed: the cop in him had reacted, but it was quickly being forced out of him by the husband. "Eh?"

"The Department's appropriation was cut this year – the last year of the Mayor's term. If he gets back in tomorrow maybe we'll get some new transport."

"We'll need it, Captain," said the driver, a white patrolman as old and stout as Jefferson. "We couldn't catch a kid on a pushbike in this one."

"That's fast enough for me, Stan. I'm no speed bug." He looked at Malone. "When I first started on the beat we never got a ride anywhere unless some punk had broken your leg while you were trying to bring him in. Maybe we should all still be on the beat, I dunno. We're all getting too fat, riding around. No offence, Stan."

"None taken, Captain. Maybe you're right. But I wouldn't wanna – Excuse me." The radio began to crackle. "It's for you, Captain."

The message was for Jefferson to proceed straight to City

Hall, to the Mayor's office. Jefferson acknowledged the directive, gave the microphone back to the driver and sat back beside Malone. "Let's hope they got some good news."

Malone said nothing, turned away and looked out at the street. They were pulled up at a red light; a bus wheezed in alongside them. Passengers stared down at him, their faces flattened into impassivity behind the window-glass; but there was no mistaking their antagonism. He was a cop, the enemy in occupied territory: none of them recognized him as a man who might have greater trouble than any of themselves. Suddenly he hated America and Americans: if they had killed his wife he would declare war on the country.

2

"Declaring war is not going to help Sylvia and this other woman, this – Mrs Malone or whatever her name is," said Michael Forte. "If we deploy every cop we have, call in every FBI agent in the country, all we are going to do is panic these sonsofbitches and they'll – " He stopped, unable to voice the thought in his mind. He looked appealingly at Police Commissioner Desmond Hungerford. "Des, I appreciate your efforts, but I think it would be wrong. I want Sylvia – and this other woman – back alive."

"And you're willing to pay the ransom price?" Hungerford said. "I don't mean that as a cruel question, Mr Mayor. I'm just asking."

Michael Forte leaned back in his chair, put his hand over his eyes, a habit he had developed years ago when trying to evade his father's questions. The other three men in the room, his father, Hungerford and Cartwright, from the FBI, watched him closely and sympathetically: each of them was privately glad he was not in the Mayor's shoes, either as the city's chief official or as a husband. Suddenly each of them was, for the moment, content with his own lot.

At last Forte said, "It's not just my decision, is it? Those men are held on charges – that means the law is responsible for them. I'm not the law, Des. The law is an instrument of the State."

"Forgive me saying so, Mr Mayor, but I don't think the Governor will like the decision being thrown in his lap."

"I didn't mean it would be." Forte dropped his hands on to the big desk in front of him. His programme for the rest of the day lay there: it was another life, one that he was suddenly no longer interested in. "Sorry, Des. I was only trying to evade the issue."

Samuel Forte sat quietly, alert but unobtrusive; he had never made the mistake of emphasizing in public that he was his son's mentor. Too many other men had done that and had ruined both their protégé's chances and their own ambitions. Even in this personal crisis of Michael's there were political implications just as critical and he waited, though deeply worried for the safety of Sylvia, with all the patience of a man who valued the long view above all others. Aristotle, his favourite philosopher, had called man a political animal, and Sam Forte took pride in being one of the best of the species. He knew he could do nothing personally to effect the safe return of Sylvia, so he sat and watched the two men whose responsibility it would be.

Des Hungerford had been his own suggestion to Michael as Police Commissioner; he had come to appreciate that it had been one of the few poor recommendations he had ever made. Hungerford was a tall bony man whose handsome face was spoiled by too much hair on it: a thick grey moustache and the thickest eyebrows Sam could ever remember seeing, dark furry grubs that continually twitched up and down the creased forehead. He seemed never to be without a cigarette in his mouth, always smoked in a yellowed ivory holder, and it bobbed up and down like an impatient finger waiting to make a point. He had a habit of not appearing to listen to what anyone was saying to him, only waiting for the other person to shut up, but Sam Forte knew from experience that Hungerford never missed a word of what was addressed to him. He had been an excellent cop and probably the best Chief Inspector the Department had ever known; but he had been a failure as Commissioner, and everyone, including himself, knew it. He was the sort of man, and Sam Forte had seen others, whose absolute pinnacle of potential was to be second from the top, the man who would always need another man above him to take the ultimate responsibility. Sam sometimes wondered, in the darkness of an old man's sleepless nights, if Michael would prove to be another Des Hungerford when he got to the White House. But it was something he would never admit to anyone, not even fully to himself. All he knew was that Michael was a man of higher principles than Des Hungerford, that he would never compromise when the big decisions had to be made.

"Mr Mayor, I think circumstances will decide for us what we can and cannot do." Cartwright was the Special Agent in charge of the FBI's New York office. He was a heavily-built man who continually had to watch his weight, forever conscious of the tightness of the belt round his middle; he was surrendering to age, hole by hole in a strip of crocodile leather. His present mood was not helped by the knowledge that today's kidnapping had taken place right across the street from his own office; so far, Commissioner Hungerford, no friend of his, had not mentioned the embarrassing fact. "We have very little to go on. We know there is a young guy involved – blond, Caucasian, thin, maybe in his early twenties. And there's a woman – the one who phoned you. What sort of voice did she have – I mean, did she have an accent or anything?"

"Not that I remember." Michael Forte gestured helplessly. "I don't think so. I was too shocked to take any notice – "

Cartwright nodded sympathetically. "Why had your wife no protection, nobody riding with her?"

"She usually does when she goes in one of our own or a City car. A detective from Headquarters rides with her or trails her in an unmarked car. This morning she rode with my father." Michael Forte carefully avoided looking at his father; this was no time to be scoring points off him. "We haven't had any threats for over three months, not even from the usual cranks. I'd begun to think maybe the cranks and criminals wanted me re-elected." He tried to smile, but it was just a pain around his mouth.

"We know a grey delivery truck was probably used to transport your wife and Mrs Malone," said Hungerford. "The man who drove down into the garage as they drove out gave us a rough description – but it *was* rough. We have the garage attendant over at Headquarters going through our mug shots, but he already says he will only be guessing. The guy who hit him had the collar of his coveralls turned up around his ears and jaw, and the dark glasses just about obliterated the rest of his face. He says he could have been a young guy who came in looking for a job two weeks ago, but he's not sure."

"I take it your men are working with the FBI?"

"Naturally, sir," said Cartwright, and looked at Hungerford, who nodded. "That's only newspaper talk, that the Police Department and the Bureau don't get on together. Des called me as soon as you gave him the news. Normally we aren't called in for at least twenty-four hours, not unless a State line has been crossed. We have no evidence that the kidnappers are even out of Manhattan, but Des thought we should pool our resources at once."

Sam Forte had never met Cartwright before, though he had seen him once or twice at official functions here at City Hall. The FBI had almost nothing to do with city politics, wisely staying well away from them, and Sam Forte, not wishing to crowd a muddy pool, had not encouraged Cartwright. The FBI, he had always thought, was something for the future, when Michael was in the White House. But he was glad to see Cartwright here now: they would need all the help they could get to get Sylvia back. Oh, and the other woman, whatever her name was.

There was a knock on the door and Michael Forte's

secretary put her head in. "Mr Mayor, Captain Jefferson is here with Inspector Malone."

As soon as Malone walked into the big room he knew that he and Jefferson were very much the low men on this totem pole. The handshake Mayor Forte gave him and the nods from the other three men were friendly and sympathetic enough; but he recognized at once that he – and Lisa – were never going to be anything more than supporting players in this drama. Nothing was said, but Malone, badly infected twice before by the virus, already sensed politics.

"Inspector Malone, I can't say how sorry I am – " Then Michael Forte shook his head in mild disgust at himself; and Malone recognized that this man at least was an honest one. "No, that's not what you want to hear, is it?"

"No, sir," said Malone, equally honest. "All I want to hear is what is being done to get my wife back."

"Nothing right now – nothing constructive, that is. We are groping, Inspector – as a policeman you will probably know what I mean by that."

"I don't think that's entirely fair, Mr Mayor – " Hungerford's cigarette holder stuck up like a challenging tusk.

"It's fair enough, Des. But you give him your version."

Hungerford took the cigarette holder out of his mouth, told Malone all they knew. "The woman who made the call said they would call back at three o'clock to see if we agreed to their demands."

"You *are* groping then," said Malone, and looked back at Michael Forte. "What are their demands, sir?"

"They don't want money, Inspector – I wish it were as simple as that." Forte had got up and come round his desk to meet Malone; since then he had been walking restlessly about the room. Now he stopped by the seated, unmoving figure of his father; Malone had a sudden clear impression of the contrast between the two of them: patience somehow had begat impatience. "We have five anarchists held in The Tombs, our detention jail, on conspiring to set off a bomb –

51

actually, it went off two months ago and killed two policemen – "

"I know about them. Captain Jefferson told me this
morning. What have they got to do with this?"

"They are the ransom fee – their release and a plane to
take them to Cuba. The deadline is noon tomorrow."

Malone felt the sick weakness come back on him. He
looked at Jefferson, the only face in the room familiar enough
for him to read, and saw the sudden pessimism in the dark
weary eyes. Puzzled, but not sure why, he looked round the
other faces, then back at Michael Forte.

"Go on, sir."

Forte looked at the Australian shrewdly, for the first time
really appreciating that this man had as much at stake in
the kidnapping as himself. "What do you mean, Inspector?"

"You hadn't finished. You've implied that you're not
prepared to agree to the kidnappers' demands."

"The Mayor didn't say that!" snapped Hungerford,
snatching his cigarette holder from his mouth.

"I know he didn't. But I'm a policeman, like you, Commissioner – I don't have to have things spelled out for me. I
don't care a bugger about your anarchists – all I want is to
get my wife back!"

"If you are a policeman, you'll realize the consequences."
Then Hungerford stopped and looked towards the door as
there was a knock and a small dark-haired man looked in.

"Joe Burgmann is here, Mr Mayor."

"Bring him in, Manny." Michael Forte was still standing
by his father; he suddenly put a hand on the old man's
shoulder and squeezed it; but Sam Forte's expression did
not change. Michael then went back behind his desk as the
small dark-haired man, dapper as a head-waiter, brought
in a burly man with thinning grey hair and hard bright eyes.
They were introduced to Malone as Manny Pearl and Joe
Burgmann.

Burgmann looked Malone over cursorily, decided he was
no voter, and turned back to Michael Forte. "Manny's put

me in the picture, Mr Mayor. Jesus, I can't say how sorry I am – " Malone caught the swift glance from Michael Forte, but there was no flicker of expression otherwise on the Mayor's face. "It's a real dilemma, a real dilemma. Anyone come up with any suggestions?"

"None so far, Joe."

"I have," said Malone. "I've suggested you give in to them. My wife – and yours too, Mr Mayor – are more valuable than a bunch of anarchists, no matter what they've done."

Burgmann had not turned round, just looked over his shoulder at Malone as if not interested in any comment from *that* ward: Malone was to learn in a moment who the burly man was and how he thought. "That's easy for you to say – "

"Nothing is easy for me to say," snapped Malone, "not when my wife's life is in danger."

"Okay, Joe – " Michael Forte motioned to Burgmann, then looked at Malone. "Mr Burgmann is my campaign manager – you know we have an election coming up to-morrow. I've always been a strong proponent – perhaps *too* strong – of law and order, but in tomorrow's election my principal opponent has chosen to make an issue of it. If I agree to the ransom demand – as you say, Inspector, you're a cop, you don't have to have things spelled out for you."

"Maybe I do," Malone said slowly. He knew now why he had sensed the atmosphere of politics as soon as he had entered the room; he had just not identified the correct strain of the virus. "What's more important to you – your political reputation or getting your wife back?"

At once there was an angry murmur from several of the men. Michael Forte stiffened, his face flushed and one hand balled into a fist. Malone poised himself, wondering if he had gone too far but determined not to back down. Then Sam Forte, a veteran of such moments, spoke for the first time.

"Inspector Malone has asked the proper question, I think. There will be a lot of people, Michael, asking where you stand on law and order when you're confronted with this – this dilemma. All you've said in the past will look pretty hollow if – "

Malone looked gratefully at the old man; but Sam Forte ignored him. Christ, Malone suddenly realized, I don't mean a thing to him: he's only intent on protecting the bloody image of his son! He had an abrupt urge to spin round and stride right out of the building, but he knew that would achieve nothing. If he was to get Lisa back safely, he needed these men in this room. All at once he felt more ragingly helpless than he had ever felt in his life before.

Then Manny Pearl said, "The reporters have guessed there's something wrong, Mr Mayor. I think you'll have to make a statement."

Michael Forte looked at Hungerford and Cartwright. "Will that endanger the lives of my wife and Mrs Malone, do you think?"

"Did the woman who called you say anything about *not* telling the papers?" asked Cartwright.

"No. Come to think of it, she didn't even say anything about not telling the police. That's one of their usual demands, isn't it?"

"Most kidnappers hope we'll be kept out of it. Telling the newspapers may result in these people thinking the pressure is being increased on them, but that is a risk we have to take, Mr Mayor." Cartwright then looked at Malone. He felt sorry for the Australian, who looked angry and bewildered by what must sound to him like a lot of empty, delaying talk. But maybe things were simpler in Australia: Cartwright already sensed the complications ahead, coming up like the hurricane from the South. "Do you agree, Inspector?"

Malone, his emotion under control again, thought, Here's one bloke who's on my side. "If we have no real clues of our own, then we may have to rely on the public, hope there's an outside chance that someone saw something that will help us."

He's a worried husband but he hasn't forgotten how to be

a cop, Cartwright thought. He turned again to Michael Forte, who looked just as worried but less decisive than the Australian. Is he the sort of man who'd panic when the chips were down? He'd make a hell of a President if he is. But then how many Presidents have been faced with a personal dilemma like this? A real dilemma, as the voting machine that went by the name of Burgmann had said.

"I think we may need the newspapers, sir. If Commissioner Hungerford agrees, I think you should make a statement."

"What do I do? Just issue a statement or call the reporters in here?"

"If I can make a suggestion, Mr Mayor, I think you should have 'em in here, right in here." Burgmann, Malone was beginning to realize, was an important man in this room; he showed some deference to Michael Forte himself, but none at all to the other men, least of all to Malone. "Some of these guys have been very much against us the past coupla months – they oughta be given the chance to see how you're suffering in this dilemma."

"Joe, I don't want to have to answer a lot of questions – "

"Okay, no questions. Just a statement. Where's some paper?"

Malone felt his anger rising again; he wanted to smash his fist into the face of the campaign manager. But Burgmann was a man whose job didn't allow him to consider what other people thought of *him*: his sole concern was to promote his candidate. He scribbled in a large hand on two sheets of paper, never stopping to grope for a word, then handed the statement to Michael Forte.

"Okay?"

But without waiting for any assent from the Mayor, he had already moved to the door, opened it and told the secretary outside to bring in the newspapermen. They came trooping in, five reporters and two photographers, all of them with that mixture of boredom and alertness that Malone had seen on the faces of newspapermen back home who had to cover the same beat day after day. They seemed to suggest that news was no more than a necessary evil, that they felt the world would be better off if its ignorance was not reduced by anything they might write.

"Gentlemen, I have some bad news – bad, that is, for Inspector Malone and myself – " Michael Forte introduced Malone, then baldly and without emotion read out the statement.

Shock replaced the boredom on the newspapermen's faces; but they were all veterans and they soon recovered. Shock was grist to their mill and they reacted as Malone had expected them to. As they moved in on the Mayor, Malone wanted to turn away, get out of this room before his disgust, anger and frustration made him erupt.

"Where'd it happen, Mr Mayor? What time?"

"That ransom, Mr Mayor – how does that tie in with your concept of law and order?"

Michael Forte's jaw tightened, but all he said was, "No questions. Not at this stage."

"It's been a terrible shock to the Mayor," said Burgmann. "Come on, boys. We'll fill you in later – "

"How do you feel about the ransom demand, Inspector?" Everyone in the room looked at Malone as one of the reporters put the question. "As a cop, you must be concerned for law and order."

Malone felt the floor suddenly rumble beneath him. He looked down in puzzlement, then Michael Forte said, "It's just a subway train, Inspector. City Hall isn't going to fall down."

Malone looked up, staring hard at the Mayor. He didn't know whether any of the newspapermen read the message in the words, but he quite clearly understood what Michael Forte meant. *Tell the truth if you like, Malone, we don't need you. But you sure as hell need us.*

"I'm a stranger in this city," said Malone. "I have to take the advice of Mayor Forte."

Out of the corner of his eye he saw the relief on the faces

of Burgmann and Manny Pearl; but he was still looking at Michael Forte. For a moment the Mayor all at once seemed another man; the dark eyes softened and Malone suddenly realized that Forte was not solely and unalterably a political animal. For the first time the two men looked at each other with the recognition that no one else here could feel the pain and worry that was common to them both.

"Commissioner Hungerford has every available man in the Police Department already at work," Burgmann was saying to the reporters, "aided, of course, by the FBI – "

But not aided by me, the one law and order officer in this room who has the most to lose. Again the explosive anger brought on by frustration simmered in Malone. He could not be expected to sit on his arse while other cops worked on this – *his* case. He had to do something to get Lisa back – but what?

3

"That's Alexander Hamilton up there," said Michael Forte, nodding up at the portrait hanging above the mantelpiece. "Have you heard of him?"

"Vaguely." Malone munched on his roast beef sandwich, looking up without interest at the painting. Hamilton stood with one hand on hip, the other held out in front of him, palm upwards. Was he putting a point or asking for a pay-off? But Malone kept his cynicism to himself; his sudden sourness with America wasn't going to be any help in the situation in which he found himself. "He was something to do with the American Revolution, wasn't he?"

Forte put down his half-eaten sandwich and pushed it away from him: he had no taste and no hunger, like a man who had gone beyond the recovery point in starvation. His only sustenance was words, to keep him from thinking of the worst. "We Americans assume that everyone knows our national heroes."

"Australians don't go in for national heroes, not political ones. Bushrangers and jockeys stand the best chance."

"Bushrangers?"

"Old-time outlaws. Ned Kelly was the best known. I've had crims I've arrested bless themselves and say prayers to him."

Forte wasn't sure if the Australian was putting him on; he had a laconic dryness to him that could have been poker-faced humour or morose hostility. Forte nodded back at the painting. "That was painted posthumously – Old Alex finished up the loser in a duel with another of our heroes, Aaron Burr. Or maybe neither of them was a hero, except to their campaign managers. You have no time for Joe Burgmann, have you?"

The abruptness of the question caught Malone off guard; he took delaying refuge behind his coffee cup. Unexpectedly Forte, when the meeting had been breaking up, had invited him to stay behind and share a sandwiches-and-coffee lunch; and Malone, intrigued now by this man with whom he had to share a common anguish, had accepted. He had not expected to be called upon to answer leading questions such as this one.

"In these circumstances, no," he said at last.

Forte stared down at the red carpet beneath his feet. He and Malone were sitting on chairs at one side of the room, a low table between them and a television set against the wall opposite them. On the table, beside the tray of sandwiches and coffee, were copies of the morning papers and the first edition of the afternoon *Post*. He smiled up at himself from each of the front pages: yesterday's man. The photograph that would be in the later editions of the *Post* and in the *Times* and *News* tomorrow morning would be of a worried, more honest man.

"You have to try to understand him, Inspector. I don't think Joe is without feelings – he has a wife and kids and I'm sure he loves them. But all his life he's been in politics – he began when he was still in high school, running messages for a ward boss. He sees everything in terms of votes."

"I wouldn't want to understand him," said Malone stubbornly, "if that's the way he is."

Forte sighed, then looked up. "What's your wife like? You didn't tell the reporters much. How long have you been married?"

"Eight weeks."

"Then you're still getting to know her, aren't you? I've been married eighteen years – I have two kids, a boy sixteen and a girl fourteen. I don't know which is worse – to lose someone you've become accustomed to or someone you're still finding out about."

"You think we're going to lose them?" Malone had put down his own sandwich and now put down his coffee.

"Jesus, I don't know!" Forte put his hand over his eyes and for a moment Malone thought the other man was going to weep.

Then there was a tap on the door and Manny Pearl came in. He was a sad-eyed little man who seemed to wear his smile as a badge of rank: it was his job to keep his boss happy. Malone was not quite sure what Pearl's official title was, but it was obvious that he had Forte's trust. He waited patiently and without embarrassment till the Mayor had recovered his composure, then he said, "The news is already on TV and radio. Just flashes, nothing more. All the networks have been on to me asking if you'd do a spot for their main news shows tonight, but I took it upon myself to say No. Okay?"

Forte nodded, then looked at Malone. "You don't want to be bothered by them, do you?"

"No. I don't think they're interested in me, anyway." Then he stopped.

"I'm not offended, Inspector. If anyone has the right to be offended, it's you." Again there was the glance of recognition between them, then Forte looked back at Pearl. "What else is happening, Manny?"

"I've taken some phone calls for you. A few people, some organizations. Gerry Farrelly called with a message from the Knights of Columbus. He read it out as if he was saving the price of a telegram. *We shall pray for you today and vote for you tomorrow.* I thanked him on both counts."

"I'm a lapsed atheist," Forte told Malone; for the first time he showed a trace of humour. "You might say I've been reconverted by three million Catholic voters – they got me back into the Church quicker than the Vatican ever could. With a name like Malone, are you a Catholic?"

"My Old Lady says I am. Until I married, when she still did my ironing for me, she used to damp my shirts with holy water." But Malone grinned this time and Forte learned a little more about the man opposite him: at least he seemed to have a sense of humour. "I don't know that she pressed much faith back into me. Except in the last hour and a half I've noticed I've been doing some praying."

"Me too." As if to relieve the slight embarrassment of his confession, Forte looked up at Pearl and smiled. "Manny is trying to get me on the side of Judaism, too."

"Over a million voters in New York alone," said Pearl, but he couldn't manage a smile and he gave up. "Sorry. It's not funny, is it? Jokes aren't gonna help."

Malone wondered if Lisa, wherever she was, was finding anything funny. He tried to remember how she had looked when she had gone out of the hotel: he could not remember what she had been wearing, but yes, she had been smiling, but it had been with love not humour. Abruptly he said, "Christ, do we have to sit here and do *nothing*!"

"What can we do?" But Forte got up and illustrated his own frustration by moving restlessly about the room. "I have to stay here for that next phone call. Did you cancel all my appointments for this afternoon, Manny?"

"Not all." All his life Manny Pearl had had an adjustable focus on the world: sometimes you took the long view, but you also played every moment as it came. Nothing was ever gained by cancelling appointments well in advance that could be cancelled at the last moment. "I've cancelled everything up till four o'clock. At four you are supposed to shake hands with the United Nations delegation that is looking over City Hall – "

"Jesus, do I have to do that?"

"It seemed to me the least demanding of your appointments. It will show you are carrying on with your job."

"Always the goddam image! You disappoint me sometimes, Manny."

"I'm sure I do," said Pearl, unruffled; and went on, "At four-thirty you were supposed to start touring the campaign offices, thanking your workers for what they've done for you. I'll just send out a message to each of the ward captains in your name. I hate to say it, but we can't postpone the election tomorrow."

"I could withdraw my name – " But the threat was half-hearted and Forte knew it. So, too, did Malone and Manny Pearl.

"What's the point, Mike?" Pearl suddenly stepped out of the role of personal assistant, became a friend, looked twice as worried. "Sylvia could be back with you this evening – and your wife, too, Inspector – " Pearl was not being diplomatically polite when he glanced at Malone; his sad eyes were too full of honest sympathy. "I think we have to be optimistic – "

Sharp at three o'clock the phone rang. By then Sam Forte, Hungerford and Cartwright had returned. They came in individually, with the air of men come back to hear a doctor's diagnosis that they feared. Michael Forte took the phone.

"Who are you? It was a woman who called this morning."

"We're partners – don't worry which one of us makes the calls, Mr Forte." There was a chuckle at the other end of the line, almost a giggle. The woman this morning had been soft-voiced, almost polite; but this man's voice had a ragged edge to it and Forte heard danger. "The message is the same, you hear? We want those five guys outa The Tombs soon's you like to let 'em go. You made up your mind what you gonna do?"

"I can't release them at once – there's a legal procedure we have to go through." Hungerford, listening on an extension, gestured to him to keep talking. In the outer office police technicians were taping the conversation and trying to trace the call. Forte tried to keep talking, to keep the kidnapper on the line: "You gave us till nine o'clock tomorrow morning. How is my wife – can I speak to her?"

"No, man, you can't." There was a note of grating satisfaction in the man's voice. He's already chewing on small triumphs, Forte thought: how is he going to celebrate if this thing goes through to the climax he wants? The question, unanswerable, had its own terror. "Is that guy Malone there with you? Let me talk to him."

Forte motioned to the Australian, handed him the phone. "Malone here."

"Your wife says you're a cop. Right? I'd sooner deal with someone else, but this time I'm not gonna hold it against you. You're just lucky, man, you ain't American – but pigs are the same all over. Listen – you tell the Mayor he's not gonna see his wife again and you're not gonna see yours, unless he lets those guys outa The Tombs. Right? That's all for now. There'll be just one more call from us."

"What time? Where – here?"

There was a chuckle, a gritty sound Malone did not like. "We'll find you. Nobody's gonna be more available than you and the Mayor. You just expect to hear from us. And pass on that message to the Mayor. We don't want to hurt your missus, but we got her and she's in the same boat now as Mrs Forte. It could get awful rough for her."

Chapter Three

The room was small but comfortably furnished; Lisa knew, from what Scobie had told her, that prison cells were a good deal less comfortable than this. Yet this was her and Sylvia Forte's cell. There was a white carpet square on the polished floorboards, two Colonial-style single beds, a chest of drawers and a dressing-table in the same style, a built-in wardrobe with louvred doors, two easy chairs with blue denim covers and an electric convector heater that stood against one wall. It was a room that Lisa guessed was similar to thousands of others all over America. Except for two things: the window was boarded up from the inside and three pictures had been removed from the walls, leaving oblong shapes that were slightly cleaner than the rest of the white wallpaper.

"We're in a cottage of some sort, I think," said Sylvia Forte. "I used to have a room very much like this in a house we had on Fishers Island."

"I wonder why the pictures were taken off the walls?"

"I don't know. Unless they were pictures that would have identified those two outside."

They had been in the room an hour and they had become accustomed to their surroundings. At first, recovering from delayed shock at what had happened to them, they had hardly spoken. After their initial words to each other in the back of the delivery truck, they had fallen silent as they had slowly begun to appreciate the frightening potential of their predicament. Their growing apprehension had not been slowed by the sullenness of the girl in the back of the truck with them. As she had stared at them it seemed to Lisa that behind and below the dark glasses the girl's face had hardened into a mask that showed no hint of mercy for them.

After three-quarters of an hour's travelling the truck had slowed, turned and pulled up. Lisa and Sylvia heard the driver get down, then a few moments later he came back, got into the truck and drove it into a garage or large shed. Lisa had found herself listening for sounds of identification that she had never taken notice of before: the amplification of the noise of the engine as the truck drove up a narrow driveway between two houses, the opening and then the shutting of garage doors, the sudden silence in the garage as the engine was shut off, and then the shouts of children somewhere outside.

The back doors of the truck were opened and Abel, smiling widely, looked in at Carole. "So far so good. You make the phone call, while I look after these two."

Carole got out of the truck, stumbling a little as she stretched her cramped legs. Abel steadied her, looking at her solicitously. "Careful."

"I'm all right." She kissed his cheek, put her gun back in her handbag and slipped cautiously out of a side door of the two-car garage. As Abel had said, so far so good. But the real reward was going to be from now on.

Abel gestured to Sylvia Forte and Lisa. They got out of the truck, both of them stumbling a little as Carole had done; but Abel made no attempt to steady them, just pushed them up against the side of the second delivery truck, a black one, parked in the garage. He wanted to spit on the two women, to humble and degrade them, but he feared that might only provoke an argument with Carole. And that he could not bear.

He opened the back doors of the black truck, took out two white hoods. "Join the Ku Klux Klan."

Lisa and Sylvia took the hoods, hesitated, then slipped them over their heads. There were no eyeholes, but a hole had been cut in the material at mouth level and Lisa found she was able to breathe quite easily. The young man moved close to her, tightening the slip-cord round her neck. She could feel the heat of his body, from excitement or anger, and when his hand touched the skin of her neck she felt the sweat on it. She tried to pull away, but he tightened the cord round her throat.

"I'm not gonna hurt you," Abel said gently. Carole had taught him how to be gentle with a woman and there were odd moments when a sort of rough charm, that he himself had never suspected he had, came out of him. "You just behave and we'll get along fine."

He moved away from her to Sylvia Forte. The latter was standing quite still, but as soon as Abel touched her her hands flew up to push him off.

"Keep still!" There was no gentle charm in him now; his voice was a hard snarl. "It wouldn't take much to make me pull this cord real tight!"

Lisa put out a hand, groping blindly, found Sylvia's hand and held it. They clung to each other, strangers who suddenly needed each other.

They were bundled into the back of the black truck, then they heard the girl come back into the garage, closing the side door after her.

"I spoke to him," Lisa heard her say. "The next call to him is three o'clock this afternoon. You can make that."

"It'll be a pleasure. Let's go."

The girl got into the back of the truck and the doors were closed. A minute later they were back on the road, moving more quickly now as if there was less traffic to hold up the truck. Lisa, sitting close to Sylvia Forte, felt the other woman reach for her hand again, felt the fingers digging into her palm.

"Don't worry, Mrs Forte." Carole sat watching the women with cold amusement. For the past hour she had felt uneasy; she had never done anything like this before, never even broken the law in a minor way, and it was not in her nature to get a thrill out of what they were doing. She had planned the whole project right down to the smallest detail, but because she could remember every detail she knew how many things could go wrong if there was the slightest accident. The only accident so far had been Mrs Malone, but she might prove to be a bonus. The climax of the operation had been reached when she had spoken to Mayor Forte himself and told him her terms. From now on the show was to be enjoyed, for she had no doubt that the Mayor would agree to her demands. He had no alternative.

"I'm suffocating in this thing – "

"No, you're not. Just relax and you can breathe quite easily through that hole. I tried it myself."

"It's not the breathing. I suffer from claustrophobia – " Lisa could feel the nails digging into her, knew Sylvia's growing panic was not faked.

"You'll just have to put up with it," said Carole. "I'd have thought a woman in your position would be accustomed to claustrophobia. All those hangers-on you find in politics – don't they crush the life out of you?"

Sylvia made a strenuous effort to relax; Lisa could feel the paradoxical tension in the hand in hers as the Mayor's wife tried to regain control of herself. "They don't try to blind one – "

"That's a debatable point," said Carole. "But in our case it's necessary. When we get out of this truck you're going to be out in the open for a moment or two – I don't want you to recognize where you are."

"Am I likely to?"

Carole smiled to herself; though they could not see her, both Lisa and Sylvia *heard* the smile in her reply: "Probably not. It isn't your territory, Mrs Forte. But I can't take any chances."

Sylvia was silent; Lisa could feel the tension slowly draining out of the other woman's hand. Then: "I heard you say you had spoken to *him*. Was that my husband?"

"Yes. I told him our terms and if he agrees to them you will be back with him by tomorrow afternoon. Maybe before."

"What are your terms? How much are you asking for us?"

"Money, you mean? None at all. All we want are five

other people in exchange for you, that's all. Two for five, that's a bargain in these inflationary days."

"Who are the five people?"

"Five men held in The Tombs. Parker, McBean, Fishman, Ratelli and Latrobe – " Carole knew the names as well as she knew her own, even the one name among them that she knew was an alias.

Lisa felt Sylvia's hand stiffen again, but she made no reply. The truck sped along; faintly through the partition that backed the driving compartment there came the sound of a radio. It was the housewives' hour, a time for romance and nostalgia: Perry Como, a voice from the past, sang of the past: housewives dreamed with him over their kitchen sinks and their unmade beds. All one had to do, an everyday feat, was catch a falling star.

Then at last the truck had arrived at its destination. As they had got out of the truck Lisa had felt a rising wind, smelled salt on the air. They had been hustled out of the garage into which the truck had been driven and quickly across a small yard into the cottage; Lisa had felt sand and short spiky grass beneath her shoes. But she had heard no sound of traffic, no cries of children, no radios playing. Wherever they were, their surroundings seemed to be deserted.

When they had been pushed into this room where they were now, they had been enclosed in the hoods for almost two hours; when the hoods had been removed it had taken them almost half a minute to accustom themselves to even the dim, shaded light hanging from the ceiling. Lisa had felt giddy for a moment and had sat down on one of the beds.

"You all right?" She had been surprised at the sudden solicitude in the girl's voice.

She nodded. "I'd like a glass of water."

The girl went out, locking the door behind her, and Lisa, all at once weak and frightened, lay back on the bed. Sylvia walked once round the room, almost like a woman trying to make up her mind whether to stay or to leave; then suddenly she stopped by the other bed and fell on it, face down. Lisa turned her head, but said nothing. For the moment the two women were separated by a greater gap than the distance between the two beds; each was concerned only with herself, afraid and selfish for her own safety. Pity was suddenly one's own mirror.

Then Carole came back with two glasses of water. "I'll make you some lunch soon. It won't be much, but then this isn't Gracie Mansion."

Sylvia did not move, continued to lie face down on the bed. Lisa got up, took both glasses of water and put them on the dressing-table. Carole stared down at Sylvia, then abruptly she went out of the room, slamming the door hard and locking it again. As soon as she was gone Sylvia rolled over and sat up.

Lisa handed her one of the glasses of water. "Do you think we are going to gain anything by ignoring her?"

"I'm trying to get myself straightened out. I'm afraid just now that I'll try to hit her if she speaks to me again. And that might be dangerous for us – for you as well as me."

Lisa looked at her with interest. "Despite the red hair, you don't strike me as the sort of woman who'd have a temper."

"Oh, I have," said Sylvia. She sipped the water, seemed to be much more relaxed now. "Or *had*. I've been controlling it for years – though there have been times when I've been tempted to let fly. At some of those hangers-on that girl mentioned." For the first time Lisa saw her smile; it was an attractive smile that took some of the cool severity out of the beautiful face. "I was a brat as a child. My daughter has the same temper – though I hope she is not a brat." The smile died and her eyes appeared to cloud over. "I hope she and Roger, that's my son, don't worry too much."

"They will," said Lisa. "So will our husbands. Poor Scobie, he will – " Then she turned away, almost on the point of tears: she felt the pain of love as tangibly as if she had just been hit a solid blow.

The door opened again and Carole came in with the two women's handbags. "I had to check you had nothing lethal in them. I've taken out your nail files, but everything else except your cigarettes and lighters is there. I'm afraid there'll be no smoking while you're here, just in case you get some ideas about burning the house down."

"A cigarette would help steady my nerves," said Sylvia.

"I didn't think you had any," said Carole. "Try a little yoga or something. Aren't you president of the Make America Healthy movement?"

Lisa turned round, recovered again. "I'd like a wash. I feel sweaty and dirty after being in that hood."

"Later. But don't start asking for too much, Mrs Malone. I'm not your servant."

"I didn't suggest you were." Lisa felt more composed, though still apprehensive; it was not going to help her own or her captors' nerves to be at loggerheads with them all the time. "Mrs Forte and I will be more satisfied – *guests*, if you like to call us that – if we can feel clean and comfortable."

Carole twisted her lips beneath the dark glasses, then smiled ruefully. "You have your nerve, Mrs Malone. Do Australians always demand such service when they're – *guests*?"

"I'm only Australian by adoption. It's the Dutch in me that you're talking to now."

"The Dutch were imperialists, just like the British. Those days are over, Mrs Malone." Carole turned quickly and went out of the room.

"I've been accused of a lot of things," said Lisa, "but never before of being an imperialist."

"I'm of Dutch extraction. My family came here in 1660."

Lisa made no comment, but she thought that the extraction by now must be pretty tenuous; she wondered if the American Pretoriouses, if there were any, looked back that far to Marken, the island village where the name was still heard and respected.

"Where do you think we are?"

"I think we're on Long Island somewhere, probably a long way out. I smelled the salt air as we came in."

"Are they likely to find us here? The police, I mean."

"I doubt it. Unless we try to attract attention somehow – " She looked inquiringly at Lisa.

Lisa shook her head. "I don't want to be a heroine – not yet."

"Neither do I," said Sylvia, and sounded relieved. "But I'm worried for my husband. I hope he believes I'm still all right."

Lisa suddenly sat down on the bed. Did Scobie know by now that she had been kidnapped? She looked at her watch; he would be back at the hotel, waiting for her, wondering what had happened to her because she was always so punctual. She lay back on the bed, sick for him and afraid, as if he were in more danger than herself. The two women lapsed into silence and it was another half-hour before they spoke to each other again. It was then that Lisa, still lying on the bed, had made a comment about their prison cell.

"Do you think this might be that girl's home?"

"Her summer home, perhaps."

"What about the boy?"

"He has me puzzled. He's not her – *class*, if you like. Would you think so?"

"I don't know I've always been taught that America is a classless society, though I don't believe that."

"It isn't," said Sylvia with an almost arrogant lack of apology; she had never seen any virtue in egalitarianism. "That girl has had the advantage of *some* money – and she's obviously educated. But the boy – " She shook her head. "I've been trying to put my finger on his accent. It's not New York. Though perhaps it is – " She looked at Lisa, said, with still no attempt at apology or false democracy, "I don't meet too many like him, not even as the Mayor's wife."

"I don't like him," said Lisa, and shuddered. "I wonder what she sees in him?"

"Politics make strange bedfellows," said Sylvia, and

thought of the dormitory of disparate characters and egos in City Hall. "An old but very true cliché."

2

Carole sat in the living-room of the cottage fighting hard against the memories that pressed in on her like the revived symptoms of a long dormant disease. She had made a mistake in choosing this place as their hide-out, but nowhere else had seemed better. And perhaps subconsciously, she thought, there had been the desire for the sense of security afforded by the familiar. She had lived for too long in limbo.

She had taken off the dark glasses and the wig, and the removal of the disguise, simple though it was, only served to identify her more with this room. She rubbed her eyes, wondering if she should put the glasses back on. Here, away from the curious gaze of the two women in the bedroom, she did not need the camouflage. But they did help to cloud the past, to dim the memories that distracted her.

She looked at her watch, wondering how much longer Abel would be. Perhaps she had made a mistake in letting him go to make the second call to Mayor Forte; but she knew his temperament, or thought she did, and knew he thought of himself as her equal partner in this job. Job: it sounded a mundane word for an act of revenge. But she had been determined all along that she would not allow her approach to the . . . the *job* . . . to become overheated. Coolness had always been her forte (she giggled like a schoolgirl; how would Michael Forte like that?) and she knew the value of it. One didn't wait four years to avenge your husband's death and then blow it all by letting anger and rhetoric, the faults that Roy himself had never been able to contain, spoil the execution of it.

Abel should be arriving back within the next ten minutes. They had timed the trip three times; she had been surprised how much pleasure she had got out of planning the details of the operation. (Operation: that was a better word. She would use it in future, even if it might make her sound like a female general.) She could recite every detail even in reverse order; she had overlooked nothing. She just hoped that Mayor Forte would overlook nothing in the part of the operation that she had assigned to him. She was not going to enjoy killing the two women in the next room, even though their deaths might be forced on her. A memory shook her, Roy lying lifeless in her arms, and she got up quickly, desperate for something that would distract her.

Then she heard the car drive up beside the cottage, heard Abel get out, open the garage doors and drive the car in. Then he was letting himself in the back door and she went out into the kitchen to greet him, clutching at him with an eagerness that surprised and delighted him.

"It's all *right*, baby." He held her to him, kissed her brow. He took off his dark glasses, was once again amazed at how beautiful she was and that she had chosen him from among a dozen guys who would have let her trample over them. "No trouble at all. It's gonna rain, though."

"Just the edge of the storm." She could hear the wind blowing through the stunted trees that surrounded the house, the trees that her father had kept because he valued privacy and which she was now thankful for. "We'll be all right."

She kissed him, ashamed of herself. He would never know what a poor substitute he was for Roy, that when this was over she was going to disappear from his life; but he had been the only man she had met in four years whom she felt she could trust. But she wondered if in their love-making he sometimes became aware of her remoteness, if he realized that the fierceness of her passion at times was no more than a disguise like the dark glasses and the wig.

"Did you talk to Forte himself?"

Abel nodded, still enjoying having her in his arms; he would hold her forever like this if she would let him, not even wanting to screw her, just hold her. "And the other

72

guy – Malone. Forte was hedging, playing for time, but I let him know we're not gonna be fu – " She shook her head and he grinned. "Messed up."

"You kept it cool?"

He leaned away from her, hurt. "Baby, trust me. I'm not gonna spoil it for us, you know that."

"I'm sorry." She kissed him again, gently disengaged herself from his arms. "You dumped the truck okay?"

"In Flushing. It could stand there in the street for a week before anyone looks at it. Nobody's gonna trace it to us. You're not starting to worry, are you?"

Carole smiled, shook her head. They had been extremely careful about the vehicles they had used in the operation. A week ago, on successive nights, Abel had stolen the two trucks and brought them to the house with the two-car garage she had rented in Jamaica. Her own car, with its Missouri plates, had been left in a garage in Flushing; Abel had picked it up from there this afternoon when he had dumped the black truck. The grey truck, minus plates, was still in the garage at the house in Jamaica, but she had rented the house under a false name and she would never be going back there. In less than twenty-four hours everything would be over, one way or another, and they would be on their way, leaving not a clue behind. Leaving the last remnant of her life behind too.

"How're they?" Abel nodded towards the bedroom door. "I think we better feed them now."

"Why bother?" But he saw the sudden stiffening in her face and he grinned quickly. He had taken off his blond wig and under his own dark hair his thin face looked older, the blue eyes warily sensitive to changes in feeling towards himself. The grin revived the boyish look and he was relieved when she smiled back at him. He kissed her cheek. "I was just joking. What'll we give 'em?"

Carole busied herself with cans, making a noise with them as if trying to exorcise the ghosts that had been troubling her over the past hour.

"Lobster soup – why the hell did I buy that?"

Abel showed a glimpse of the shrewdness that had attracted her in the first place, that had made her think of him as a possible accomplice; but sometimes he could be embarrassingly shrewd: "Looks like you're trying to prove to Mrs Forte that you're as good as she is. You don't have to, baby. You're better."

She looked at him curiously, catching a reflection of herself in his words that was another reminder of her parents: their influence was still with her. "You really think so? Why should I want to do that?"

He hesitated before replying. "Baby, I don't know anything about you – " Again there was the stiffening in her face, and he held up a placatory hand. "Okay, I *know* – you'll tell me all that in your own time. But I'm not blind – you don't come from the same sorta neighbourhood I do. You've had – *privileges*. You belong to the sorta people I been hating all my life."

"Do you hate me for that?"

He touched her jawline tenderly with one finger. "I'll never hate you – for *any* reason. But that don't say you've forgotten where you came from – all *this*." He waved a hand at their surroundings. "When you were a girl here, it meant something to you, didn't it, that your mom put on a party as good as your friends threw? Am I right?"

It was her turn to hesitate, then she nodded. "Some day I'll tell you all about it."

They put on their dark glasses and wigs again, smiling at each other as they did so: they were still new enough to the game to be amused by parts of it. They took in soup, sandwiches and coffee to the two women in the bedroom. Sylvia, ear pressed to the door, had heard the conversation that had gone on out in the kitchen; the cottage was not large and the walls were thin. As soon as the door was opened, Sylvia said to Abel, "Did you talk to my husband?"

Abel nodded. "He didn't say much, but it seems like he

isn't hurrying himself. Maybe you're not the number one priority."

"I don't believe that!" Sylvia turned her back, her face going white and taut. Then after a moment she said, "Put the tray over there."

There was a rattle of cups and saucers as the tray shook in Abel's hands, but Carole put a restraining hand on his arm. She shook her head at him, then said, "Don't start giving orders, Mrs Forte. I've warned you once. You keep on this way and you'll get no food at all. It doesn't matter to us whether you're fed or not."

Sylvia still had her back turned. "That's up to you. I am not going to kow-tow to you."

"Kow-tow? Is that what you get when you go down to Chinatown soliciting votes for your husband, patting all the kids on the head, being Mrs Goody Two Shoes?"

Lisa, standing by her bed, watched the three Americans; this was not her war. She wanted to take the tray from Abel, usher him and the girl out of the room, placate Sylvia Forte; but she sensed that all three might turn on her. Outsiders were never welcome in a civil war.

"You're very different from your public image, aren't you?" Carole had taken over the baiting, aroused in her turn by Sylvia Forte's arrogance. "All that devotion to good works, all that bit about wanting to show New Yorkers their heritage –'

Sylvia turned back slowly, looked the two kidnappers up and down. Oh God, Lisa thought, don't start fighting them, just let them go! "Do you belong to the Weathermen?"

"I belong to nobody but myself," said Carole, suddenly stiff with her own cold dignity.

"And to me, baby," said Abel.

Carole relaxed, smiled. "And to you."

Lisa, watching Sylvia's face, waited for some sarcastic remark; but Sylvia was not stupid, knew the right moment when to concede. She moved away, sat down in a chair and put a hand over her eyes, borrowing Michael's strategy. It was a strategic withdrawal, not a surrender. She would never kow-tow to these people, but she realized nothing was to be gained by antagonizing them. The boy might be provoked into blind anger and that might be dangerous. The girl would remain cold and nothing would alter the course she had planned for herself. The horrifying discovery was that she had glimpsed something of herself in the girl. They both knew what they wanted.

Then Lisa said quietly, "May we have the tray? We're both very hungry."

Carole looked at her for the first time. "You sound as if you are going to be sensible, Mrs Malone."

"How is my husband? Does he know that I'm here?"

"He's okay," said Abel. "He understands what's happening. He's not gonna be any trouble."

"I didn't think he would be." Lisa smiled with rueful irony; but the image of Scobie was in her mind and she smiled also with love. "He's like me. All we want is to go home."

Sylvia lowered her hand from her face and looked up. "Why don't you let Mrs Malone go? You don't want her."

"No, that's right," said Carole. "And I'm sorry we had to bring you here, Mrs Malone." She looked at Lisa, at the innocent stranger who would have to die tomorrow if the ransom demands were not met, and felt sick and sad. Violence had its own impetus: that had killed Roy. And as soon as she thought of him all pity for anyone else, stranger or not, disappeared. Abruptly she went out of the room, saying as she went, "Your husband had just better work on the Mayor, that's all."

Abel stared at the two women, his face bony and hard behind the dark glasses, then he went out, locking the door again. The wind had risen and they could hear it rattling the shutters outside the boarded-up windows, like some beast trying to get in at them.

"They're going to kill us," said Sylvia.

Chapter Four

Malone got out of the police car, waited for Jefferson to ease his bulk out of it. "We could've walked over here," said Jefferson, "but I gotta keep in touch on the radio, just in case. Stick around, Stan. Anyone wants to give you a ticket, tell him you know a cop."

"I'll do that, Captain," said the driver with the tired smile of a man who had listened too long to tired jokes.

Malone had been looking about him, at the towering block of the Manhattan House of Detention, The Tombs as it was called, above him, at the shabby bail bond shops across the narrow street. The shops surprised him. He hadn't known what to expect, perhaps upstairs offices with small brass signs by their doors: the shops, with large signs painted across their windows, somehow reminded him of pawn-shops. But of course that was what they were, shops where men pawned their liberty.

A figure went by, long-haired and covered from neck to ankles in a huge shaggy fur coat. Jefferson looked after it and Malone said, "What do you do? Root it or shoot it?"

"I dunno, I try not to be too square, but I guess I got old-fashioned eyes or something. I have to keep *telling* myself to accept 'em, that they're today and I'm just a bit of yesterday that's left over." As they crossed the sidewalk he said, "I hope I did the right thing in asking you if you wanted to come over here with me."

"It's better than sitting on my bum back at the hotel."

"That's what I thought."

After the second phone call to Forte's office and the subsequent discussion which had been only words going in circles, Malone had wanted to escape from the ornate room and the stifling atmosphere brought in by the men who surrounded Michael Forte. He had realized that the Mayor himself had wanted to escape, if only back into his official routine. Malone could not understand why the kidnappers' demands could not be met at once, but he knew he would get no answer to such a question if he asked it in the company the Mayor kept. He would have to wait till he was alone with Michael Forte again. But then he would not make it a question: it would be a demand.

He had come out of the Mayor's room escorted by Manny Pearl. "I suggested to the Mayor that it might be better – for you, for all of us – if you moved out of your hotel and went up to Gracie Mansion."

"I'll think about it," said Malone.

"It would save you from being pestered by the press. And – " He glanced at Malone, wondering how sensitive the Australian was. "And maybe you and the Mayor can be of some comfort to each other."

"He would be more comforting if he agreed to release those blokes you are holding."

Then John Jefferson had come down the carpeted corridor to them. "I'll take the Inspector off your hands, Mr Pearl. I'm on my way over to The Tombs. Maybe he'd like to come."

"What's happening?" Pearl asked.

"We gotta work quietly – that's all we can do for the time being. There are two guys from the Department over at The Tombs now with an FBI man – they're questioning Parker and the other men we're holding. I thought you might like to listen in, Inspector."

"Is that usually allowed?"

"No. But so long as you promise not to interfere, we'll be glad to have you. It might help convince you we're trying to do *something* to get your wife back."

Now, as they crossed the sidewalk to the entrance of the detention house, Jefferson said, "You're not gonna be impressed by this place. We got no excuses – except lack of money. We're the richest country in the world, but we never seem to have enough money to solve our worst problems. There are worse prisons in the world than this one, I guess, but that doesn't excuse what you're gonna see now."

Malone had never been in a jail in which one stepped immediately in off a city street. Jefferson tapped on a door and it was opened by a uniformed guard. Malone at once recognized the sour smell that was prison stink and felt the tension; yet behind him a boy and girl were passing by, arms wrapped round each other, and across the narrow street two old women, eyes rejuvenated by malicious envy, went clucking by like ancient fowls. The guard clanged the door behind Malone and Jefferson and opened another door to allow them into the main lobby, a narrow hall crowded with guards who had the same air about them as Malone had seen on prisoners, a boredom laced with tension. The guards in this crowded building were as much prisoners as the men they guarded.

"You carry a gun?" Jefferson asked.

Malone, surprised, shook his head. "This far from home?"

"I'm never without mine. That's what life's like nowadays – I put it on before I put my pants on." He checked his gun with the duty officer in the tiny cubicle in the corner of the lobby, signed a book, introduced Malone to the duty officer, then stepped up to the bars that separated the entrance lobby from a second, inner lobby. A guard opened a door in the bars and Jefferson and Malone stepped through.

"Hi, Jack. How's it been?"

"Same old routine, Captain." The guard, like most of the men in uniform in the cramped lobby, was black. Though he could not have been more than thirty he had the battered, slightly abstract expression that Malone had seen on the faces of old prize-fighters, men who had spent all their lives having hell knocked out of them in the preliminaries. This guard would never rise above his present job, would never get higher billing, and he knew it. "We had another two suicides last night. Maybe if enough of 'em did that, we could solve the accommodation problem."

"This place was designed in 1933 to hold 900 inmates," Jefferson explained to Malone. "It was designed in the immediate post-Prohibition era, when the whole approach to crime was punitive and when practically all criminals were white. Today the average day to day population is between fourteen and fifteen hundred. It's an overloaded pressure cooker."

"How long do you keep men here?"

"It varies. Some guys come and go in a day, depending on their charges. Others – " Jefferson shrugged. "If they got smart lawyers, ones who can keep getting remands, they can be here a year, maybe two. Only thing is, the lawyers prove too smart – their clients usually go crazy."

The guard came back and led them into a side room. It was the sort of room familiar to Malone, designed to eliminate all cheer and encouragement, sterilized even of hope. Three men were there, two of them sitting on the metal chairs, the third resting his behind on the bare table. They all stood up as Jefferson and Malone entered; but Malone had the feeling they had not done it out of deference but only to relieve the tedium of whatever they had been doing for the past hour. They were introduced to him as Captain Lewton and Lieutenant Markowitz of the Police Department, and Special Agent Butlin of the FBI.

"We're getting nowhere so far, John." Lewton was a tall, thin man with an unhappy mouth and eyes yellowed with ague or bitterness. "The bastards won't see us."

"They don't have to," Jefferson told Malone. "Since they haven't yet been convicted, they still have most of their rights. One of them being that they can refuse to be questioned on anything that doesn't concern them. And they're claiming the kidnapping has nothing to do with them."

"But the ransom has!" Malone, suddenly affected by the atmosphere of the jail, had the feeling that doors were being slammed on him; from somewhere beyond the closed door of the interviewing room there came the loud clang of iron against iron, a sound as cold and dead on the ear as that of doom itself, and abruptly he was as without hope as any of the prisoners in the building. Anger shook him as he thought of Lisa held prisoner somewhere, possibly already dead (the thought was there in the dark corners of his mind like a plague-carrying rat). The world was standing still and waiting with its hands in its pockets; and some anarchists somewhere in this building who did not believe in the rule of law were invoking it to wash their hands of the lives of two women they had never met. Suddenly he wanted to tear this bare, negative room to pieces. He felt like an innocent man just condemned to life imprisonment. He thumped the table with his fist. "Jesus, can't you *drag* them down here? We're trying to save the lives of two women – what rights do these bastards have against that fact?"

"I don't know what the law is in Australia," said Lewton quietly, "but in this country, since the Supreme Court decided in its wisdom that the guilty have as many rights as the innocent, we work with our hands tied."

Malone, despite his emotional state, recognized the sour hyperbole and understood it. Only in police states did the police ever think the law worked for them: there had been times back home when he had thought he had been wearing the handcuffs and not the lawbreaker he had brought in. He simmered down, aware again of doors clanging outside: he had to find some way of surviving in this cage of frustration that enclosed him.

Then a door behind Lewton opened and a grey-haired white man in uniform came in. With him was a young black guard and a second black with an Afro hair-do and wearing a red-and-black *dashiki* over his blue jeans and his white T-shirt.

"McBean has said he'll listen to you." The grey-haired man was introduced to Malone as Warden Canby. "I told him, Inspector, that you might be coming here. That was when he said he'd come down."

"Just to show you your side doesn't have a monopoly on compassion," said McBean.

Canby looked over his shoulder at McBean, casually as he might have looked at a man he had known all his life. "Our side doesn't have a monopoly on anything. Don't get sanctimonious on us – we got enough do-gooders on our own side."

McBean suddenly smiled; evidently there was some rapport between him and the Warden. "Stick around, Warden. We'll find a place for you in our system when we take over."

Canby, dark lines gullying his grey face like the tribal marks of experience, turned back to Malone and the others. "He's all yours. Officer Robinson will stay with you. Good luck."

"That's what you gonna need – luck," said McBean, and sat down at the table, arranging his *dashiki*. "You like my outfit, Captain? A marriage of two cultures – Africa and Seventh Avenue."

The Warden shook his head and went out of the room, and Lewton said, "What do you mean, Eddie? Why are we gonna need luck?"

"Because there's nothing I can tell you about this kidnapping – nothing."

Malone found himself at the opposite end of the table from McBean; the two men looked at each other down its length and Malone saw nothing in the broad blue-black face that afforded him any hope. But they had to start somewhere if Lisa was to be found before it was too late. If it was not already too late (the rat gnawing away in the dark, the plague spreading through his mind).

"I don't know what the other guys have told you," said McBean. "I haven't seen 'em since I come in here – they don't let conspirators fraternize, you know that? Afraid of conspiracy, I guess."

"Do you mind if we cut out the jokes?" said Lewton patiently. "I don't think Inspector Malone is in the mood for laughing."

McBean looked down the table again at Malone. He had not yet been convicted, but if he were he would still be defiant: he was a man whose pride lay in *doing*, as if he had already conceded that victory for his cause was doomed. But, as he had said, he was not without compassion. "You're one of the pigs, man, and internationally speaking you're all the same. But this isn't your scene and I guess you deserve some sympathy."

"Thanks," said Malone, not attempting to keep the irony out of his voice: he knew this man would not be offended by it. But McBean sounded like an echo of the kidnapper who had spoken to him on the phone less than an hour ago.

"Like I said, I dunno anything about your wife or the Mayor's wife. I dunno, if I *did* know anything, that I'd be co-operative about the Mayor's wife. She's part of what we don't believe in and we don't owe him anything." He glanced around at the other men. "But you know that, don't you?"

"That's why you're here," said Lewton.

McBean shook his head, smiled. "Let's be specific, Captain. I'm here on a bomb conspiracy charge and you have to prove I had anything to do with it." He looked back at Malone. "Man, believe me, I know nothing about your wife and I'm sorry you got to suffer."

"Thanks," said Malone again, and this time there was no irony in his voice.

Then Butlin leaned forward. "Mr McBean, we are not suggesting you had any hand in this kidnapping. But you must have some idea who amongst your supporters would dream up such a bizarre scheme."

"Not bizarre, man. It looks to me like a stroke of genius."

"So if we agree to the demands of the kidnappers, release you and send you to Cuba, you'll go along with it?"

"You crazy? Wouldn't you?"

"I'm not in your position, Mr McBean."

McBean's laugh was one of genuine amusement. "I got imagination, man, but not that much – you in my position!"

Butlin sat back, flushing slightly under his sun-lamp tan. Malone, watching everyone at the table carefully, well aware that they were the ones on whom he had to depend to get

Lisa back, had remarked the deep, healthy colour of the FBI man and wondered if he had just come back from an assignment somewhere in the sun. Then he had seen Butlin's pale hands and knew the tan on the man's face had come from a lamp; like so many lamp-users, Butlin had forgotten his hands.

So far Lieutenant Markowitz had said nothing. He was a burly, balding man of middle height, with intense dark eyes and a nervous impatience that seemed to exhaust him as he tried to control it. He did not lean forward now as he spoke, but his body was strained as if he were bound by invisible cords to the back of his chair. "McBean, we'll be candid with you. We got nothing, no record, on any of you but old Fred Parker – "

"Oh, Fred," grinned McBean. "The daddy of us all."

"We know him – he's been around for years. But the rest of you – you're all strangers. None of you have even had any visitors while you been in here – "

"You think that's strange? They come here, right away you pigs gonna be leaning on 'em. No, man, they know enough to stay outa this scene."

"Would you blame us for leaning on them? You killed two of our men – "

McBean shook his head. "Not guilty. You heard our plea."

Mankowitz took a deep breath, looked at Lewton. The latter looked at Jefferson and Malone, then nodded at the guard standing by the door. "You can take him back. Thanks, McBean."

"For what?" McBean stood up, the bright *dashiki* catching the light, adding a note of frivolity that seemed indecent in the sour atmosphere of the room. "I'm sorry, Malone. I hope your wife is okay. But like I said – you're gonna need all the luck you can get."

When McBean and the guard had gone Jefferson said, "What do you reckon?"

"He knows nothing," said Lewton. "I'm sure of it."

"Where do we go from here?" All four men looked at

Malone, and Lewton's eyes narrowed at the grating harshness in the Australian's voice. International boundaries were being drawn, but Malone was too worried for Lisa to be concerned with diplomacy. At the best of times, even on cases dealing with strangers, he had never been noted for it. "What about the other four bastards? If they won't come down here, let someone go up and see them."

"Inspector – " Lewton began; but Jefferson, rising from his chair, interrupted him.

"I'll explain it to him, Ken. Inspector, let's go back to Headquarters. Maybe something's been happening while we been away."

Malone stood up, all at once feeling stiff, exhausted and depressed to the point of sickness. He was at the door when he paused and looked back. "Sorry, Captain. It's just the frustration of doing bugger-all – "

The three men still at the table nodded, their faces for a moment softening with sympathy. When he and Jefferson were outside in the street Malone said, "Maybe I shouldn't have come down, Captain – "

"Call me John. I think you and I might be spending a lot of time together." He went across to the car, checked with the driver that there were no messages, then came back. "Let's walk – Scobie, isn't it? I always like to get the stink of that place out of my nose. It's not really a smell, it's – well, you know what I mean?"

"I know," said Malone, all at once glad of the black detective's company. "I once picked up a vagrant back home, a Pole who'd been in a concentration camp in Europe. He said that freedom had a smell all its own and he'd become an addict of it. I thought he was having me on, then I realized he was fair dinkum."

"Fair dinkum?"

Malone grinned. "On the level. I'll stick to English."

"Looks like Hurricane Myrtle is gonna drop in on us after all."

Jefferson looked up at the darkening sky. A wind had

sprung up, ambushing people as they came to corners. Papers blew along the gutters like derelict birds; a wino sat on the kerb surrounded by a whirling aviary; he clutched at the flying papers and giggled like a child. Other citizens narrowed their eyes against the grit in the air, looked more bad-tempered than usual, bumped into each other and snarled like sworn enemies. A fire engine went by, charging through the traffic like a red rhino, the firemen riding it with faces turned back away from the wind, looking like reluctant heroes. The city had abruptly begun to show its nerve-ends.

"Someone will stay there with those anarchists," said Jefferson, "just in case one of them decides he knows something. But I think in the end the Mayor's gonna have to agree to the ransom demand. We could be beating our heads against a wall for the next twenty-four hours."

"Do you think he will – agree to the demand, I mean?"

A headline flew by in the air: 2 DEAD. Jefferson caught the newspaper, screwed it up, dropped it into a bin they were passing. "He'd agree, I think. I dunno – sometimes I think he's not as ambitious as the people around him. His old man, for instance – and his missus, come to think of it. She's in the news as much as he is. Look there." The wind had flattened the front page of the *Post* against a wall: Sylvia Forte smiled at them as from an election poster; then her face wrinkled, the wind played another trick, and the sheet was whipped away. "That'd be the early edition. She'll be on the front page of every paper in the country by tomorrow morning."

"The reporters asked me if I had a photo of my wife. I've got one in my wallet, but I didn't want to part with it."

"I don't blame you. But I might have to ask you for it, run off some copies. Our men don't know what she looks like, other than your description. Tall, blonde and good-looking. Could be a million women. Can I see it?"

They stopped on the corner of a street and Malone took

Lisa's photo out of his wallet. Jefferson, turning away from the wind, looked at it carefully. "You downgraded her. She's beautiful."

"I think so, too. But I couldn't say that."

"I know. I used to think my wife was beautiful – she's dead now – " He was silent for a moment: he could have been waiting for the traffic light above them to turn green. When it did he stepped off the kerb, going on, "Maybe other people thought she was no more than pretty. She was black, darker than me, and that don't appeal to everyone. Can I keep this a while?"

"Be careful of it."

"I will, Scobie. I'll have some extra copies run off for you, if you like."

"No, the original will do." It would be too much like tempting fate to ask for extra copies, as if he were storing up mementoes of Lisa against an empty future. The Celt in him was rising, as gritty and depressing as the wind swirling about him.

2

Police Commissioner Hungerford looked up as Sam Forte came into the Mayor's office. The old man took off his velvet-collared coat and laid it carefully on a chair, sat down, arranged the creases of his trousers, then at last gave his attention to Hungerford.

"Michael still upstairs at the reception?" Hungerford nodded. "So in the meantime, what have you got for us, Des?"

"Nothing." Hungerford jammed a cigarette into his holder, lit it and blew out a cloud of smoke. "We're up against it, Sam. In every way."

"Which ways do you mean?" But Sam Forte did not sound curious or ignorant, only as if he wanted confirmation of what he already knew.

"First, getting Sylvia and this other woman back. That's the main thing, of course."

"Of course."

"But there's the other aspect – " Hungerford chewed on his holder. "If we release Parker and those others, it could mean losing the election. It'll certainly make a laugh of what Mike and I are supposed to stand for – law and order."

"We'll forget the election for the moment," said Sam Forte, taking the long view. "The law and order principle is the one we have to sustain."

He wiped his lips with the silk handkerchief from his breast pocket. He had been a fastidious dresser from the very first day he had escaped from work on the construction gangs. He still remembered driving over to Manhattan in the Packard, parking it outside Sulka and Company in the days when one could still park on Fifth Avenue, going in and ordering a dozen silk shirts and a wardrobe of other clothing that had at once established the image of him for the years ahead. From that day on he had never again been dirtied by grit and dust and mud; and he had built a corporation that, at book value, was worth several hundred million dollars. In a land that, he had come to learn, placed such a high value on appearances, he had achieved the appearance of the chairman of such a corporation. And, if he should last long enough, and he hoped God would be willing, no one would be able to say that he did not look like the father of a President.

"We still have time on our side, Des."

"Not much." Hungerford looked up at the ormolu clock on the mantelpiece: like all cops, he hated a deadline.

"But some. And I think we must use it. My own first impulse was to do anything they asked, so long as it got us back Sylvia and this – this Mrs Malone." Sam Forte had an infallible memory for the names of voters and political workers and business contacts; but this unknown Australian woman was beyond his ken and he had difficulty in giving a name to a faceless stranger. "But I think I can persuade Michael that we should ask for some proof from the kidnappers that the two women are still alive. Pat Brendan is certainly going to ask for that sort of guarantee."

Brendan was the District Attorney. "Have you suggested it to Mike?"

"Yes. He wouldn't give me an answer. I think he has to hang on to the belief that Sylvia *is* still alive."

"What about the other man – Malone?"

"He has no cards at all to play. I'm afraid he will have to go along with us."

You callous old bastard. "They said they won't be calling back till – God knows when. What if they don't call back till five minutes of nine? It could be too late then."

"Michael can go on television, make an appeal to the kidnappers to give some proof that Sylvia is still alive, and hope that they are watching."

"They will be. Or listening to a radio. But what happens if they don't give us any evidence?"

"Then we don't release Parker and the others."

"But what happens if the women *are* alive and the kidnappers just ignore Mike's appeal? When we don't release Parker and the others, what happens then?"

Sam Forte shivered in his chair as if he were suddenly cold. He put his hand to his mouth; when he took it away there were deep fingermarks in the soft flesh round his jaw. He had shut his mind against the thought of the worst happening to Sylvia, but Hungerford, with the brutal facing of truth born of his job, had forced the possibility of the fact on him.

"I think we shall have to set ourselves a time limit. Give ourselves till say seven o'clock tomorrow morning. If we have made no progress by that time, then we release Parker and his gang."

The door opened and Michael Forte came in. He paused to give some instructions to Manny Pearl behind him; then he shut the door, crossed to his desk and sat down. His father and Hungerford sat across the room from him, saying nothing and waiting for him to recognize their presence. At last he glanced across at Hungerford with an inquiring look.

The Commissioner shook his head. "Nothing. The garage attendant found nothing in our files on the young guy who hit him. And the last I heard we were getting nowhere with Parker and the others."

Michael Forte could feel the beginning of a severe headache, something he had not had since he was in his teens, when he had occasionally suffered mild attacks of *petit mal*. Even over the past four years of crises, savage criticism and the civilized assassination that was called political comment, the old malady had never recurred. But now the headache was attacking him and soon, he feared, there would be the odd feeling of detachment, the sensation of being removed from everything that was happening to him. He hoped he would not faint as he had done two or three times when he was young.

"I've just been upstairs talking to an Arab sheikh. He told me that where he comes from, kidnappers are beheaded and their heads stuck on a pole in the public square for a week. He thinks advertisement is a good deterrent."

"Insensitive bastard," said Hungerford.

"No, I think he was trying to be sympathetic, in some roundabout way. He appreciated that a head stuck on a pole in the middle of City Hall Park wouldn't get me many votes." He swung his chair round, stared out the window for a while at the darkening sky, then turned back. The other two men saw how close he was to breaking and they kept quiet, not wanting to push him any closer to the edge. At last he said, "I'm no longer interested in law and order or votes. The next time the kidnappers call I'm going to tell them they can have Parker and his gang."

Sam Forte was aware of Hungerford's quick glance in his direction, but he didn't acknowledge it. He got up, moved across past his son to the window and looked out at the trees, their leaves dying and being whisked away by the wind, the seasons appearing to change even as he looked at them. He wondered if Sylvia had a window to look out of wherever she was being held; he felt an abrupt wave of pity for his daughter-in-law. Then he wondered if she would understand his efforts to save what he could of the career they had both nurtured so patiently all these years.

By leaning forward he could see the statue of Horace Greeley, bald head flecked with the dandruff of bird dung. There was another man who had run for political office, had been vilified, who had lost his wife just before an election, though she had not been kidnapped but had died. *I am not dead, but I wish I were*, Greeley had written; and Michael already had that same look of hopeless despair that must have been on Greeley's face when he had penned those words. Hope must still be kept alive, Sam decided; not just for the safe return of Sylvia but for success in tomorrow's election. He looked at his watch: they still had sixteen hours to the absolute deadline, fourteen hours to the deadline he had discussed with Hungerford.

"Michael – " He kept his voice soft and sympathetic while he told his son of the need for some proof from the kidnappers that Sylvia and the other woman were still alive. "I don't think you can surrender at once – "

Michael shook his head, put his hand to his eyes as the pain increased. He felt sick and he suddenly swung his chair round and put his head down between his knees. At that moment there was a knock, the door opened and Manny Pearl stood there with Malone and Jefferson.

"Mr Mayor – " Then Pearl was across the room in a swift pattering run, was on his knees beside the still bent-over Mayor. "Mike! Mike, are you all right?"

Michael Forte slowly straightened up, leaned back in his chair. He blinked, saw Pearl; then a ghastly grin slipped across his mouth. "Okay, Manny – I'll be all right."

Manny Pearl stood up, his face as white as that of his boss. "Jesus, you had me scared!" He looked around at the others, his concern for Michael touching because it was so sincere and unexpected by the other men who knew him. "He's so goddam healthy and fit – You're sure you're okay?"

Michael nodded. "Get me a drink, Manny. Maybe the others would like one – ?" Only Hungerford nodded, and Pearl moved across to the drink cabinet in a corner of the room. Michael, his head still aching but his composure recovered, looked at Malone and Jefferson. "Any luck over at The Tombs?"

"None," said Malone. "What's been happening here?"

Malone meant it as a general question, but from the expressions on the faces of the two Fortes and Hungerford he guessed at once that there were several answers. It was Michael Forte who said, "We've decided to hold off releasing those men until seven o'clock tomorrow morning. I'm going to make a broadcast, ask the kidnappers for some proof that our wives are still alive. Do you agree to that?"

"I have no vote in this city," said Malone.

3

"That was a pretty low blow this afternoon." Michael Forte pushed his steak, hardly touched, away from him. "You don't seem to appreciate the fix I'm in."

"Look," said Malone, pushing his own steak away. He picked up the beer he had asked for with his dinner and sipped it; compared to the stuff back home it tasted like aerated water that had a hop or two dunked in it; maybe Americans made their beer the way they made their tea, with beer-bags in a glass. "Look, I'm not a boneheaded bastard – or at least I try not to be. I'm not a stranger to politics – I've had one or two brushes with it back home. One of our Police Commissioners once told me never to expect to outlive politics – I think he also meant never expect to beat them, either."

"You think that's all I'm considering – politics?"

"Isn't it?"

"No, it damn well isn't!"

"I don't care what your considerations are – " Malone put down his glass, stared at Forte across the table between them. "If I don't get my wife back, and your politics or whatever has been even part of the reason, I'll take you apart bone by bone!"

Forte stared back, then slowly he relaxed. "I think you would, too," he said quietly. "But only because I wouldn't fight back."

Malone, after more persuasion from Manny Pearl, had decided to leave the hotel and move up to Gracie Mansion. He had not seen Michael Forte till they had sat down to dinner, just the two of them, and then Forte had made his comment on what had happened down at City Hall that afternoon.

"My kids are due home some time tonight. They're going to ask the same sort of questions you've been asking."

"What are you going to tell *them*?"

"Lies, I guess. You see, releasing those guys isn't just up to me. The District Attorney is the key man – and like me, he's got people behind him leaning on him. He's got political ambitions – next time around he'd like to run for Governor. But he's the one who'll have to effect the release. He'll come to some arrangement with the judge who's going to preside on the bomb conspiracy case and have a motion made to dismiss it. He's not a callous son-of-a-bitch, but he's even more hard-nosed than I am about law and order. And he knows those anarchists better than I do. He figures if we let them go free, go to Cuba, they'll be back in the United States within six months. They're fanatics and they're not going to give up their fight. You want something else to eat?"

"Just some of this fruit." Malone took an apple from the bowl on the table.

"Fruit for dessert is an old Italian custom. My mother never believed in apple pie or angelfood cake or all those things Americans are supposed to fight wars for."

"Were your parents born in Italy?"

"Only my mother. Her name was Verrazano. My father claims she is a direct descendant of Giovanni da Verrazano, who was the first European to sail into New York Bay – we have a bridge named after him."

"That must have been a help when you first ran for Mayor."

"It was when I first ran for Congress too."

"Does your wife mind you being in politics?" Malone suddenly realized he was talking about an absolute stranger, a woman he had never even seen.

"No. Does yours mind you being a cop?"

Malone chewed on the slice of apple in his mouth. He could not taste it, but the peeling and slicing of the fruit gave him something to do with his hands. Any minute diversion was a relief from the agony that filled his mind each time he thought of Lisa. "I don't think she understands the – the politics of it, if you like. When it comes to law and order she tends to think of everything in black and white. Most people do, I guess."

"You're looking at our present situation in straight black and white."

"I think you are too – when you forget you're the Mayor."

"Maybe. But nobody lets me forget I am the Mayor."

Then the two Forte children arrived, brought home from their respective schools. Roger, red-haired, sixteen and already taller than his father, shook hands with Malone. "Glad to meet you, sir."

"It would be better in other circumstances," said Malone, and the boy, after a moment's puzzled blink, then nodded.

Pier Forte freed herself from her father's embrace. She was as dark as her father, already a beauty at fourteen, and Malone had the immediate feeling that she was going to cope with this situation better than either her father or her brother. She is not only Michael Forte's daughter, he thought, she is very much Sam Forte's granddaughter.

"I am sorry for you, Inspector. But I am sure my mother will do her best to see that the kidnappers don't hurt your wife." The speech sounded almost rehearsed, yet Malone knew the young girl had had no expectation of meeting him, had not known that he would be here.

He glanced at Forte, then back at the young, composed face. "I'm sure they'll both be all right."

"When are you releasing the anarchists, Dad?" Roger had picked up a banana from the table and was peeling it; without being greedy he looked like a boy who would always be eating, never able to fill the frame that was too big for him. "There's a guy at school who's one."

"One what?" his father said.

"An anarchist, for Pete's sake – "

"They're everywhere," said Forte drily to Malone; but his humour did not reach his eyes. "Roger goes to Portsmouth Priory, it's supposed to be one of the top Catholic schools in the country. When I was there we were only interested in two things – dodging prayers and catching girls."

"Some of the Catholic girls at St Tim's are saying prayers for Mother," said Pier; then added, and Malone did not know whether she was being truthful or just gracious: "And for Mrs Malone too, Inspector."

The mention of prayers reminded Malone of his own mother; he tried to remember the time gap between New York and Sydney, wondered if she and his father and Lisa's parents down in Melbourne had yet heard the news. Christ, he thought, I'm so bloody concerned with myself. "Mr Forte, I wonder if I could make a couple of phone calls to Australia?"

As soon as he uttered the words they sounded ridiculous in his own ears: on the rare occasions back home when he had made a trunk call to Lisa's parents in Melbourne, he had counted the pips as if they were gongs of doom. But Forte was a man accustomed to his overnight guests asking if they could make international phone calls: "Ask Nathan to place the calls for you. He'll get you priority, if it's needed."

As Malone went out of the room he heard Forte say to his children, "You're to go down to Grandma Veerkamp's – "

"We want to stay here!"

Malone heard no more as, out in the hall, he found Nathan the butler, who led him into a small study, got the Melbourne number first and handed the phone over to Malone. "I hope it is a good line, sir."

The line was almost too clear: Malone heard Lisa's mother gasp as he spoke to her. It was ten o'clock in the morning in Melbourne and the news of the kidnapping had been on the early morning radio news. It's already tomorrow out there, he thought; her parents and mine are probably out of their heads trying to work out the actual time of the deadline. It had always confused him that Australians and Americans had two different dates for the bombing of Pearl Harbor, almost as if history were echoing itself on successive days. He tried to sound reassuring to Lisa's mother and to her father, who soon took over the phone from his wife; but distance and Malone's own despair exposed his words for the sham they were. He wanted to hang up, but that would be too brutal. He did not know Lisa's parents well and he had no measure of their capacity for pain.

Then he realized that Jan Pretorious was comforting *him*. "Scobie, all we can do is trust in God. I wish we could be there with you. If the worst – " his voice faltered for a moment: ten thousand miles of painful silence separated the two men " – if the worst happens, we'll fly over at once. Will you call us again?"

"As soon as I have something definite."

While he waited for the call to Sydney to go through he looked at the books on the shelves in front of him. They seemed to be all political biographies: Presidents stood in ranks at eye-level before him: some books looked as if they had been handled more than others, some Presidents taken down and scrutinized to see what example they offered. On the desk on which the phone stood was a brand-new book, but Malone had to look twice to make sure he had not mistaken the title: *Baedeker's United States, 1893*. He leafed through it, the phone still held to his ear. In that year one could stay at the Waldorf-Astoria for four dollars, including meals; Los Angeles was still trying to drag itself together as a city; Las Vegas sold wool and nothing else. He wondered who in this house had bought the book, who was so tired of the present and afraid of the future that they wanted to retreat so far into the good old days. He could guess who it was; and he understood. He wondered what Australia had been like in 1893, felt his own desire to escape into nostalgia.

The line to Sydney was, inexplicably, a bad one. Only Brigid Malone was at home and she keened as if at a wake. He could see her in his mind's eye, holding the phone almost at arm's length, shouting into it as if she were on a direct line to Hell: "Wait till I get me glasses – I can't see you for weeping!"

"Mum!" He found he was yelling too, chasing her down the thousands of miles as she went looking for her glasses. Then he realized what he was doing, where he was, and he began to laugh almost uncontrollably. He was still laughing when she came back on the phone.

"Is it good news you have, then? Is the poor girl safe?"

"No, Mum." The keening started again, made worse by static; it was time to hang up. "Mum, I have to go. I'll call you again tomorrow – "

"What?" she shouted across the world, unable to believe he was so far away from her when he needed her so much. "I'm having a Mass said for the poor girl – "

She's already buried Lisa, he thought: the Irish dig graves while other people dig gardens. He shouted goodbye to her again and hung up, knowing she would still be there yelling comfort to him into the dead phone for minutes after he had gone. When he went out of the study Nathan was in the hall.

"How do I pay for the calls, Nathan?"

"I think the City of New York can afford them, sir," said the butler with a slow sympathetic smile.

Malone grinned. "I wonder if the City of New York could afford me a drink?"

"Another beer, sir?"

Malone shook his head: he needed something stronger than American beer to get him over what he had just been through. "A Scotch and water."

Forte was waiting for him in the living-room. Rain had begun to pelt against the windows and outside the wind was finding the weak branches in the trees. "I have to go out – I have to take the kids down to their grandparents, then I have to go to my campaign headquarters down at the Biltmore. Do you mind being left alone or would you like to come with me?"

"Will there be reporters down at your headquarters?"

"Dozens of them, I'd say."

"I'll stay here." Then the cop in him said, "What about your kids? I mean, in case someone tries to snatch *them*?"

Forte looked grateful for his concern. "That's been taken care of. There'll be a police guard staked outside my in-laws' apartment. But thanks for thinking of it."

Malone nodded, feeling a slowly growing rapport with the other man. There would never be time for them to become friends, but Malone's life was milestoned by friends he had never made, men whom he understood and who understood him but whom he had never had time to stay with; friendship was a continual siren call in a policeman's life, always desired but always suspect or inconvenient. He would be gone from here in a day or two, with or without Lisa, and Forte would be another one of those he had liked but would never really know.

Then the butler came to the door. "Mr Frank Padua wishes to see you, sir."

"Padua? *Frank* Padua?" Forte's brow came down in puzzlement, then he shook his head. "Tell him I can't see him."

"I think he anticipated that, sir. He said to tell you it was to do with Mrs Forte."

Malone looked sharply at Forte. The latter said, "Tell Mr Padua to wait a moment," and the butler went out. Forte lowered his voice. "I don't know what the hell this is all about."

"Who's this Padua?"

"A wheeler-dealer, he's in everything in this town that will make a buck – and he's made a lot. But as far as I know he's respectable. I'd better see him alone."

"If he has any news of your wife, then he'd know something about mine. You can't expect me to step outside – "

When the butler brought Padua into the room Malone recognized his type at once. He could have been an old-fashioned banker, a gentleman whose larceny would be gentlemanly and courteous. Yet Malone sensed this was a man whose money was not as old as the man himself, who was not quite sure of the power of money and would therefore, when the pinch came, rely too much on it. Sydney, like New York and affluent cities everywhere, was full of them, the robber barons who wanted to be accepted at court.

"I wanted to see you alone, Mr Mayor." Padua, like Sam Forte, had worked hard on his voice; but he was twenty years behind Sam and the rough times in New Jersey were still there in the voice that was hardly more than a whisper. "Perhaps Inspector Malone will excuse us?"

Malone shook his head and Forte said, "I understand you wanted to see me about my wife. Inspector Malone's wife is with her – he and I are in the same terrible situation."

"As you wish. May I sit down? I have had a very busy afternoon – ever since I heard of this dreadful business." He sat down, carefully arranging the creases in his trousers. He pulled down his shirt cuffs and Malone caught the glint of gold; he had the feeling that Padua had dressed specially for this call. Forte sat down opposite Padua, but Malone, suddenly on edge, wondering what the news of Lisa and Sylvia Forte might be, remained standing. "As you know, Mr Mayor, I have a lot of connections in our city – "

"So I've heard. I have some myself – they go with the job."

The irony was not lost on Padua; he smiled appreciatively. "True, true. But from your demeanour I assume your connections have not been as helpful as mine have been – "

"Padua, for Christ's sake get to the point!" Forte's voice did not rise, but Malone saw his body stiffen.

"Mr Mayor, I believe I may be in a position to effect the return of your good ladies." He looked up at Malone, acknowledging him at last. His prim posture in the chair, his over-formal way of speech, brought on another image in Malone's mind: the bishop from the wrong side of the tracks, the priest who knew all the cardinal's sins. There were no such bishops in Sydney, or if there were the Criminal Investigation Bureau hadn't yet been called in; but Italy and the older Catholic countries, he had been told, were full of them. And Padua was an Italian, a different sort from Michael Forte: all his expensive conservatism could not hide his inborn talent for intrigue. "That is why I have been so busy this afternoon. My connections – "

"What connections?"

"Ah, I am not at liberty to say, much as I should like to take you into my confidence. However – "

"Padua, have you come here with any definite information on my wife and Mrs Malone? Or are you just flying a kite?"

Padua spread his hands palms upwards, the Italian answer that was no answer. "That depends. Are you interested in kite-flying?"

Forte sensed rather than saw Malone's angry, impatient movement; without looking at Malone he waved a restraining hand. "All right, Padua. Keep talking."

"I shall be honest with you – I do not wish to raise your hopes unduly. I do not like to see suffering any more than I care to endure it myself." He took a gold watch from the fob pocket of his waistcoat. "I should need probably seven or eight hours – can you give me that much time?"

"First, I want to know who your connections are. Are they

political connections? I just don't believe Tom Kirkbride would try to make capital out of something like this."

"Mr Kirkbride has nothing to do with this, I assure you."

"Then who are they?"

"Just connections."

There was a loud crack from outside, the gunshot sound of a branch being snapped off by the wind. Forte looked up at Malone, then back at Padua. "Are your connections the Mafia?"

"What is the Mafia?" There was no surprise at the question on Padua's smooth thin face; it was as bland as an over-exposed photograph. "Mr Mayor, you are Italian like me. You know we don't admit any more that there is such a thing as the Mafia. It offends our patrial sensitivities."

"I didn't know I had any till I came into politics. But it is the Mafia we're talking about, isn't it?"

"Connections, that's all I have. But I think they can be very helpful."

"For a price?"

Padua spread his hands again. "I haven't talked about such a thing with them. My desire to help you is just that of a citizen who thinks such things as this dreadful kidnapping should not happen in our city."

I'm going to king-hit the oily bastard in a moment, thought Malone. But he restrained himself and said, "Mr Padua, you're not being helpful at all. I don't know what Mr Forte thinks of your offer to help, but I think you ought to be kicked up the arse for coming here giving us false hopes and then trying to make some sort of deal. If you came into a police station and tried that same sort of caper, I'd lock you up."

Padua stared coldly at Malone for a moment, then he stood up. "I can help you, Mr Forte. Here is my card. Call me at home if you think I'm honest in my offer and that Inspector Malone is wrong in his opinion of me. Goodnight. I'd just warn you – you don't have too much time."

He went out, walking with practised dignity. Malone took

a step after him, but Forte stood up and grabbed his arm.

"Let me bring him back! Christ, he's the only lead we've had so far – "

"Nothing doing." He waited till Malone relaxed, then he let go of the Australian's arm. He looked at the card in his hand, then dropped it on a small side table. "If he was here sounding out the chances of a deal with the Mafia, I wouldn't want to listen to him. I've never connected Padua with them before, but it's no surprise."

"Have you had any trouble from the Mafia before? Padua said you were Italian like him – "

Forte's mouth stiffened. "Never. There are quite a few Italians who'll have nothing to do with them. Most of them are Sicilians and my old man, like a lot from northern Italy, has no time for them."

"If Padua came up with some proof that he knows where Lisa and your wife are – would you do a deal with him?" Malone was still chafing with anger at being held back: he had wanted to grab Padua by the throat and force the man to tell them if he knew anything.

"Jesus, how do I know what I'd do!" Forte whirled round, working off his own sudden anger; then he regained control of himself, turned back. "Look, these guys have their price for everything. That explorer I mentioned, Verrazano, he went on down to Brazil and the Carib Indians ate him as a main course. If I made a deal with Padua, his connections would do the same with me. Except I'd be the hors d'œuvres and they'd take the city as a main course. I can't take the chance – not yet."

Malone sat down in a chair by the window. Outside, the wind and rain had risen now to a full storm: Hurricane Myrtle was making her presence felt. He could not comprehend the power of the Mafia; he had read of its strength here in America, and an Antipodean branch had tried its luck in Melbourne but without much success. Sydney was not without its corruption, but it was fragmented: politicians, aldermen, policemen, all looking for graft for their own ends:

there was one organization that aimed at an empire among the city's clubs but so far it had not reached the headlines. There was another loud crack from outside: the trees were being demolished limb by limb.

"Christ, how did I get into this?" He leaned his head back against the chair, exhausted by dread, hopelessness and anger. He sat there a moment, then abruptly he stood up. He grabbed up Padua's card from the small table. "I'm going after him! I don't care a bugger about you and New York – "

Forte stood in front of him. "You stay where you are! You try to go see Padua and I'll have you picked up and held – "

"Held? *Arrested?* What for?"

"Disturbing the peace, suspicious behaviour – you're a cop, you've used the same excuses whenever you've wanted anyone held. I'll do it, Malone," he emphasized, when he saw that the Australian didn't quite believe him. "I'm sorry about your wife, but my wife's in this too. And we'll play it my way till I know there's absolutely no alternative but to give in on the ransom terms!"

"That may be too bloody late – "

Then Roger and Pier came in, wrapped up against the storm outside. They paused at the door, sensing something was wrong. Then Roger said, "We're ready, Dad. But I wish to hell we didn't have to go down to Grandma's. We'd rather be here – just in case they let Mother make a call – "

Forte hesitated, looked at Malone, then back at the children. "Okay, stay here. Look after Inspector Malone, keep him company." He looked back at Malone. "And remember – I meant what I said!"

4

"Mother and Dad are on TV tonight," said Pier.

Forte had gone, and for the past half-hour Malone had held a desultory, awkward conversation with the two children. Roger, gauche in his attempt to sound older than he was, not helped at all by Malone's inability to find a level with him, had soon lapsed into silence. Pier, more at ease, had tried to keep the conversation going by asking about Lisa; Malone, appreciating her effort, had done his best to reply in something other than monosyllables. But he was well aware that when he was in the company of anyone under the age of eighteen he was about as loquacious as an aborigine who had had the bone pointed at him. If the Irish were supposed to love children, he had been overlooked when his ration of charity had been handed out. Kids bored him, even ones he felt sorry for.

Pier led the way out to the study where Malone had taken the phone calls. Roger, unwinding himself like a young giraffe getting to its feet, followed his sister and Malone into the room, switched on the television set mounted in the wall, then fell into the nearest chair. Malone looked around for chairs for Pier and himself.

"Let Roger get them, Inspector." The young girl looked at her brother. "On your feet, you slob. Your manners are execrable."

"Ex-who? Jesus, what sorta words do they teach you at St Tim's?" But the boy got to his feet, dragged two chairs up level with his own. "Sorry, Inspector. I guess I'm not functioning too well tonight."

"Who is?" said Malone, but he smiled at the boy and for the first time there was some rapport between them.

"The segment was taped last week." Pier arranged herself in her chair. *Arranged* is the word, Malone thought: she wasn't *sitting* like himself or *sprawled* like her brother. "Mr Cronkite was here when I phoned Mother from school."

"Who's Mr Cronkite?"

The television screen almost cracked; certainly Roger's face splintered. "He's just about the biggest name in television news in America! Don't you have TV in Australia?"

I must sound like someone from the Arunta tribe; they're probably wondering why I haven't got my boomerang and spear with me. "Yes, but we're still showing lantern slides on it."

Roger stared at him, then abruptly grinned. "You're okay, Inspector."

But Pier wasn't smiling. "When I phoned Mother, that was the last time I spoke to her." She looked down at the hands folded in her lap and Malone, watching her closely, saw the fingers tighten. His own hand went out of its own volition, touched her arm. She looked up at him, blinked, then said quietly, "Thank you, Inspector. I'm going to be all right."

Then Malone all at once felt at home with the two children; the three of them settled back like a family for a night's television viewing. Mr Cronkite, the stranger to Malone, was already on the screen, green-hued enough to have passed for St Patrick; Roger got up, adjusted the colour tone, then flopped back in his chair. Malone listened to the introduction to the Fortes, wondering why all American commentators sounded like ventriloquial dolls for the voice of God, then the film of Michael and Sylvia Forte began to run.

The children both sat forward, something Malone was sure they had not done other times they had seen their parents on television. Roger's face was wide open and very young, his love for his mother exposed through the cloak of sophistication that was several sizes too big for him; and Pier's eyes were brimming with tears, her hands in her lap now held in the attitude of prayer. I wonder how much would show in my face, Malone wondered, if Lisa were also there on the screen?

But Lisa was not there and so he looked at the woman he had never seen but whose fate was linked so tightly now with Lisa's, who, blameless as she might be, was the reason Lisa was in danger. He now dimly remembered seeing a photograph of Sylvia Forte in *Time*, but it had not done her justice: he would have remembered her better if she had looked as she did now on the screen.

"Your mother's beautiful."

"Yes," said Pier, and her brother nodded. "But she's more than that. Dad loves her so much – you can see it even there."

It was true: Michael Forte turned and smiled at his wife and there was a moment of intimacy between them when the camera suddenly was an intruder. Cronkite was interviewing them, but Malone was not listening to the words: the sound could have been turned off for all the notice he took of it. He stared at Michael and Sylvia Forte, and as he did, like a double image, he saw the ghosts of himself and Lisa behind them.

The phone rang. Malone, lost in the nightmare fantasy on the television screen, jumped nervously but recovered at once. He looked anxiously at Roger as the boy picked up the phone; then tried to tell himself that a hundred calls a day must come into this house and there was no reason why this one should be any different from all the others. Then he saw the puzzled look on Roger's face.

"What is it?"

The boy put his hand over the mouthpiece. "It's some dame wanting Dad – "

Malone took the phone. "This is Inspector Malone – "

A man's voice answered. "This is Lieutenant Denning, Inspector. We've set up an emergency switchboard here, just in case something like this happened. We've told the woman the Mayor's not here. Do you think we should tell her where she can get him? She could be just a crank – "

"Put her on," said Malone. "If I keep her talking, can you trace the call?"

"We can try, sir. We're linked through to Headquarters and they've alerted the telephone company."

The woman's voice was soft and pleasant, but Malone could notice the faint undertone of tension in it: whoever she was, he would bet she was not an old hand at this game. "I understand Mayor Forte is not there. Who is this?"

"Malone. You're holding my wife with Mrs Forte."

Behind him he could feel the strained attention of the children. Roger had taken hold of Pier's hand, the first sign the boy had shown of any concern for his sister. The sound on the television set had been turned off, but Michael and Sylvia Forte still walked in the garden of the house, laughing at each other in the happy past of a week ago.

There was silence for a moment, then the woman said, "I am truly sorry about that, Mr Malone. We'd rather not have her with us, but we had to take her."

"Is she still all right? Both of them?" The children leaned forward; he could almost hear them holding their breath. He stared at the screen: Sylvia Forte was there in close-up, alone, a frown of amused puzzlement on her face as the unseen Mr Cronkite asked her a question.

"They are both well, Mr Malone."

"Can you give us some proof of that? Can I speak to my wife? To both of them?" He had no real hope that the woman would grant him his request, but he had to keep her on the line: somewhere the electronics experts were seeking to pinpoint the call. "We want some proof that you're going to carry out your part of the bargain – "

"Oh, we'll carry it out, Mr Malone. But there may be a hitch – " Oh Christ, he thought, what's gone wrong? Have we buggered up things at our end? "This storm – planes might not be able to get off the ground tomorrow here in New York. What happens then?"

"You name it. We'll do whatever you say, just so long as we get my wife and Mrs Forte back safely." He looked at the children, nodded reassuringly; but there was no reaction on their faces, they would believe nothing till the silent smiling ghost on the television screen was a live reality in the house again.

"You've decided to release Parker and his friends?"

"Yes." She had asked him if *he* had decided: he was not speaking for Forte and the politicians who surrounded him.

"We'll be back to you." The tension went out of her voice; she sounded – relieved? he wondered. "If the storm keeps up, we'll tell you our other plans. We'll call again first thing in the morning."

"Wait!" How could he keep her on the line? Had they succeeded in tracing the call yet? Michael Forte was now on the screen, looking directly into the camera, silently pleading for last week's cause, whatever it had been: law and order? Then Malone said, "What about Frank Padua?"

"Who?"

"Your go-between – " He hoped he sounded convincing. "He was here an hour ago, said he was acting for you – "

"Padua?"

"I don't know him. He's a – a political acquaintance of Mayor Forte's – "

There was silence for a long moment, then a click. A man's voice came on the line at once: "She's hung up, Inspector. We traced the call, but I'm afraid it's not gonna be much use. It was a phone booth out on the Island, at Patchogue. We've sent a coupla squad cars to it, but we'll be lucky if she's still there."

Malone hung up, turned back to the children. He shook his head in answer to their silent question. Then Nathan, the butler, came to the door.

"Captain Jefferson is here, Inspector. He says he has something for you."

Chapter Five

Carole hung up the phone, stood staring at the wall in front of her. Something was wrong; and once again she felt the uneasiness grip her. It had clutched her this afternoon when the wind had come battering at the cottage; it was the first warning that things might not go exactly as she had planned. She would have to find out who Frank Padua was, do something about him. She had no idea what could be done, if she did find him, but no outsiders could be allowed to interfere with her plan.

She ran across the sidewalk to her car, got in and drove down the deserted street. Neon signs glimmered like watery fires through the rain-swept windscreen; the lighted windows of stores splashed the pavements with gold that ran off into the gutters. A huge truck, loaded with potatoes, overtook her, riding alongside her for a full block, flinging up mud and water against the window beside her. She cursed the truck driver, urging him to get quickly by her. She did not see the two police cars speeding down the other side of the street, nor did they see her.

It had been a mistake to come out on such a night. But she had had to escape from the cottage; she had become as much a prisoner there as Sylvia Forte and the Australian woman. It would have been useless to explain to Abel; the only memories he retained were the ones he wore like a hair-shirt. He would never understand that pleasant memories could, in the sad realization that the experiences that had prompted them had gone forever, turn into a form of torture. Childhood and girlhood had scratched at her, raising welts of memory: Julie Birmingham had not been buried after all.

"You're crazy, baby, wanting to go out *now*!" Abel had said.

"I *have* to. I – I think we ought to call them, tell them the storm may change our plans." It was as good a reason as any, though she had had to invent it.

"The hell with them!" Abel was angry; he did not like the thought of her leaving him even for a couple of hours. "If they want the dames back, they're gonna let those guys go, don't matter what the weather's like."

"We've got to think of Parker and the other men – we can't risk their lives by insisting that the plane take off for Cuba regardless of what the weather's like. No, I'm going into Patchogue, honey – "

It was part of their plan that they should make no phone calls any closer than thirty miles to the cottage. There was a phone here in the living-room, but they had agreed it was to be used only in the utmost emergency; she had been pleased to find that her mother hadn't changed, had, with her usual vagueness, forgotten to have the phone disconnected when the cottage had been closed up. The first call by herself had been made from the house in Jamaica; the second, by Abel, from a call-box in Flushing; so long as they spread the calls the police would have difficulty in pinning down their location. She would be safe enough driving into Patchogue: anywhere would be an escape from what was beginning to torment her in this cottage.

Unguardedly she said, "I need to get out – "

He had a trick of looking from the corners of his eyes, half-suspicious, half-frightened; as a small child he had learned not to trust anyone or anything, the helping hand had too often turned into a fist. "You getting tired of me?"

"Honey!" She put almost too much protest into the endearment; she leaned forward and kissed him, hoping he wouldn't see the truth in her face. "That's a terrible thing to say – we're only at the beginning of things – "

He put his arms round her, pulled her to him. "Sorry, baby. I love you so much – too much, maybe – "

"Never too much. You can't love too much – " But maybe if she had not loved Roy too much her life would not have ended four years ago, she would not be enduring this husk of an existence . . .

As she drove out of Patchogue she debated whether she should stop and phone Abel; then she decided against it, exhausted even by the thought of the argument that would go on over the phone. He worried too much for her and, she had begun to realize only after she had driven away from the cottage, he too had made a prisoner of her.

She drove as fast as the storm would allow her. Several times, when she had got on to the parkway that led to Manhattan, she slowed, wondering if she should turn back. But each time she picked up speed again, driven on by the determination to find out who Frank Padua was, to stop him, if she could, from ruining her plans.

She knew where Michael Forte had his campaign head-quarters and she reasoned that would be the best place to start looking for information on Padua – "he's a political acquaintance of Mayor Forte's," the Australian had said. Once in Manhattan she had very little trouble finding a parking spot; tonight was a night for sensible people to stay at home. She got out into the wind and rain, staggering a little under the force of them, buttoned her raincoat to her neck and tied her rainhat firmly under her chin. Her wig and her dark glasses were in the glove compartment of the car, and this afternoon she had changed out of the suit she had worn this morning into a tan sweater and brown skirt. She was taking a risk going to the Biltmore Hotel, into Michael Forte's very own territory. But she knew she would merge easily with those who were working for the Mayor; the newspapers had been full of stories of the number of young middle-class people he had gathered about him. And she had been middle class almost all her life.

The lobby of the Biltmore was thronged: sensible people might stay at home on such a night, but campaign workers and kidnappers were not sensible people. She smiled to herself at the thought, and a passing young man, a *Forte for Mayor* button in his lapel, stopped beside her to help her off with her raincoat.

"You're a real worker to come out on a night like this. You've lost your button, though."

She smiled up at him. "Where can I get another?"

He took the button out of his lapel. "Be my guest. I haven't seen you down here before – how about being my guest later on for a drink or something? I'm Bill Brewer."

She looked him up and down, keeping her smile friendly. Does he know how much he is one of *them*, the ones Roy so despised? she wondered. Straight Ivy League: it was the image her parents had wanted for Mark, her brother. He had rebelled, turned his back on the image; but this smiling, good-looking man with his Brooks Brothers suit and shirt would go to his grave exactly as he was now, conservatism personified. The image of her own father . . . "I'll think about it. First, I have to find Mr Padua – Frank Padua."

Brewer frowned. "Frank Padua? I don't think you'll find him around here. But you might try up in one of the rooms – someone up there may know."

As soon as she got out of the elevator on the floor that had been taken over as campaign headquarters, she was afraid; but the elevator doors had closed and she was trapped in the loud rapids of the crowd surging down the corridor. Then she heard the yells for *Quiet!* and she saw all the heads turn towards the far end of the corridor.

Four girls were standing on a bench against one wall; before she could protest one of the girls had grabbed her arm and pulled her up beside them. "You want to see our hero? God, the poor man! Doesn't he look sick and worried?"

Michael Forte was coming down the corridor, a phalanx of aides pushing their way through the crowd ahead of him like the prow of a boat over-populated with figure-heads. Carole stepped down from the bench, suddenly realizing how conspicuous she was. Then all at once the crush of people in front of her thinned out and she was face to face with the Mayor. She saw the strain in his face, the dark exhaustion in his eyes; but he was smiling and reaching out with both hands to those around him, going through the motions of a wound-up political doll. He reached towards her and, suddenly laughing, she took his hand and pressed it.

"Good luck!"

"Thanks – thanks for working for me – " He smiled at her, but she knew he could not see her; the faces in the crowd were not registering on the dark, worried eyes. "We'll win tomorrow – thanks a lot – "

He passed on, the crowd closing behind him, claiming him, and she moved in the opposite direction through the rapidly thinning wake. She found herself opposite a doorway, looking into a room in which a man, weary-faced and dishevelled, sat with his feet up on a paper-strewn table. He looked up at her and grinned tiredly.

"Thirty years I been a volunteer for this sorta thing. My old lady asks me what's in it for me and I can never give her an answer. Every time it's been like it'll be tomorrow night – the same old debris – " He waved a hand at the posters, already torn and crinkled, hanging from the walls like the papering of a room waiting to be demolished. "The faces and the names change, but every time I finish up in here with just a mess of paper. Maybe I'm working for pollution, you think?"

She smiled, humouring him. If he had been in politics for thirty years, even just as a campaign volunteer, he should know who Frank Padua was. "I'm looking for Mr Padua – Frank Padua."

"Frank *Padua*?" He looked at her curiously, the weariness abruptly gone from his face; and she felt suddenly afraid. "You a friend of his, miss?"

She shook her head almost too vigorously. "Someone must be playing a trick on me – they told me to report to him here – "

He relaxed, smiled again. "They are, they are indeed. People do it to relieve the strain – like sending a kid out for a can of striped paint. I haven't seen Mr Padua around these headquarters in, oh, maybe two or three campaigns. He used to be known as Stabber Frank. He'd stab you in the back – figuratively speaking, of course – if he could make a political point for himself. But I understand he's retired from politics now. He's either rich and respectable or he ran out of knives."

"Well," she said, smiling at him, the poor bastard who had been coming here for thirty years, working for a system that he only half-believed in, the volunteer slave for what was euphemistically called democracy, "I guess my friends were putting me on."

"Yeah," he said, ignorant of the tricks being played on him: won't they ever open their eyes? she wondered. "I'd go back and give 'em hell, miss."

"I'll do that. Good luck."

"It's not me needs the luck. It's our candidate." He looked up and around at the posters; a dozen Michael Fortes smiled at him from the walls. "In more ways than one, eh? Terrible business about his missus."

Carole found some back stairs, made her way down and out a side entrance to the street. The wind and the rain hit her at once, pushing her back against the hotel wall; a policeman went by, head bent into the storm, walking like an oil-skinned robot. Then he stopped and came back, stood threateningly in front of her.

"You want a cab, miss? Over at Grand Central is your best bet."

Rain ran off her face, streaking it beyond recognition: she looked directly at him, daring herself as much as him. "Thanks, officer, but I have my car."

"Driving on a night like this? Be careful."

"Oh, I will be."

He went on, leaning into the storm, all law and order and helpfulness, and she hated him for being so solicitous of her. But she followed him, heading for Grand Central and a phone booth. It was going to take her hours to drive back to Sunday Harbor and she knew Abel would never forgive her for letting him worry for so long.

2

Abel angrily hung up the phone, cursing Carole for her stupidity. But what had gone wrong, what had taken her all the way into Manhattan? "I'll explain when I get back. It may be nothing, but I had to check. Don't worry – I'll make it back okay."

Don't worry! Sweet Jesus, what did she think he was made of? He turned off the small lamp in the living-room where he had been sitting, went out through the dark kitchen to the back door. There was a porch outside the door and he was able to step out on to it without the rain reaching him. But the wind hit him like an invisible wave, and at once he retreated into the house, slamming the door shut against the battering wind. In the darkness of the kitchen he leaned against the door, sick at the thought of Carole driving all the way out along the Island in that bitch of a storm. Hurricane Myrtle had not been included in their plans, simply because when they had made their plans and committed themselves to the timing of them, the hurricane had not been born. Part of their plan was to leave here tomorrow by ferry and cross the Sound to Bridgeport; Carole's car, stripped of its plates, was to be dumped and they were to buy another in Bridgeport. But now they might have to take the risk of driving back to Manhattan if the storm kept up.

He cursed again, went into the living-room and turned on the light. All the shutters were up outside and all the windows had been blanketed. Even though this outer section of Sunday Harbor was made up entirely of summer cottages closed for the fall and winter, they had done everything they could to ensure that nothing would expose their presence to any casual passer-by in a car. The only risk they had taken had been their arriving here in daylight and then his taking off to dump the delivery truck; but that had been unavoidable in view of the timing of the kidnapping forced on them by the Forte woman's dental appointment. He was sure no one had seen them during the day and he was even more certain that no one was likely to be out tonight and catch a glimpse of Carole driving back this way. But what had gone wrong, had taken her into Manhattan of all places? Jesus, she must be out of her head to take such a risk!

There was a knock on the door of the bedroom across the narrow hall. "We want to go to the bathroom."

He crossed the hall, stood outside the door. "You both went a coupla hours ago."

"It's damned cold in here," said Lisa. "If this heater was stronger, perhaps we shouldn't trouble you so much."

He was about to unlock the door when he remembered his dark glasses and wig were on the table in the living-room. He went back and put them on, took the gun out of his belt and returned to the bedroom door. He had had very little to do with guns, but each time he held one he got the same thrill, a sexual one. It was a thrill he had never described to Carole and he didn't think he ever would. In lots of ways she was as much of a square as the two women in the bedroom.

"One at a time. And like I told you – no tricks."

When both women had been to the bathroom he followed them into the bedroom, sat down in one of the chairs, the gun held loosely in his lap.

"I'm real sorry there isn't enough heat," he said affably. "Maybe I'm used to the cold more than you. But this'd be a nice place in the summer. I didn't know any places like this where I come from."

The old Polish neighbourhood near the Loop in Chicago had had no citizens who could afford a summer cottage; as a kid you spent your time looking for fire hydrants to turn on as your only relief against the heat. In the winter the family apartment never had enough warmth, but his old man had never spent any money to improve the heating system. Always and forever talking about how much worse things had been in the goddam Old Country.

"Carole – " said Sylvia.

He stiffened, his hand tightening on the gun. "How'd you know her name?"

"You haven't been too careful about your names, either of you." Sylvia was watching the gun carefully. "When we first got into the truck, she called you Abel."

"You're too fucking smart – "

"All right, watch your language!" said Lisa; then she looked at the gun in his hand. "Sorry. That sounded ridiculous, considering."

He looked down at the gun, then back at them. He smiled and relaxed. "Yeah – ridiculous. But if that's the way you want it – okay, no language. Carole doesn't like it either, you know? She says they degrade the language, there's no eu-eu – "

"Euphony?"

"Yeah – no euphony in four-letter words. I tell her where I come from euphony would've dropped dead before it was born."

"Carole has obviously had a better life than you," said Sylvia. "Do you resent the luck she's had?"

"Luck? You're right there – I mean for guys like me. But how much have you had to depend on luck? The day you were born everything was mapped out for you. We did a lot of research on you, you know? Maybe we know more about you than you do yourself."

"Perhaps," said Sylvia, and wondered how many pages she had left unopened on herself.

"The day I was born," said Lisa, "the Germans came into the house next door and shot dead a man and his three sons. They were going to shoot my father too, but my mother got out of bed and told them to shoot her and me as well, that she wouldn't want to live without my father. I was lucky that the officer in charge of the Germans was a family man."

"Why were they gonna shoot your father?" Abel knew very little of *that* war: it was ancient history to him, fought and done with five years before he was born.

"Reprisal. The Resistance had killed a German soldier. The local commander always operated on a ratio of five to one as a punishment."

"You *were* lucky, then." Sylvia had barely been touched by that war: her father had been too old to go to it, she had had no brothers who had fought in it. She realized how lucky *she* had been and she looked at Lisa with new interest.

"I believe in it," said Lisa. "I believe it affects everyone. It was pure luck that I met my husband."

She lapsed into silence when she mentioned Scobie; Sylvia, and even Abel, caught the sudden sadness in her. Abel, to divert himself, stared at Sylvia, the woman for whom he would never have any sympathy.

"Nothing like that ever happened to you, eh?"

"When did it ever happen to you?" Sylvia demanded with some spirit.

Abel smiled, unruffled. "Nothing like a war, I'll admit – I run away from them. They were looking for me for Vietnam, but they never caught up with me. But I've met plenty of pigs who believe in punishment like the Nazis – someone causes some trouble, they pinch five guys just to make sure. They call it keeping law and order."

Sylvia had a sudden moment of insight. "Is that part of the reason we've been kidnapped? You don't like my husband's ideas on law and order?"

You'd never understand even if I told you, he thought. All his life authority had been a stifling weight pressing down on him from above: his old man, the nuns, the priests, the cops. His old man had believed in an ordered system: authority had to be obeyed or everything collapsed. He had exercised his own authority in his family with a leather belt and occasionally his fist; Abel had run away from home the day he had finally flattened his old man in a fight. The authority of the nuns and priests had just been something to jerk his thumb at, but that of the pigs had been another matter. You didn't jerk your thumb at cops in Chicago and get away with it.

"They're all the same." The affability of a few minutes ago had gone; the thin face behind the dark glasses had the same cold, bony look it had had this morning. "Nobody's got any say but them. That's the way they see it."

"You're wrong – "

"No. *You're* wrong. Because *we* got the say now and if they don't listen to us – "

Abruptly he stood up and went out, locking the door behind him. The two women, sitting on their beds, each wrapped in a blanket, looked at each other. The temperature was not as low as they believed, but fear and hopelessness had reduced their resistance; no matter what the temperature was, they felt cold and would remain sleepless because of it. The lash of the rain against the shutters outside only added to their feeling that this room was an ice-box. That and the hate-filled man who had just left the room.

"I don't understand why we're still here," said Lisa, and tried not to sound petulant. She looked up at the boards covering the window, suddenly feeling as claustrophobic as Sylvia must have felt in the hood when they were in the truck. It occurred to her that she had never spent any length of time in a room with no view; even to look out of a window across a narrow street gave one some sort of perspective. She was a long way from becoming completely unnerved, but she was beginning to understand how some people could go insane when faced with nothing but four walls. One needed an occasional glance at the world outside: even strangers seen at a distance had their uses. She looked back at Sylvia, still half a stranger to her. "Surely they've released those men by now."

"I'm sure my husband is doing all he can." Sylvia, in her turn, tried to sound patient. "But it isn't just up to him. He has to go to the District Attorney and the Court."

"You sound as if you know the whole procedure."

"I've been working it out while we've been here. I know City Hall backwards. My whole married life has been political, one way or another. My husband was a junior Congressman when we married. He was only twenty-six. Perhaps we should have stayed in Washington," she mused. "Life would have been much simpler."

"I don't understand the American political system – why would your husband leave Washington to come back here to New York? I've read what a terrible job it is. Isn't it supposed to be the worst job in America, worse even than being President?"

"I think so." Then she said half-jokingly, "I'll tell you if my husband ever gets to be President."

"Would you like to be in the White House?"

Sylvia was too shrewd to let her ambition show in her face. "Why do you ask?"

"I read that some Presidents' wives never wanted to be there. Mrs Truman, for instance."

But what of the dozens of wives who loved every minute of their husbands' Presidency? And I'd be one of them. She closed her eyes, was warm for the moment with the dream. "I think it would depend on the times and the circumstances. If it could be a trouble-free time, no foreign war to worry about, no economic recession, no law and order crisis – " She opened her eyes, realizing she was taking the dream too far: Paradise already had its Chief Executive. "But no President for the next ten years is going to be *that* lucky."

"Would your husband like to be President?"

No: how often had the accusation been there on the tip of her tongue to fling at him. Ambition and love had several times almost torn her apart; Michael and she had fought and he had never really understood what had spurred on her fury. She did not answer Lisa's question but asked one of her own: "Do you and your husband have any secrets from each other?"

"I – I don't know." The question had exposed something

of the Fortes: *they* had secrets. "I suppose in a way we don't really know each other yet, so there are bound to be secrets. Perhaps there always will be. Are there?"

"You mean after you've been married for years? Yes, I think so. They're not always deliberate – " She lay back on her pillow. She felt suddenly penitent for everything she had not told Michael: love should have no secrets. And she did love him, had never even thought of another man after she had met him.

"What are you thinking about?" Lisa was massaging her jaw as her tooth, forgotten for most of the day, began to ache again. If only I'd listened to Scobie, got the hotel desk to recommend a dentist, I'd not be here . . .

"Myself. Doing a little self-examination."

"That's what prisoners are supposed to do, aren't they? But if they do, why don't they all come out better men?" Lisa was silent for a while, absent-mindedly stroking her jaw. "I've been thinking too. Wondering if we'll come out of this alive."

"Don't!"

They faced each other across the space between their beds. "It's possible, though, isn't it? That boy Abel hates us."

"My husband will give them what they want – "

"You said he would have to go to the Court? What if they refuse to release those men? What if they say the system of law is more important than us – our lives?"

"No – " But she knew the maze through which Michael would have to fight his way.

Lisa said slowly, "I think we should try to escape from here. I don't want to trust to the luck of what's happening back at City Hall."

Chapter Six

"It's only your wife's photo," said Jefferson, handing the photograph to Malone. "I'm sorry. I shouldn't have told the butler to tell you I had something for you. You were expecting some news, weren't you?"

Malone nodded, looked at the photo of Lisa, then put it carefully away in his wallet. "Did you run off the copies?"

"They've gone out to all the newspapers and wire services and TV stations. Trouble is – "

"Yes?"

"By the time they appear, your wife and Mrs Forte should be safe."

"Should be?"

"*Will* be." Jefferson looked at the Forte children standing in the doorway of the study. "We'll have your mother back here first thing in the morning. We're making progress – "

"I'd like to talk to the Captain," said Malone, and led Jefferson towards the living-room. He glanced back and saw Roger and Pier still standing in the doorway of the study, their young faces aged with suspicion, the faces in every cop's gallery. Christ, don't they trust me? Have they forgotten I have as much to lose as they have? He closed the door of the living-room. "Did Denning tell you about the phone call just then?"

Jefferson nodded. "I wouldn't count on anything coming of it."

"A bloke named Frank Padua came here tonight, tried to offer a deal to the Mayor. When I asked the woman who rang if she knew Padua, she hedged."

"Did you get the impression that she knew Padua?"

"I couldn't tell – I'm not very good at reading voices over the phone. I was trying to keep her talking, so I told her that

Padua said he was their go-between. That seemed to hit her – she said nothing for quite a while, as if she were thinking about it, then she just hung up."

"Did the Mayor give you a rundown on Padua?" Malone nodded. "What was the deal?"

"They didn't get down to specifics." Malone outlined the conversation with Padua. "The Mayor thought Padua was flying a kite, but I don't know. From the reaction of that woman, maybe Padua does know something, does have a connection that can help us."

"Padua with the Mafia? It's possible, I suppose. I don't know him well. He was never in my precinct and by the time I got down to Headquarters he'd sort of retired from politics."

Malone picked up Padua's card from the side table where it still lay. "That's his address. I'd like to go and see him."

"Officially or unofficially?"

"Here, I'm very unofficial. I'm not even an ordinary citizen with a vote."

"Don't be sour with me, Scobie. I'm on your side."

John Jefferson over the past year had almost lost interest in being a policeman; all he looked forward to was retirement. When he had first joined the force he had had no ambition beyond reaching Sergeant; he had surprised both himself and Mary, his wife, at how well he had done in the examinations for promotion. But even when he had reached Lieutenant he had not thought he would get beyond it and had been content. He had not first at appreciated it, but his lack of ambition had been the reason for his popularity and also the reason why Commissioner Hungerford had promoted him to Captain and brought him into Headquarters as a special assistant. But he had soon realized that he was no more than window-dressing, another black face with its propaganda value; the job had been given to him because the really ambitious, black or white, would not have wanted it. He was a twenty-thousand-dollar-a-year reception clerk, a widower who had too much time to think about his dead wife, to think about politics, to wish for escape into a retirement that might be dull but would at least not call for a blind eye to principles.

"Enough to come with me?" Malone told him of the Mayor's threat to arrest him if he tried to see Padua.

Jefferson chewed on his bottom lip, then shrugged. "Why not? Sure, I'll come."

Malone, having invited him, now looked at him carefully, not wanting to bring the other man out on a limb that might break off under them. "Officially or unofficially?"

Jefferson sighed. "I don't really care. I been sitting on my ass for four years – now they got me on my feet, they can't be too surprised if I sometimes walk into the wrong house."

Malone grinned, the adrenalin of optimism running in him again if only because he too was off his arse and on his feet. "I'll get my raincoat. It sounds a bastard of a night."

"It could get worse."

Malone told the Forte children he was going out but did not say where.

"Are you going to see this Mr Padua?" said Roger.

"Are you trying to be a detective?"

"No offence, Inspector, but a cop is the last thing I'd want to be – none of the guys would speak to me." Malone and Jefferson exchanged resigned expressions. "But you didn't answer my question, Inspector."

"Okay, yes, I'm going to see Mr Padua. But I don't think you'd better tell that to anyone, least of all your father."

"Good luck, Inspector," said Pier, cool and political. "We want Mother back any way you can find her."

Malone and Jefferson went out a side door, avoiding Denning, who was in a small waiting-room off the main hall. As they got into Jefferson's car he said, "I came off duty at eight – I'm due back at eight in the morning, an hour before the deadline. Another guy and I are splitting the liaison duty between us."

"So it's going to be an unofficial visit after all?"

"Isn't a cop supposed to be always on duty?"

"Will it get you into any trouble?"

"Depends what results we get. You get the right result and up top they'll always turn a blind eye to how you got it. You better slide down out of sight till I get away from here. There are some newspaper guys parked across the street. They wanted to come in, but Denning wouldn't let 'em. He hates 'em and they hate him. Makes for a nice little rapport in a situation like this."

Malone slid down in the seat, feeling ridiculous, even criminal. "I'm beginning to feel like Ned Kelly."

"Who's he?"

But Malone didn't want to go into that again. "Feller I knew back home. Okay to come up?"

"All clear. Jesus, what a night! They've closed all the airports between Washington and Boston, did you know that?" Jefferson drove the car across to Second Avenue and headed downtown, driving carefully and leaning forward to peer through the windscreen that seemed to be dissolving under the amount of rain hitting it. "I dunno where the hell we're gonna have to take those jerks to put them on a plane for Cuba."

Malone sat quietly in the corner of the seat, now and again flinching instinctively as water was flung up by a passing car. Still flashing on his memory were the images of the Fortes and behind them Lisa and himself. Worry had gone further, into deep loneliness; without admitting the surrender he was already accepting the possibility that Lisa might not return; this was the delayed repayment for that month of windfalls. The optimism he had felt as he had come out of Gracie Mansion had gone as suddenly as his hat might have been whipped away from his head by the wind. This short trip through the storm-distorted night was only a diversion, something to distract him through the sleepless hours till they brought him the final dreadful news. What was it he had thought about his mother and the Irish digging of graves?

"You don't want to give up hope," said Jefferson.

Malone looked up, puzzled and surprised. Were the blacks, like the Celts, also digging graves before they were needed? "I'm still hoping," he said defensively.

"Not then, you weren't. I've seen that look on too many other faces, Scobie. You'd recognize it yourself if you looked in a mirror."

"Would you be optimistic if you were in my place?"

Jefferson pulled the car up at a red light: it glowed like a bleeding eye through the water running down the windscreen. "If you want the truth – and I think you do – no, I wouldn't be optimistic. Kidnappers are a different breed of criminal from any other. For one thing, there are practically no professional kidnappers, guys who make a career of it. Professionals at anything usually act to a pattern, it's part of being professional. They apply logic and that's the main thing that helps us cops – you can always apply logic against logic and come up with some sort of answer. With kidnappers – " The blood turned to crème-de-menthe; and Jefferson drove on. "You never know what the bastards are gonna do. Especially political kidnappers."

"So why did you tell me not to give up hope?"

"What else did you expect me to say?" Jefferson glanced at Malone and the latter understood the look and the question: the black man was offering his friendship.

Then Jefferson turned the car down a cross-street, slowed to look for a parking spot, found none and finally double-parked. "I don't think there'll be any squad cars out on a night like this handing out tickets. One of the advantages of being a police captain is you can always get traffic violations fixed. My small contribution to corruption."

"I do the same thing back home," said Malone, making his small contribution to friendship.

Jefferson wound down his window, peered out through the rain. "That's the address. Padua's doing all right if the whole house is his. You own a town house in this area, you're paying maybe a quarter of a million bucks for it. Even the taxes would break me."

They ran up the few steps through the rain, huddled against the grille guarding the front door. Malone could not see much of the house, but it did not look large; for a quarter of a million dollars he would have expected Buckingham Palace or maybe the Vatican; not a house that looked no more than thirty feet wide and seemed to be no more than three or four stories high. And had no garage: a suburban man, he shook his head at such a lack.

The front door opened and a young, white-jacketed man-servant looked cautiously out at them through the grille. Jefferson introduced Malone and himself, showed his badge; the manservant surveyed them suspiciously, then let them into the narrow hall and went away to see his master. Jefferson looked after him. "I thought he was gonna leave us out there in the rain. They don't like us."

Malone didn't know who *they* were and he didn't know whether Jefferson, when he said *us*, meant blacks or a cop. "Who are *they*?"

"Puerto Ricans. He's one."

And I think I've got problems back home: at least there the dislike of a cop is simple and all of one colour.

The manservant came back, face as blank as the back of his hand, told them Mr Padua would see them and led them upstairs to the most sumptuously furnished room Malone had ever been in.

Sumptuous was not the word Malone thought of; but even he, a man of not much taste, who judged rooms only on the comfort of their beds or chairs, knew that someone had gone too far in the furnishing of this particular room. There was nothing in it that was garish, but somehow he knew there was too much of everything: too many pictures on the walls, too much rich comfort in the chairs and sofas, too many valuable ornaments, too much *expense*. This is a rich man who has let someone else spend his money while he thinks he's been buying advice. Then Malone grinned at himself, the count-the-pennies big-time spender who knew when other people spent too much. Then he remembered Lisa's gentle ribbing of his stinginess and the memory was too poignant; he acknowledged Padua's greeting with a brusque nod and turned his face away. Padua stared at him for a moment, then looked at Jefferson.

"Is this an official visit, Captain? Did Inspector Malone suggest it?"

"No – on both counts, Mr Padua. But I can call up Headquarters and have them make it official if that's the way you want it."

"Let's see what you have to say first."

Padua gestured them to chairs, but remained standing in front of the big marble-surrounded fireplace. The wrought-iron grate held small logs of wood that looked to Malone as if they might be taken out every day and dusted, but there were no smoke stains around the fireplace and he wondered when a fire had last been lit in it. A fire would only have been another unnecessary ornament to the room: the central heating was much too warm for Malone's comfort.

Jefferson looked at Malone and the latter took the hint: since their visit *was* unofficial, maybe he'd like to do the talking. "Mr Padua, after you left tonight I talked to one of the kidnappers – a woman."

"What did she have to say?"

I'd hate to play this bloke poker: he'd play his cards from inside his pocket. "I mentioned your name to her – "

He waited for a reaction, but Padua's face was as smooth and cold as the marble behind him. "So?"

"She said she was not prepared to have you or your connections come into the act unless you were going to help her and her partner. Otherwise – " Malone glanced at Jefferson, but the latter was looking at Padua, not a hint on his big dark face that he felt any puzzlement or surprise at Malone's lie. Talking about professionals, Malone thought . . .

"Otherwise?" said Padua, another professional.

"She implied they had not let off their last bomb." Christ, what am I saying? I am borrowing threats from people who hate the society I am supposed to respect, I'm graduating by proxy to guerilla warfare to get my wife back. And yet why not? What else did he value in life more than Lisa?

For the first time Padua showed some reaction. He had long ago lost any fear of physical violence; he had been inoculated against it in boyhood. Unlike Sam Forte he often looked back. Sometimes in early spring, when bitter nostalgia ran in him like a fever, he would call for his car and be driven downtown to Battery Park, the eyepiece to the telescope back to the past. He would look south and over towards the Jersey shore: there in the cold March winds he had worked with his father, taking their boat out as soon as word came in that the shad were running. There had been fights with other fishermen, with no quarter given for his being only a boy; at fourteen he had had his skull laid open by a bailing-hook wielded by a man old enough to be his grandfather. His father had died violently, shot in the back in a waterfront brawl. Frank Padua had been sixteen then and, covered in his father's blood, he had carried the body to the parish church so that the priest could administer the last rites to Angelo Padua before his soul was as cold and useless as his body. Frank Padua then and now did not fear for anything that might happen to himself.

Himself personally, his body or his soul: but he feared for his possessions, for his house and his respectability that was as new and expensive as any of the furnishings that surrounded him. A bomb planted outside his front door would be something he could never hope to survive. The Establishment might be marked for destruction by the urban guerillas (he knew the battle lines as well as any war correspondent; any real social climber today had to be a military historian), but the bombing of his house would not admit him as a welcome refugee into the Establishment. He was still on a temporary visa from his past.

He was fifty-eight years old and he had been twelve when he had first seen Manhattan as the future: the telescope had been turned the other way around then. Boys on the Jersey shore had had their heroes: Dutch Schultz, Jack Dempsey, Babe Ruth; he had yearned to be like Mayor Jimmy Walker and the bosses of Tammany Hall. He had crossed the water from Jersey to Manhattan in 1930, a bad year to be going anywhere, and within six months he had discovered there were other, bigger men than the politicians, rich old-family men who were a law unto themselves. *They* had become his heroes and he had determined that some day he would join them. But for a poor fisherman's son from New Jersey the way uptown was far tougher and longer than a mere subway ride. He had had to make commitments along the way: even Christ, he supposed, had had his debts when they finally nailed him to the cross.

"Why should they want to threaten me like that?"

"I don't know." Malone knew he had scored with this wild punch; but where was he to go from here? "Unless you know more than you think you know."

Padua looked at him sharply. "What do you mean by that?"

Malone shrugged; the remark meant as much to him as it did to Padua. I've worked in the dark before, he thought, but I've never been bloody blindfolded too. "If you told us what you know, maybe Captain Jefferson and I could take them off your back."

"I am only the go-between," said Padua. "My connections asked me to see the Mayor – "

"Put us on to your connections."

"I can't do that – "

Suddenly all the anger and frustration of the long day burst out of Malone. He grabbed Padua by the front of his jacket, stood over him. "By Christ, I'll do you, Padua! Tell us who they are!"

Padua, unafraid, looked at Jefferson. "Captain – "

But Jefferson did not move and his dark face remained expressionless.

Malone, blind with fury now, raised his hand and

whipped the knuckles across Padua's face. Padua fell back, jerking free of Malone's grip, and fell over a small table. A vase fell to the floor and was shattered. There was a gasp from Padua as his foot crunched into a piece of the vase; he staggered back as Malone came after him. They were up against the fireplace now; Malone swung wildly to grab Padua again, missed, and his hand swept a small figurine from the mantelpiece and it, too, shattered as it hit the floor.

"No! No!" Padua stopped, let himself be snatched at by Malone. "Don't break anything more!"

"Tell us who your connections are!"

Malone hit Padua again. He had never been as blindly savage as this before; but before this he had never lost anyone as dear to him as Lisa. Jefferson still remained unmoving as Padua was pushed across the fireplace. Padua's arm came up to protect his face as Malone hit him again, his elbow swept along the mantelpiece and three more figurines were knocked to the floor.

"No – please! No more! I'll call them! Please!"

Malone let Padua go and the latter stepped away, his foot again crunching on a piece of china. He looked down dazedly at his broken treasures, then up at Malone.

"I could have you killed, you know that?" Padua's voice was still soft, but his own anger was as furious as that of Malone.

"I'm sure you could," said Malone. "Your connections would fix that for you. But that's a risk I'm willing to take."

"You better tell us who they are, Mr Padua," said Jefferson quietly. "Otherwise Inspector Malone is likely to wreck all this room of yours."

"The Mayor might not like cops acting the way you two are." A note of resistance, a whistling into the wind, flickered in Padua's voice.

"The Mayor knows as well as you and I do that he doesn't run the law," said Jefferson. "And I don't believe you'd complain to him, anyway. Come on, Padua – !" Abruptly his voice sharpened. "Who are your connections?"

Padua hesitated, then said, "I'll have to call them – "

Malone picked up the phone on the table beside the fireplace. "Here!"

"I'd rather be alone when I call them – "

Malone shook his head. "Come on – get on the phone!"

Padua took the phone reluctantly. He stepped on another piece of china, heard it crush beneath his heel, and he shut his eyes as if in pain, as if the shard had gone right in to cut his foot. He opened his eyes again, looked at Malone with hatred, then dialled a number.

Malone, his anger dying down, reason returning, lifted a hand and looked at it. The knuckles were skinned and a trickle of blood ran down the back of his hand. He stared at it in surprise, then looked at Jefferson as if asking the cause of it.

"It got what we wanted," said Jefferson quietly. "Sometimes it's the only way."

Padua spoke into the phone: "This is Frank Padua. I've had a visit from – from one of our friends." He glanced at Malone, smiled thinly; he was recovering his composure. "He wants to see someone . . . Anyone, I guess – " He looked at Malone again.

"Not *anyone*," said Malone. "The top one. The bloke who sent you up to see the Mayor."

Padua sighed, spoke into the phone again. "He insists on seeing the top man." He waited, looking from one policeman to the other. Once he looked down at the shattered pieces of china on the floor, bit his lip, then glanced around the room at what he still possessed. Then he held the phone close to his ear again: "Okay. They'll be there as soon as they can."

He hung up, scribbled an address on the pad beside the phone, tore off the sheet and gave it to Jefferson, ignoring Malone. "Someone will be waiting there for you."

"They're prepared to see both of us?" said Jefferson.

"I don't know. You'll know that when you get there."

When the two policemen had gone, Padua remained

standing in front of the fireplace looking about him. He put his fingers up to the weal across his jaw where Malone had hit him, but the pain there was nothing to the other pain he felt. He knelt down, picked up the largest piece of broken china. Now he had regained his composure he knew that not only the Australian was to blame for what had happened.

There were others, the ones who had never forgotten that his father was a Sicilian. The ones who had done him favours years ago when he had first crossed to Manhattan, who had waited all these years before asking for repayment. Men like Don Auguste Giuffre, a voice from the past that had called today and mentioned an old debt.

2

"Where are we going?" Malone said.

"Staten Island. We'll go over the Verrazano Bridge from Brooklyn."

Verrazano: the man who had been eaten by cannibals. "John, are you sure you want to see this through with me?"

"I'm sure. Only when we see these guys, don't get rough. They won't stand for it the way Padua did."

They had driven across from Manhattan through the Queens Midtown Tunnel, out along the Long Island Expressway, then turned on to the Brooklyn – Queens Expressway. Malone could see little but watery auroras of neon off on either side of the expressway; for all he knew they could have been passing through the Brooklyn tundra, if there was such a thing. They saw three cars piled up on the side of the expressway, two police cars and two ambulances parked behind them; but Jefferson drove past without a glance at the accident, his mind intent only on the interview ahead. He knew he was laying his head on the block by accompanying Malone on these "unofficial" visits to Padua and whomever they were going to see in Staten Island, but he liked this phlegmatic Australian and he knew how he would have felt if any jerk had ever kidnapped Mary. There were times when the job was of no importance at all except for the clout it could give you.

They crossed the Verrazano Bridge, the storm blasting at them, threatening to sweep them off into the Narrows beneath. "If they release those guys from The Tombs, they're gonna have to drive them to Cuba. I can't see any planes taking off tomorrow, not unless this storm blows itself out all of a sudden."

"I'll drive the bastards there myself," said Malone, "if it means getting my wife back."

They came down off the bridge on to the Staten Island Expressway, turned off and headed south. There was less neon out here; they were in the suburbs of darkness. Then Jefferson slowed, began peering out at street signs; finally he turned right and pulled up in front of a tavern. There was a small neon sign in the window, offering *Beer and Cocktails* to the traveller in the storm.

They got out of the car and went into the bar, a dingy stall staffed by a St Bernard in a dirty apron. Before they had time to speak to him a thin young man in a black raincoat and a plaid cap got up from one of the booths.

"Mr Malone?" He had a pleasant smile and he looked to Malone like one of the youngsters one used to see in the films they no longer made any more, the quiet dark boy who was the buddy of the college hero. There's something wrong: this kid looks too square to have anything to do with Padua or his connections or the kidnapping. "You have a car? We'll go in that, if you don't mind. Mine is an MG, it might be a squeeze for all of us."

Once in the car he gave them directions, then sat back, occasionally passing casual remarks about the weather. "I was sailing only yesterday, out on the Sound. Now look at this – " Then he leaned forward. "That's the place."

It was a closed-down picture theatre standing in a line of dark locked-up stores, some of them with their fronts boarded up. As they got out of the car, the wind and the rain still lashing at them, the young man said, "We are waiting for this section to be re-zoned. Eventually, we hope, we'll have a development of better class homes and apartments here."

"Are you in real estate?" Jefferson asked.

"I'm still at college studying business administration. But I was the one who saw the possibilities here." He said it with almost shy modesty, as if he were ashamed of being so precocious. "This way, please."

"Do I come too?" said Jefferson.

"That's up to you – Captain Jefferson, isn't it? Mr Padua rang back after you'd left, just to say you were with Mr Malone. Are you here officially or unofficially?"

"Unofficially," said Jefferson. "Very."

"Then there's no problem."

He slid back a grille across the front of the theatre, opened a door and led the way across the lobby. The place was in darkness, but by the light of the flickering street lamps outside Malone had seen the posters peeling off the billboards on the walls. A torn and mangled Shirley MacLaine smiled at him, and behind her dozens of other stars were leaning on her as they peeled off the wall. The posters, Malone imagined, might go right *through* the wall: Tom Mix might be buried somewhere there in the peeling sheets, pushing Lillian Gish out of the way to smile at the public who had gone forever. The young man opened another door into the picture theatre itself.

Malone paused, all at once realizing how far they had come, aware of the unknown danger that might lie ahead. "Why do we have to come to a place like this?"

"Privacy, Mr Malone. You'll have to trust us. We don't want trouble, any more than you do. We're just trying to be civic-minded, Mr Malone."

"That's all you guys are these days," said Jefferson. "Nice harmless civic-minded people."

"I get your point, Captain," said the young man with a smile. "But would you believe – I've never heard the word *Mafia* spoken in our family?"

"How about *Cosa Nostra*?"

"Fairy-tales." The young man smiled again, but now there was just a slight coolness to his voice. "But is this the time to be asking such questions?"

Then he led them into the theatre, down an aisle between the rows of empty seats. Malone, eyes alert, saw the four men standing in the shadows, one to each corner of the big cavernous barn. He saw Jefferson undo the button of his jacket, making it easier to get at the gun in his shoulder-holster if the emergency arose. Then they had stopped by an elderly, heavily-built man sitting in an aisle seat.

"Grandfather, this is Mr Malone and Captain Jefferson." The young man gestured at the old man who was wrapped in a dark overcoat and was wearing a black homburg hat. "My grandfather, Don Auguste Giuffre."

"Wait at the back, Ralph. In case we have some other customers." He chuckled, waited till his grandson had gone back up the aisle. Then he raised his hand, waved it in a dismissal gesture. The two men down at the front of the theatre moved up the side aisles, joined their partners at the back and the four of them disappeared through the door into the lobby. Then, and only then, did Don Auguste Giuffre look up at Malone and Jefferson. "I own this movie house. Once I come here with my family every Saturday night – two features, three shorts, a newsreel, all for fifty cents. Pete Smith was my favourite. Now – " He made a gesture of disgust. "I could keep it open, make money by showing dirty movies. But my grandchildren, the young ones, not Ralph back there, they might come here. Not good. Sit down, gentlemen."

Malone looked over his shoulder towards the back of the theatre. The four men had disappeared, but Ralph Giuffre stood by the door. The two policemen moved into the row in front of the old man, faced him with their buttocks perched on the backs of the seats behind them. The lights along the side walls were on, but they had been dimmed: the show was about to start. Two features, three shorts and a newsreel, all for fifty cents: Malone wondered what price the old man was going to ask for what he was about to offer them.

"What can I do for you, gentlemen?" Giuffre's accent was rough, as ineradicable as a birthmark; but his manners were impeccable, he took his position as *don* of his Family as seriously as any president or prime minister. "Our friend said you were having some trouble – "

"Mr Padua – " said Malone.

Giuffre held up a hand. "No names, please. Is better that way."

"All right, no names." Malone had decided he would do the talking; it was too long since he had been a junior cop, keeping his mouth shut, and, besides, he could take the questioning further than Jefferson could. If he could think of the right questions . . . He would begin with a lie, not always the best approach but one that had, accidentally, had its effect on Padua: "The kidnappers have threatened your friend. They said they would plant a bomb outside his house if you interfered."

"Did they say that?"

"They implied it."

"Implied – what's *implied*? I do not have the education my grandson has."

"They hinted – suggested – "

"You mean that's what you think they meant?"

This old bugger may not have gone to college, but he is educated all right. "No, that's what I'm *sure* they meant."

"I think you are bluffing, Mr Malone." The old man took off his hat, put it on the seat beside him. He was bald, with white wings of hair that stood out above ears that seemed almost at right angles to his head; the effect was to broaden his whole head, like primitive masks Malone had seen in museums. Now that Malone's eyes had become accustomed to the dim light he could see that the old man's face was mottled, as if his skin had been tie-dyed. At certain moments and in certain moods, Malone decided, Don Auguste Giuffre could be downright ugly. But so far his temper and his voice were even. "The kidnappers do not know who our friend represents."

I can be cunning too. "If they don't know who he represents, how do you know who they are? I think you are bluffing too, Mr Giuffre."

Giuffre sat very still in his seat for a long moment, then he shifted his bulk, took out a handkerchief and blew his nose. "Every year, this time, I get a cold. I never get used to the New York climate."

"You should go home to Sicily," said Jefferson, shifting his own bulk on the back of the seat.

The old man shook his head. "Nothing there, Mr Jefferson. Everybody I know is dead. Stupid vendettas – " He looked back at Malone. "You think I am bluffing, Mr Malone? That is insulting."

"My wife is in danger," said Malone. "I didn't come here to watch my manners. I'm sure if Mrs Giuffre was in the same situation, you wouldn't be too bloody polite."

"My wife is dead, Mr Malone. But you are right – " He looked down to the front of the theatre, to the big blank screen, defaced by a large rip in it, that still hung there. He was not an imaginative man and the screen remained blank for him: he did not see there the scenes that had mirrored this clandestine meeting with his enemies, the police. Edward G. Robinson, Joseph Calleia, Eduardo Cianelli: he had never come to see movies that had featured Italian gangsters: to him they had been as dirty as the sex movies of today. He had never condoned even the amount of flesh that was shown in Italian-made movies; but Mama, God rest her lately departed soul, had liked Sophia Loren and Gina Lollobrigida. If anyone had ever attempted to kidnap Mama, he, personally, would have cut the heart out of the son-of-a-bitch. "I am trying to help you, Mr Malone. And the Mayor."

"How?"

"Everybody has the wrong picture of us Italians. The Negroes also, eh, Mr Jefferson?"

"At least you're the right colour."

"You think so? An olive skin, dark hair, a name like Giuffre or Rapelli or Gasperi, you get into trouble with the police, and what they say? Who you know in the Mafia?" He looked around as if searching for a place to spit. "When I come to America sixty year ago, nobody talk about the Mafia. My father and me, we had an oyster lease in those days. There were coloured folk there too, nice peaceful people from the South, and we got along fine. The oyster leases, they nearly all gone now, everything muddied up. What they call it – polluted? Anyway, when I first come here nobody heard of the Mafia. Men with Italian names get into trouble with the police, lots of them, but nobody say anything about the Mafia."

Jefferson said nothing, his dark face an asset in the gloom: Giuffre could read nothing in it. Over this past year or two he had heard this plea so often he could recite it by heart. The honest, decent Italians were entitled to resent being classed as all related to the Mafia, but that did not say there was no Mafia.

"Why do they call you *Don* Auguste?"

Giuffre shrugged, shifted again in his seat. He should have had the meeting up in the circle, where he and Mama used to sit in the old days: the seats were wider and more comfortable up there. "Just respect, Mr Jefferson. And a little pride for me, too, I suppose – it's a title. Like yours. Why do they call you Captain?"

"Maybe because I earned it."

"Me, too. I have done much good in this parish – ask the priests and the sisters, ask anybody. Now I want to do some good for the Mayor."

"Why him?" Malone asked.

"The Mayor, he is not gonna stay in City Hall. If we have an Italian in the White House, nobody is gonna say all Italians belong to the Mafia. Mr Forte, everybody respect him. I would like to see him in the White House, the first Italian President. The Greeks got a Vice-President, didn't they? What the Greeks ever do for the world? They invent something called democracy and they sit on their asses ever since."

So much for Greek history, Malone thought; but his own education could not add much to it. "All right, then, help us. But don't let's waste time." He held up his watch, looked at it in the dim light. Though he always wore a watch, in the past he had rarely looked at it; but now time had become a growing sore, like a skin cancer on his wrist. "If these people stick to their deadline, every minute counts."

"I got information on all those men in The Tombs. Maybe more than you got, Mr Jefferson – " For a moment there was a twinkle in the dark eyes; they had seemed as dull as black olives to Malone. "You try Fred Parker, ask him about San Francisco and Pasquale Parioli. Maybe he tell you something?"

"Do *you* know something?" Jefferson asked.

The old man smiled, put his hat carefully on his head. "If I tell you, Mr Jefferson, maybe you think you owe me something. Is that what you want?" He stood up and Malone was surprised at how short he was; he had looked a much taller, bigger man in the seat. He stepped out into the aisle, looked down with distaste at the litter. "Was a very clean place when we ran pictures here. Everywhere. Up there – " he gestured at the screen " – here, everywhere. It's a dirty world now."

3

"He should know," said Jefferson as they got into their car. "It's his kind has made it dirty. I just never understand the split in their characters. They lead blameless family lives – they go to church, bring their kids up strict, protect and respect their women. Yet that old bastard has ordered more contracts – "

"Contracts?"

"Orders to kill. He's handed out more of those than I can count – but we've never been able to lay a finger on him. He runs the drug racket in South Brooklyn and there isn't a bar or restaurant for miles around that he isn't leaning on in some way or other. He's got the prostitution game sewed up and he runs two union locals in the construction business. He sure knows it's a dirty world."

"I'll worry about my conscience later – when I get my wife back."

Malone watched Giuffre, his elbow held solicitously by his grandson, cross the sidewalk and get into the big black Cadillac drawn up in front of Jefferson's car. The Cadillac drove off into the night, its tail-lights lost almost at once in the driving rain. A moment later it was followed by another car containing the *don*'s four bodyguards. Malone looked across at the flapping, shredded posters beneath the theatre marquee. A sticker had been pasted across the posters: *Last Week Ever*: behind the obituary notice *The Love Bug* rode into oblivion.

"Were the good old days really that good and innocent?"

"Maybe not innocent, but a goddam sight better than today." But Jefferson wondered if he spoke the truth. Nostalgia was only an escape and everyone had his own exit; but it could never be proved that the past had been better, memory could never be trusted to be objectively selective. He started up the car. "Do we go and see Fred Parker at The Tombs?"

They drove back to Manhattan through the almost deserted streets; the storm seemed to have worsened. It was almost a relief to get inside the detention building; at least the storm gathering in here had not yet broken. But in the hard light reflected from the yellow walls none of the guards looked relaxed. Malone noticed, as he had this afternoon, the tension under the casual, gum-chewing attitude of the officers; this hurricane they policed might not blow itself out for years, not till the whole prison system was changed. Jefferson signed himself and Malone in, checked his gun with the guard in the duty cubicle, then led Malone into the Warden's office.

The Assistant Warden, a black about Jefferson's age, was on duty. "I can't let you see them this time of night, John. What authority have you got?"

"I'll sign a DD24, if you want it."

Davidson, the Assistant Warden, pondered a moment, then nodded. "Okay, just to keep my own nose clean. Parker? I dunno he'll come down to see you."

"Just tell him Don Auguste Giuffre sent us."

Davidson's eyebrows went up. He had prematurely grey hair and eyebrows; Malone thought he looked like a negative of a white man, but he knew he would never voice the description. He had noticed that Davidson had barely glanced at him since he had entered the room.

"The Mafia? Are they in this?"

"What's the Mafia?" Jefferson made an Italian gesture with his hands; both blacks smiled at each other. "Just do me the favour, Phil. We're trying every angle we can to get Inspector Malone's wife back. And the Mayor's."

Davidson looked at Malone seemingly for the first time. Then he nodded. "Okay. But if Parker won't see you, I'm not gonna press him. We got enough to worry about here without worrying about what's going on outside."

That's it, Malone thought. He doesn't care one way or the other about me, whether I'm white, brindle or striped. I'm just an outsider, someone who doesn't belong to his world, The Tombs. He and all the other guards are the long-term prisoners here.

Malone and Jefferson went out to one of the interview rooms, sat there for ten minutes before the door finally opened and a grey-haired man, his face still cobwebbed with sleep, came in with a young black guard.

"Curiosity got the better of me, Captain." Fred Parker sat down at the table, lit a cigarette and blew out the smoke. Malone tried to guess his age, but it was impossible: too many years had been crossed out on the lined calendar of his face. Once he might have been heavily built, but passion and God knew what else had worn all the flesh off him; the fingers that held the cigarette were the thinnest Malone had ever seen on a man, no more than claws of bone. Yet there was an air of tired tranquillity about Parker, as if the tightly wound spring of the years had finally rusted and fallen apart. "Who the hell is Don Auguste Giuffre? Is that the name you sent up?"

Jefferson considered the other man for a moment, then said, "I do believe you honestly don't know. You live in a world all your own, you anarchists, don't you?"

"Everyone needs his escape, Captain. But don't quote me." He looked over his shoulder at the young guard behind him. "Especially to my young friends upstairs."

"Giuffre is a Mafia *don*, one of the top three in the New York area."

"Ah, then that's why I wouldn't have heard of him." He glanced at Malone and smiled; several of his teeth were missing, yet it was still a not unattractive smile. "We anarchists, Mr Malone, are the only political party in America who have no connection with the Mafia."

"You should try campaigning on it," said Malone. He had had no experience of anarchists. Somehow Australians, among the world's most conservative rebels, had bred very few; Australians had always had very little tolerance for eccentrics, especially for political rat-bags. "But Giuffre said he knew a lot about you. More than Captain Jefferson and his mates know."

"Captain Jefferson and his – *mates* have a file on me they tell me is that thick – " He held his hands apart. "I think Don Auguste Giuffre has been putting you on, Inspector."

"He said to mention San Francisco and a Pasquale Parioli."

Parker drew on his cigarette, but Malone did not miss the slight tremor in the bone-like fingers. "What else did he say?"

"Let's just take that for starters. Who is Pasquale Parioli?"

"Don't you know?"

"No," admitted Malone. All the years of questioning had developed a sixth sense in him: he knew this man was on the verge of talking. "But we can go back to Giuffre, if that's what you'd prefer."

Parker said nothing, staring down at the smoke curling up from between his fingers. Somewhere outside a steel door clanged and he lifted his head, not quickly but like an old dog recognizing a familiar sound, a door that had been opened and shut many times. He was dressed in a cheap blue suit that could have been twenty years old and a tie-less white shirt that was in need of laundering; Malone didn't know how the other anarchists, except McBean, dressed, but he guessed Parker must be the square amongst them. He looked like the crumpled newspaper picture of some clerk in the Fifties who had been arrested on a charge of petty embezzlement. Except for his face: there was too much agony, too much exhausted idealism there for a man caught only with his hand in the cash-box.

"Jesus, they never let you go!" His hand quivered and he took another drag on the cigarette, coughing on the smoke this time. When he had recovered he looked at Jefferson. "There's a prologue to that file on me, Captain. You want to hear it?"

"If you want to tell it." Both Jefferson and Malone were quietly casual: they were dealing here with a man who was not going to spend the night waving polemics at them. Fred Parker, they were beginning to realize, had grown tired of carrying banners and shouting slogans.

"None of this gets to the kids upstairs, okay? I'm not gonna split on them, but I'd just sooner keep a piece of myself to myself, you know what I mean?" Jefferson and Malone nodded, waiting patiently; this was not the time to be counting minutes, because what they might learn might save them hours. Parker lit another cigarette, sat back in his chair. "Pasquale Parioli was my old man. He was the top lieutenant for the *capo* of one of the Families in 'Frisco. That was back in the Twenties and Thirties – I was seventeen years old before I found out how he made his dough, and I only found that out because someone chopped him down, with a Thompson gun, right outside our front door. That was in – 1932. Yeah, 1932." He closed his eyes for a moment, shutting out the present, trying to look back at the years he had tried to forget. "My old lady knew what my father did – I dunno whether she condoned it, but she never made any excuses for him. They were both from Sicily and maybe she believed in the Mafia and the way it went about things. I dunno – I never stopped to ask her. I ran away from home the day they buried my old man and I never went back, never saw my mother or my sisters again." He had been talking with his eyes downcast, as if memory were something he had laid out on the table in front of him; but now he looked up. "You're not taking any of this down?"

"Not unless you want us to," said Jefferson. "That file doesn't really concern Inspector Malone and me. Not to-night, anyway."

Parker nodded. "Maybe it's all only what they call extenuating circumstances and I don't think the powers-that-be want any of that. They've already made up their minds about me." There was no bitterness in his voice nor in his thin smile. "What they'd never believe is that I became an anarchist because I didn't believe in a society that had room for characters like my old man. I'm a very moral man – I even believe in God. I've read 'em all and preached 'em all – Bakunin, Kropotkin, Malatesta. But I believe in God and – maybe I should've been a priest – I think Christ preached a better brand of propaganda than any of them. But don't tell that to my friends upstairs – they'd think I was a Jesus freak and I sure as hell ain't that."

Malone, without lifting his arm from the table, stole a glance at his wrist-watch. "What happened after you ran away from home?"

"America, that's what happened. All of it." Parker put his head back and for a moment his eyes were those of a young man. "Jesus, it was a country then! Lots wrong with it – but still it had something. If we could have taken it over then – " He stubbed out his cigarette in an ashtray filled with the butts of the day's visitors, the brown and white ends of other people's nerves. "But I'm tired now – "

"Keep going, Fred," said Jefferson, his impatience showing for the first time. "You can't stop now."

Parker smiled again. "You misunderstand me, Captain. I mean I'm tired of what I've been doing all these years. The kids today are different – I don't even speak their language. I had nothing to do with that bombing we're in here for. Okay, okay – " He held up a hand. "I *know*. You're not the one I'm supposed to plead before. But if they offer me a ticket to Cuba tomorrow, I'm gonna take it. Do you think the Mafia operates there?"

"What has the Mafia got on you?" Malone asked.

"Nothing." Parker opened his hands in the gesture Malone had seen several times that night. "I don't even know what they know about me. But they must have kept tabs on me all this time. How, Christ knows. I changed my name three times after leaving 'Frisco – it was 1936, '37, before I became Fred Parker. When the file started – " He grinned at Jefferson.

"Parker," said Malone carefully, "something is going to happen to my wife and the Mayor's wife if we don't release you from here and fly you to Cuba – "

"I know that, Inspector. It's not a deal I would've planned myself – I've never traded lives, women's or men's. That would only reduce me to my old man's level."

"We don't even know if their lives haven't already – been finished." Malone shut his eyes for just a moment: for Christ's sake, Malone, don't lose hope! When he opened them he saw the look of sympathy on the face of the young black guard behind Parker and he nodded gratefully. "We could sit still, release you and just wait for the women to be delivered. But we have no guarantee that that is what is going to happen. You say you're a moral man. If you get away to Cuba and my wife and Mrs Forte are never re-turned, are – *killed*, are you going to come back and help us put the finger on the muderers?"

Parker took his time about replying; then he lit another cigarette, said through the smoke, "I'd do that if I knew who they were, Inspector. But I don't know who they are. I'm as much in the dark as you are. I'm sure the Mafiosi could help you more than I can."

Malone shook his head. "They wouldn't have sent us to you. If they knew anything definite, they'd have put a price on it."

"You're learning, Inspector. Do you have the Mafia in Australia?"

"They may be there, but so far they've been no trouble." Malone looked up, feeling sick now with disappointment; he had learned nothing, except that the Mafia never lost track of even the distant members of its family. "Thanks for coming down to see us, Parker."

"Just a minute." Parker stubbed out his cigarette, stood up. He looked at the young guard. "Would you do me a favour, Mr Irving, and leave us alone for two minutes?"

The guard looked at Jefferson. "I'm not supposed to – "

"I'll take the responsibility. Do me and Inspector Malone a favour too."

The guard looked at Malone, indecision mixed with sympathy on his young bony face, then he nodded, stepped outside the door and pulled it closed behind him.

"How big are the files on the other guys?" Parker asked Jefferson.

"I looked at them this afternoon. The ones on Ratelli and Latrobe started the day they were picked up. We don't know anything about them other than their names."

"I know Ratelli. It's not his real name – I'm not gonna tell you what is – but I know a little about him. But Latrobe – he's a blank page. Try him."

"Fred," said Jefferson slowly, "you haven't got it in for the kid, have you? We're trying to save a coupla women's lives. We don't have time to help you revenge yourself on some kid who's rubbed you the wrong way."

"Have more faith, Captain. That's what anarchy is, you know, having faith in people. No, the kid's okay as far as I'm concerned. I don't even know if he can help, but I can tell you – he's the only one amongst us who could have someone on the outside working for him. The rest of us – " He shook his head. "McBean, Fishman, Ratelli, they all come from families so uptight they don't even let off firecrackers the Fourth of July. Me? You think the Mafia would want me out?"

"Why have they kept tabs on you so long then?" said Malone.

"They're another bureaucracy. They just never want to let you go." He held out the claw of his hand to Malone. "Good luck, Inspector. In a proper society there would be no need for kidnapping."

"I'd like to think so," said Malone. "You just have more faith in human nature than I have, whatever the society."

"Faith," said Parker, forty years on the road to his New World and now knowing he had been standing still all the time, "it's the only banner I got left. They just won't let me wave it in a place like this."

He went out, the door clanging shut behind him, and Malone looked at Jefferson. "Do you sometimes feel sorry for the so-called enemies of society, feel you may even be on their side?"

"Too often for my own comfort," said Jefferson. "Well, let's see if this kid Latrobe will talk to us."

But Latrobe wouldn't talk to them, refused to come down to them from his cell up on the seventh floor. Jefferson and Malone went back to the Warden's office. Davidson, his feet up on the desk, sat up as they came in, put down the paperback book he had been reading.

"*The Female Eunuch*. I think I'd rather handle what we got in here than a bunch of Women's Lib."

"Has your wife read the book?" Jefferson asked.

"You kidding? I let her read that, I wouldn't bother to go home. This would be Sunnybrook Farm compared to home."

"I don't read any of it. Come Liberation Day for women, I'm gonna let them walk right over me – it'll be easier. Phil, we want to go up and take a look at young Latrobe. Okay?"

"Just a look? Okay, but don't make too much fuss up there, John. We got some mean bastards on that floor, just waiting for an excuse to start something." He picked up his phone, gave instructions to someone on the other end. As he put it down he said, "They say everything is quiet up there now. For Chrissake, don't disturb 'em."

"Are Parker and the others on that floor?"

"No, we got 'em spread around, so's they can't communicate with each other." He picked up the book again, settled back in his chair. "Female eunuchs. I've met one or two women I thought should've had the balls cut outa them."

A guard took them up in the elevator, waited with them until another guard had unlocked the barred gate on to the bridge, the central area that joined the two tiers of cells arranged on either side of it. The door was closed quietly behind them and the guard, another young black, said softly, "Most of 'em are sleeping. I've woked Latrobe, but he ain't said anything, ain't even got off his bed."

He led them down to a cell at the far end of the bridge. In the cells they passed, open-barred cubicles that offered no privacy, Malone was aware of figures stirring, slowly rising from their beds like disturbed animals. He saw the eyes watching him and he thought, I'm in a zoo: those are cages and that's a menagerie of killers behind those bars.

"Dig Whitey." He barely heard the whisper, but it seemed to grow on its own echoes in the bare-walled chamber; it was taken up by other voices, finally rising to a scream: "Kill Whitey! Kill! Kill!"

Malone kept walking, waiting for some reaction from

Jefferson and the guard. They came to the end cell and only then did the guard say, "You and Latrobe are the only white men on this floor, Inspector. Maybe it would have been better if you'd let Captain Jefferson come up by himself."

"It's too late now," said Jefferson. He had to raise his voice above the din; the prisoners were yelling and chanting and banging on the bars of their cells. "What's the score on this floor?"

"Every cell's full, Captain, two to a cell. We got all sorts – half a dozen rapists, coupla sodomists, six on murder raps, some dope pushers, half a dozen crazies – you name it, we got 'em up here."

All the inmates were awake now, all standing at the bars to their cells, some standing quietly like men waiting to be let out, but most of them screaming, yelling, sobbing, kicking at the bars with the heels of their shoes. It sounded like pandemonium; then Malone noticed there was a rhythm to the bedlam. There was the occasional off-beat scream or thumping on the bars, but Malone guessed that came from one or two of the psychopaths. But the very steadiness of the rhythm invoked its own feeling of fear in Malone. This was controlled hatred, the intelligent use of anarchy against those like himself, the whites who ran the society they hated. No wonder Fred Parker, the out-of-date anarchist, was exhausted and finished.

The guard switched on a nearby light, looked at his watch. "I gotta call downstairs, Captain. Every ten minutes we gotta report in by phone to the control room."

As the guard walked back to the entrance gate the inmates chanted *Kill, Kill, Kill* at him, but he took no notice of them; the shouting was a gesture, like the chanting of campus demonstrators, and they had no real hatred of him. He wore the wrong uniform but he had the right colour, there was still some hope for him.

"Every ten minutes right around the clock they report in," said Jefferson. "You never know when the psychos are gonna go crazy and start trying to kill themselves or the guy in with them. Looks like we got one here."

"I am a political prisoner," said the young black standing inside the bars. He was thin and he had the biggest eyes Malone had ever seen in a man's face; they reminded him of the eyes he had seen in the faces of starving children in pictures of Asian famines. The man's hair was in paper curlers, the hair wound tightly into thin strands that stuck straight out from his head; his head looked like a black pudding studded with fancy cocktail picks. He was dressed in a yellow frilled blouse and a red-and-yellow flared skirt and he was barefooted. He's straight out of Uncle Tom's Cabin, Malone thought, a caricature piccaninny. The man's voice had a high lisping note to it: "Women's Liberation is a legitimate movement – "

"There are no political prisoners in here." Malone was surprised at the coldness in Jefferson's voice. Even though he must know he was dealing with a mentally unbalanced transvestite, it seemed to be a sore point with Jefferson that the jail was holding political prisoners. "Every one of you who is in here is here because he broke the law. Whether he broke it for political reasons doesn't matter – he broke it and that's why he's here. You're not here because of your politics."

"Bullshit," said a voice from the back of the cell.

The transvestite looked over his shoulder. "You are right, honey, but that's no language to use in front of a lady."

I'm dreaming all this, Malone thought. I'm exhausted and worried and now everything is becoming a nightmare. The chanting had almost died away and everyone in the cells was trying to hear what was being said down at the end cell; occasionally there would be a scream or a wild laugh, but the offender would angrily be told to shut up. A barred window high in a wall at the end of the bridge was partly open and through it came the sound of the storm as it tore its way through a narrow alley outside. There was a thick smell in Malone's nostrils, of sweat and ammonia and stale food and excreta, the sour smell of prison, and somewhere in a cell on the upper tiers a man was crying quietly, like a child afraid of the dark. And in front of Malone and Jefferson the thin dark head with its paper curlers swung itself back and forth on its bony shoulders.

"No respect, no respect! How can we get equality when there's no respect?"

Jefferson looked past the transvestite into the back of the cell. A white youth lay on a bunk, hands behind his head, dark expressionless eyes staring down past the lower planes of his face at the two policemen. "Mr Latrobe, we'd like to talk to you."

Latrobe said nothing, the expression on his still face remaining unchanged. Malone could not see him clearly in the gloom, but one feature did mark him: through his long dark hair there ran a broad white streak, as bizarre in its way as the paper curlers on the head of the other man in the cell.

"Oh, he don't talk, except to be insulting to me." The transvestite reached out a hand through the bars at Malone, but the latter stepped back; suddenly the black spat at him and the spittle hit Malone in the face. His immediate reaction was to lunge forward, but Jefferson put an arm in front of him. The transvestite giggled delightedly and wiggled his hips, swaying the skirt from side to side. "We fed up with *your* insults too, white honey."

Malone wiped his face with his handkerchief, looked at Jefferson. "Maybe I *had* better go downstairs. You'll probably get further without me up here."

"Why don't both of you get lost?" That was a man from the next cell, a huge brute who looked as if, were he to put his mind and strength to it, he could bend the bars that encaged him like vermicelli stalks. "You pigs stink up the place."

Jefferson ignored him, looked back at Latrobe. "You could maybe save the lives of two women, Latrobe, if you talked to us."

Latrobe still said nothing, but now turned his face to the wall beside his head. The giant in the next cell pressed his face against the bars, making himself even uglier; his small dark eyes, surrounded by scar tissue, stared out on either side of the yellow bar that split his broad face. He put a huge paw down and rubbed the front of his trousers.

"They white pussy? You saving 'em for yo'self, black pig?"

Malone suddenly knew he had to get out of this place, at once, before he tried to reach in through the bars to get at these men who hated him. He abruptly wheeled about and walked down to the entrance gate. As he did so the chanting started up again: *Kill, Kill, Kill,* a litany of hate whose echoes he knew would never die away in his ears. Cops were disliked in Australia, but he had never met anything like this: he was branded by both his badge and his skin, and the latter he could never hand in. You could not resign from your race: the men yelling and screaming and spitting at him on either side of him told him that; they knew it even better than he did. He understood their hatred of him, yet he hated them for it. If any one of the men had stepped out of his cell Malone knew he would have attacked him, would have vented all his fury on the black skin that faced and taunted him.

The young guard let him through the gate and he stood on the landing outside the elevator. A senior guard, also a black, had just stepped out of the elevator and he looked angrily at Malone.

"I dunno who you are, mister, but you asked for that." Jefferson came through the gate and the guard captain turned to him. "They should never have let you up here, not this time of night. Christ, don't you think we got enough trouble on our hands?"

"I'm sorry, but we needed some information. We didn't get it, unfortunately." Jefferson looked at Malone. "You all right, Scobie?"

Malone stood facing the wall, both hands leaning on it;

he looked like a suspect about to be frisked by the two black law officers. He was trembling, something he could not remember ever having had happen to him before; he felt cold, as if a fever had suddenly left him. The shouting and the banging on the cell bars was still going on, and behind it all was the loud mad laughter of a prisoner who had suddenly gone hysterical.

"All my bloody life," said Malone dazedly, talking to himself as much as to the two middle-aged black men behind him, "I've tried to tell myself I was tolerant, that I didn't care a bugger what colour a man's skin was. But just then, for a minute or two, I was a bloody racist. I'd have killed any one of those bastards, if you'd let me at him. Just because he was a bloody nigger." He dropped his arms, turned round, stared at the two dark faces looking at him expressionlessly. "And don't tell me you understand, because I won't believe you. I don't understand myself, not now anyway."

The two blacks exchanged glances, then Jefferson pressed the button for the elevator. "Let's go downstairs, Scobie."

The shouting and banging were dying away as Malone and Jefferson got into the elevator. They rode down in silence and when they got out Jefferson, still saying nothing, led the way to the Warden's office. Davidson, *The Female Eunuch* nowhere in sight now, was poring over some papers. He looked up as the two men came in.

"There was a ruckus up there. Captain Hemmings blew his top because I let you go up." Davidson was a tall angular man whose unflappability had been his main recommendation towards his promotion; he knew that the world, its joys and griefs, its wars and riots, would never alter its course because of anything he might do. Come Judgment Day he would be standing patiently in line, reading a paperback, while everyone else was adding up his merits or demerits. He would take neither heaven nor hell for granted, but he would accept the fact that, wherever he was bound, someone else had already booked his place for him. He accepted The

Tombs and everything in it as a fact of life. "I was just about to send up the riot squad."

"It was all just noise, nothing serious," said Jefferson, but he did not look at Malone. "Phil, could we have a look at what you took off Latrobe when he came in?"

"Sure." Davidson picked up his phone. When he put it down he said, "You get anything out of him? Nothing? Neither have we. We get silent bastards in here, but most of 'em are psychos or junkies. But he just seems to have withdrawn from the human race. Can't say I blame him, the section of it he's got up there with him on that floor.'

"Why did you put that fag in with him?"

"I had nowhere else to put the fag. I got a whole block of them on the fourth floor, but there was no room for that one. If I put him in a cell with any of the straights, they'd rape him before we locked the door. He's safe enough with Latrobe."

A guard brought in a tin tray in a cloth bag. A tag was tied to the bag: *Charles Latrobe* and the date of his admission. When the guard had gone out Jefferson ran his fingers through the few belongings in the tray.

"Not much there." A wallet, some money, a gold-nibbed fountain pen, a pearl-handled penknife, a gold signet ring. "No social security card, nothing like that?"

"That's all he had on him," said Davidson. "The wallet had nothing but those dollar bills in it, not even a driver's licence. Just as if he knew he was gonna be picked up and he was gonna have nothing on him that would identify him."

"What about the pen and ring?" Malone was almost his normal self again. The experience upstairs had almost wrenched him apart; but he had to remember that the safe recovery of Lisa was his sole objective. He tried being a cop again: "That's a pretty expensive Parker pen, isn't it? How many anarchists go around with those?"

"Fred Parker, maybe," said Jefferson, then grinned with embarrassment. "Sorry."

Malone recognized the small, poor joke for what it was: an attempt by Jefferson to tell him that the mood upstairs was forgotten. He managed a smile in return. "It was probably a present from someone. We don't do it back home, but don't you Americans give graduation presents or something?"

"We celebrate everything," said Jefferson with only mild sarcasm. "I remember when I was a kid I was sorry I wasn't a Jew – I missed out on *bar mitzvah* presents. Latrobe isn't old enough to have graduated from college. This could be a high school graduation present."

"The ring could be anything," said Davidson, holding it up to the light. "On the head of it it's just got two colours, black and gold, with the initials ZT laid over it. Those could be his initials, Z.T. Z? Zeke? Zachary?"

"Could it be a high school ring?" Jefferson took the ring. "ZT. There's the Zachary Taylor High School out on Long Island. Did anybody check this out?"

"Maybe they did, maybe they didn't. That's the job of you guys up at Headquarters, John. We just look after them when you bring 'em in. We don't get paid for playing detective."

Jefferson gave him a sourly amused look, then said, "If Latrobe was so keen on hiding his identity, why did he keep something like this?"

"Sentiment," said Malone. "Maybe some girl gave it to him, or his parents. Maybe that and the fountain pen are the only links he has with who he really is, and he couldn't give them up. He's a brave man who chops off his past. For most of us it would be like chopping off an arm."

Jefferson looked at Davidson. "*That's* why we get paid for playing detective."

"I'm very impressed," said Davidson, but he smiled, "I hope you get somewhere. But where do you go from here?"

"I think we'd do better to go straight out to the school."

"This time of night?"

"There'll be a caretaker, or someone in the neighbourhood

who can tell us where we can find the principal." He looked up at the clock on the wall above Davidson's head. "I've never been on a case where I've had to watch the clock like this. Ten hours – it's not long."

"One thing before we go," Malone said to Davidson. "That white streak in Latrobe's hair – Did you run any photos of him in the newspapers? Nobody came forward to identify him from that?"

"That streak has only come out since he's been in here. That's been two months now. It must have been dyed when they first brought him in. In daylight you can still see the streaks of dyed hair in it. The photo in the newspapers didn't show it. No, nobody's come forward. For him or any of them."

Malone nodded, then gestured towards the phone. "May I call the Mayor, just to let him know where I am. And just in case he's had another message."

Davidson waved at the phone and Malone waited for the switchboard operator to connect him. Then: "Inspector Malone? This is Lieutenant Denning. The Mayor has been trying to reach you for the last hour. He wants you to call him at City Hall."

Malone pressed down the receiver buttons, then asked to be connected to City Hall. While he was waiting he looked at Jefferson. "I'm not daring to hope, but do you think – ?"

Jefferson shrugged, but his face remained blank. "We could have been lucky. Let's hope so."

Then Michael Forte came on the phone. "Inspector Malone? Scobie – where have you been? Where are you now?" It was impossible to tell from his voice what news he had. "Get across here to City Hall as soon as you can. Something's come up."

Chapter Seven

"Why do so many American men always wear black socks?" said Lisa. "They look like a lot of defrocked priests."

"What?" Sylvia looked up from examining the ladders in her stockings.

"Nothing. Just making conversation. But I might just as well save my breath."

"I just don't feel like talking. Chattering isn't going to help us in this situation."

"I'm not suggesting we chatter. I want to *talk* – about trying to escape from here."

"I told you, I don't *want* to talk about it. We'd never get out of this room – and that boy outside would beat us up unmercifully just for trying."

"That's a risk we'd have to take. God, haven't you risked *anything* in your life? Have you always waited for everything to be cut and dried and *safe*?"

Sylvia took her time about answering. She did not think she was any less brave than Lisa; but all her adult life had been given to weighing percentages. She did not think she would lack courage if instant action were required, certainly not lack it enough to immobilize her. Years ago, out on the Sound, she and her father had been caught in a sudden storm, their small craft driven before the wind like a crippled bird. She had never been so frightened, not until these past hours; but she had not panicked, had reacted instinctively to her father's shouted instructions and had helped bring the boat and themselves back to safety. She had hated and been frightened of storms ever since, and this was part of the reason she did not want to risk the attempt to escape from this cottage: the storm outside might be less dangerous than the boy in the next room, but it still held its fear for her. It, and the certainty in her own mind that Abel would hear them escaping, were percentages she could not ignore.

"He'll hear us – "

"With the noise of the storm? And he's got the television on, too. Look how loudly we've had to knock each time we've wanted to go to the bathroom."

"You'll never get those boards off – "

Lisa had been standing by the window examining the boards. They were planks, six inches wide by an inch thick, cut to fit exactly the width of the windows to the outer edges of the frame; Abel, who had cut the boards, had allowed no room for leverage between the wall and the raised edge of the frame. Each plank was held by three big nails at either end, each nail driven right into the timber. "If we could slide something in under the end of one of the boards – "

"What, for instance?"

"Oh, for God's sake, can't you be constructive?" It was only in the past half-hour that they had begun to snap at each other. Though they were not stumbling over each other, their prison room was proving too small for them; they did not have to adapt, as long-term prisoners in a penitentiary would have to, and their nerves were rebelling against the proximity of each other. They did not know each other well enough to make allowances. They had nothing in common but their predicament and it was not proving enough, despite its seriousness. "What if your husband can't do anything for us?"

"Then will be the time to think about escaping – "

"It'll be too bloody late then!" There was an echo in her ear of Scobie: she couldn't remember using *bloody* before, it was not one of her words. Oh God, let me see him again! Get us out of here – please! She turned back to the window, began to run her fingers up and down the edges of the boards, searching for some leverage.

Sylvia stood up, lifted her head and listened: it was an instinctive habit she had, as if she could hear nothing unless she strained for it. She heard the storm outside, the rain hammering against the shutters and the wind blasting its way through trees; she moved to the door and listened to the voices on the television set out in the living-room. Then she took the belt of her suit from where it hung on the end of the bed. "Try that. That buckle is brass – it may not bend."

It was a big square buckle with the initial S worked into the centre of it. "I might ruin it," said Lisa. "That's an expensive suit – "

"Goddammit, do you want to get out of here or not? What's more important – getting away from here or worrying about my suit? Or were you just talking – just *chattering*?"

"No, I wasn't just talking! I'll damned well show you!"

Lisa turned her back on Sylvia, began looking for a gap where she could insert a corner of the buckle under one of the boards. She was trembling with temper and her fingers fumbled; then she found a slit under the bottom board. She had to get down on her knees to get at it. The end of the buckle slid under the edge of the board, but not far enough to give her any leverage. She took off her shoe.

"What the devil are you going to do?"

"I'm going to have to hammer it under the board. Are you having second thoughts about me ruining the buckle?"

"No, I'm not. I just think he'll be sure to hear you – "

They were snarling at each other like two women who had been chained to each other for months. Perhaps all prisoners went through this mood, Lisa thought. The anatomy of captivity was something she had never studied; how many prisoners employed a PR consultant? The sudden wayward thought amused her, relaxed her. She sat back on her heels and looked up at Sylvia.

"Why are we picking at each other? We already have someone else to fight – why fight each other?"

Sylvia hesitated, then nodded. "I'm sorry. What can I do to help?"

"Keep an ear to the door while I try and hammer this buckle in."

It took four heavy whacks with Lisa's shoe to push the buckle in under the edge of the board. Being tall, she never wore really high heels; she was doubly fortunate that current fashion dictated solid chunky heels designed to help fashionable women escape from boarded-up rooms. After each hard tap she stopped and looked at Sylvia; the latter, ear pressed to the door, would listen and then nod to go on. Abel, a man not given to much reading, was filling in the hours waiting for Carole by looking at an old movie on television. Pat O'Brien, machine-gun voice punctuated with machine-gun fire, drowned out the sound of the shoe heel whacking against the buckle.

Lisa did not have enough strength in her wrists and forearms to use the buckle as a lever. Sylvia came and stood over her and together they pushed as hard as they could against the makeshift lever. The nails holding the board gave just a little; then the buckle began to bend. Lisa, massaging her hands and wrists, pulled out the buckle and reversed it.

"We'll have to drag the board out at least half an inch so we can get our fingers under it."

Sylvia was also massaging her hands. "I don't think the buckle is going to hold. Bonwit Teller should put steel ones on their suits."

"That other store – Bergdorf Goodman? – is better for escape kits."

They were joking out of the hysteria of exhaustion as much as anything else; but also out of the fear that had begun to increase now they had committed themselves. Beyond the bedroom door gangsters or police, someone, went down under a storm of bullets. And on the other side of the boarded-up window the real storm, the other enemy, beat against the shutters, mocking them.

They tried again, pushing hard against the buckle. Suddenly Sylvia's hands, oily with sweat, slid off Lisa's; as they did so, her long nails, breaking off, gouged into the back of Lisa's right hand. Lisa let out a stifled gasp of pain, let go the buckle and it clattered to the floor. Instantly both women turned towards the door, Lisa holding the back of her hand to her mouth.

But Warner Brothers had come to their rescue: thank God they had made noisy movies in the Thirties. Pat O'Brien yelled at Glenda Farrell and she yelled back: in those days one never heard a pin drop nor a brass buckle, perhaps not even a house brick. Lisa, still sucking her hand, picked up the buckle.

"That's no good. We'll have to find something else."

Sylvia looked at her broken nails, then at Lisa's blood-streaked hand. "You better put something on that, in case it becomes infected – "

"What, for instance?"

"I don't know. Anything. Spit, even – "

They were snapping at each other again; frustration was smarting as much as the bloody marks on Lisa's hand. Lisa got up, began to move angrily about the room, searching – for what? She abruptly pulled up, tried to steady herself. She wanted to weep, but that would only weaken her further; she was not afraid of nor ashamed of tears, but this was not the moment for them. Pain and disappointment had temporarily made her lose her normal coherence of thought; the walls closed in on her, closing her mind. She looked about her, trying to see everything in the room individually and in its turn; she remembered Scobie telling her that it was the way a good detective worked, always dismembering everything. Then, moving towards the furniture, she began to inspect every piece in detail.

She found what she was looking for with the dressing-table: its legs unscrewed, the screw a thick threaded iron bolt. As she took off the leg, Sylvia pushed one of the chairs forward to prop up the dressing-table. The two women looked at each other and nodded, their differences forgotten again. Lisa shoved the bolt end of the leg in beneath the board; there was just enough space to get some purchase. But when they pulled on the leg the board did not budge.

"We need a fulcrum," said Sylvia. "We'll get more leverage pushing instead of pulling."

Lisa glanced at her with amused admiration. "Where did you learn that?"

"It's a political maxim," said Sylvia, and smiled at her own reply; she was beginning to feel light-hearted, almost convinced now that they *were* going to escape. "I'll unscrew one of the other legs – we can use that."

She pushed the chair in squarely against the dressing-table, took off the other front leg. It was what they needed: held underneath the leg that Lisa pushed against, it gave them enough leverage to raise the end of the board. Lisa felt the board slowly coming away from the window frame; her wrists felt as if they were cracking, but she kept pushing with all her strength. Both of them, concentrating on what they were doing, did not notice the sudden silence in the other room: Pat O'Brien and the machine-guns had been replaced by a soft-sell commercial. The board suddenly gave, lifting off the window frame with a screech of nails. And in the split moment afterwards they did hear the silence out in the living-room, then the sharp scrape of a chair on the floor.

Lisa snatched the curtains together, fell on her bed, held the dressing-table leg against her breast as she hastily pulled the blankets up over her. Sylvia had fallen on her bed, done the same: pale with fear, eyes closed, they looked like women who had finally collapsed from exhaustion. They heard the key being turned in the lock, then the door opened.

Abel stood there looking down at the two women. For the first time he saw them without their glaring back at him. They were good-looking dames, even if one of them was almost old enough to be his mother. He had seen dames like them on Michigan Avenue back home, the well-dressed bitches whose husbands ran Chicago, who never saw the poor neighbourhoods, who preferred to believe ghettos only happened in other countries but never in America. He had hated those dames he had never known and now he transferred that hatred to the two women lying here asleep.

He stared at them, suddenly excited by his power over them; then his feeling of power made him magnanimous. He'd let them get a good night's sleep: tomorrow might be their last day. He switched out the light, closed the door and locked it.

Lisa opened her eyes, saw absolutely nothing in the blackness. She sat up, turned towards Sylvia; but there was only blackness there too. Then her eyes became accustomed to the darkness and she saw the thin sliver of light under the door; but it illuminated nothing, only seemed to deepen the darkness of the rest of the room. Lisa slid off her bed, groped towards Sylvia's bed, banged her knee against it and once again had to stifle a cry of pain. She fell on Sylvia, felt her way up the latter's body, whispered in her ear, "We can't put the light on again. We'll have to work in the dark."

"Oh God, is it worth it?"

Lisa shook her, feeling the hopeless listlessness in the body under her hands. "We've *got* to! If we stay here and he finds that loose board in the morning – "

She felt Sylvia's body stiffen. "We should never have started – "

"But we *did*! Come on – help me – "

She felt her way round Sylvia's bed and to the window. She dragged back the curtains and groped for the loosened board; one pull on it told her it would come away with no difficulty. She eased it back, careful in the darkness of the long protruding nails. Then she felt Sylvia touch her.

"It may take us hours in the dark – "

"We'll take it in turns." She was feeling beneath the second board from the bottom; now the bottom board had been removed there was space to slide the dressing-table leg in between the board and the inner edge of the frame. "Where's my shoe? I'm lopsided."

She found her shoe, put it on and then began to work. It took them an hour to remove enough boards for them to be able to reach up and snap back the window catch. By that time they had barked knuckles, aching wrists and nerves ready to burst through their skin; when they spoke to each other it was only to snarl abusively. But they were committed now to the same end: escape. There was no turning back.

The sound of the storm penetrated the bedroom more clearly as they removed the boards. But out in the living-room another old movie had begun: Akim Tamiroff was dying this time to Paramount's machine-guns. Lisa gently eased the window up, drew back her head as the wind whistled in through the slats of the shutters.

"Get your jacket and your handbag. You go out first and hold the shutters so they won't bang, while I get out."

"Which way shall we go?"

"To the left, I think. I remember when Abel came back in the truck this afternoon, I heard him drive up from that direction. The road or the street must be that way. Once we're there we'll look for the nearest lights."

Though she had been listening to the sound of the storm for hours, Lisa was shocked at the fury of it when she pushed open the shutters. One of them slammed back at her, almost breaking her wrist; she had to push hard against it to prevent its banging against the window frame. Though she was now looking out of the room she could still see nothing; the whirling roaring darkness suddenly had its own terror for her. But she fought against the erupting fear in her, pushed Sylvia out of the window.

"Good luck! Wait for me – we mustn't get separated – "

She had already put on her suit jacket. Her handbag was at her feet; she reached down in the darkness and snatched it up; even at that moment it struck her that she must be one of those women whose handbag was an inseparable part of her. She scrambled through the window, hitting her head on the raised glass, slipped on the sill and fell awkwardly into a pool of water and mud, grabbing at Sylvia as she did so. They both fell, Sylvia letting go of the shutters, which at once slammed back against the side of the house with a crack like gunfire.

Lisa struggled up to her hands and knees, looked up into the lash of the rain. And instantly the darkness was gone; for a moment she thought she had been blown out of her mind. The whole side of the cottage sprang into sharp relief: the glistening, dripping white boards, the banging dark shutters like disembodied wings, the ragged, frantically dancing bush at the corner. She saw the line of scrubby trees on the other side of the narrow driveway whipping back and forth in the onslaught of the wind, saw the fence that had been blown down; then the car or truck, she couldn't see which, was almost on top of her, its horn blowing urgently and its headlights blazing at her like white furnaces. She scrambled to her feet, shouting to Sylvia to follow her, and plunged across the driveway and through the trees. She fell over the blown-down fence, hurting her knee, picked herself up and stumbled down the side of the cottage next door.

She kept going, her mind a blank, running with the instinctive urge to escape of a terrified animal. She had forgotten Sylvia; she was alone in the black tumult of the night. She ran into something, cracking her hip against it; grabbed at it and recognized it as a picket fence. She felt her way along it, came to an opening and stumbled through it. Then the ground gave way beneath her and she fell, her mouth wide open in a scream that was nothing in the fury of the storm. She landed heavily on her side, sank into soft mud, felt it close over her face. Oh God, God, don't let me die!

She rolled over on her back, clawed the mud from her eyes and mouth, felt the rain washing it away. She got painfully back to her feet, trying now to accustom her eyes to the darkness. She looked around for Sylvia but there was no sign of her; which way had she gone, had she managed to get away at all? Lisa could no longer see the car's or truck's headlights; they must have been switched off. But she caught a glimpse of the dancing firefly of a torch and she turned and stumbled away from it, making her way along the trench or whatever it was she was in, one hand reaching out to the bank on her left. She was crying with fear and pain and exhaustion, but her legs carried her on of their own volition. She slipped and fell again, falling to her right. There was no bank there and, reaching out as she lay on the ground, she felt the mud give way to a hard surface. She must be on a road.

She stood up, stepped blindly on to the concrete surface of the roadway. Turning her face away from the wind and the rain, she could see a little more clearly now. It was not that the darkness had diminished, there now appeared to be varying degrees of it. She could make out no definite shapes, but there seemed to be houses on both sides of the street, all of them darkened; away in the distance, God knew how many miles away, she could see pin-points of light that came and went like cloud-swept stars. Then she saw the closer light, the flickering yellow eye of the torch as Abel came looking for her.

She turned and began to run again, straight into the wild surf of the storm this time. She came to a bend in the roadway, did not know she had reached it till she ran right off the concrete into a dip, fell again, picked herself up and saw the big dark shape ahead of her that must be a house. She stumbled up a slope towards it, lurching across long grass and up on to a wide porch. She fell against a door, beat on it with her fists, her head turned to look back over her shoulder as the yellow beam of the torch came bouncing down the roadway. She was screaming incoherently, hurling her fists against the door; they had smashed through the wire of the screen-door and were thumping on the timbers of the front door. But there was no answer: her pounding was echoing through an empty house.

She ran along the porch, plunged off the unseen end of it into a thick bush that scratched at her like a clutch of claws. As she picked herself up a sudden, extraordinarily strong gust of wind flung her back against the side of the house, cracking her head against the timbers. Dazed, she fell on her knees again, ready now to surrender to the rain and the mud. The bush hid her from the roadway; the beam from the torch swept across the front of the house, then was gone. But she had not seen her good fortune. Blind with pain and exhaustion she half-lay, half-sat in the mud while the wind tore at her and the rain drove an army of lances at her.

Then in her clouded mind she remembered she had not been alone: she had to find Sylvia. Like an old crippled woman she forced herself up into the storm; driven by the wind, she almost ran down the slope into the roadway again. There was no sign of the torch; Abel might be as lost as herself in the wild black night. She had no idea which way to turn; help could lie in any direction. She stumbled up the road, trying to keep to the hard surface of it; another furious gust of wind hit her, sending her tumbling off into the mud. She picked herself up, looked up and saw the dim shape of a house and a smaller, darker shape beside it. She struggled up a driveway, the rain lashing against her face as if to drive her back. She fell against the smaller shape: it was a car. A car? She leaned against it, fighting for some memory that eluded her. What did the car mean? Then she remembered: they had come out here in a *truck*! This house was someone else's, someone was there only yards away who could help her!

Crying hysterically, she dragged herself up on to the front porch, stumbled along it, fell against the screen door. Somewhere she could hear a familiar sound, wood slamming against wood, but her mind was too confused for memories. She beat against the wire, breaking it, her frantic fists thudding through to pound against the front door. Then the door itself opened and she saw the dim shape in the opening.

She fell back as the man pushed open the screen door and reached down to take hold of her. "Oh, thank God you're here! I'm – "

"Welcome back, Mrs Malone."

2

"We may not be so lucky next time," said Carole.

"There isn't gonna be a fucking next time!" Then Abel swallowed his anger as he saw her stiffen. "Sorry, baby."

"I'm not blaming you, honey – "

"Jesus! Blaming me?" The anger sprung up in him again. What was she talking about? Blaming him? "You go off, you stay away half the goddam night, you leave me here like I'm some fucking baby-sitter – !"

She hit him across the mouth with her hand. He raised his own hand to retaliate and she stood in front of him, her eyes cold and hard, daring him to hit her. "Hit me, you bastard, and that's the end! I don't need you – "

He slowly lowered his hand, shook his head dazedly at what he had almost done: if he had hit her he would have gone on hitting her until she was dead. His head suddenly began to ache and he slumped down in the chair behind him. "I'm sorry, baby. Don't let's fight – "

Still unmoving, she stared at him, wondering what to do with him. She was not ungrateful for what he had done so far; she knew she could not have kidnapped Sylvia Forte without him. But she did not need him from now on and the longer he stayed with her the more difficult it would be to get rid of him when the time came. But if she told him to go now . . . She had seen the look in his eyes, had recognized the danger sign that she had glimpsed before but had told herself was only her imagination. He was not insane, she was sure of that, but his anger would some day break out of him entirely and he would not be able to control it. She had seen the same look in the eyes of the policeman who had clubbed Roy to death.

She turned away from him, went out to the kitchen and began to make coffee. She took down a cup and saucer, hesitated, then took down three more cups and saucers. It would be a simple means of letting him know that all four of them in this cottage were bound together, whether he liked it or not.

She felt rather than heard him come to the doorway, but she did not turn. "I'm making coffee."

"For *them*, too?" She didn't answer and after a moment he said, "Carole – I was worried, baby – Jesus, anything could've happened to you, you know?"

Without looking at him she said, "What would you have done with those women if something *had* happened to me?"

"I dunno." Slightly reassured by her response, he came into the kitchen, slid on to one of the stools at the breakfast bar. He had changed out of his wet clothes, but his hair was not yet dry; sleeked back and down into his collar, it made him look a stranger. "Just left 'em, I guess."

"Left them here – not told anyone?"

"They'd have got away eventually. They just got away now, didn't they?"

She turned round, sat on one of the stools opposite him. She and Mark used to sit here in the early hours of the morning, when each of them had come back from a party; the memory was too sudden and too sharp, she felt a catch in her throat. She could see the hurt look in Abel's face, but she resisted the urge to be sympathetic. Mark was the important man in her life now, even if he could never be a real replacement for Roy.

"Abel, you've got to understand – nothing is absolutely cut and dried for us. I thought it was – I thought I had planned every little detail – but things have come up that I just could not anticipate. *That*, for instance." She nodded at the curtained window; the rain beat like grapeshot against the shutters outside. "I heard on the car radio that they've closed all the airports between Washington and Boston."

Concerned only with their own relationship, it took him a moment to realize the implication of what she had said. "What are we gonna do then – I mean if they can't take those guys to Cuba?"

"I'll – we'll have to think about it." She made a concession, let him think he might help in the decisions. The coffee had begun to percolate and she got up and turned down the burner. "There's something else – someone named Frank Padua."

"Who the f – " He held back his tongue; he was still on edge. "Who the hell's Frank Padua?"

"I don't really know. He's someone in politics, but what he is, I don't know." She looked for something to eat with the coffee; suddenly she was very hungry. She had hardly eaten all day, consumed as she had been by nervous excitement, but now she was ravenous. She saw the dirty dishes in the sink and the empty cans on the draining board. "I wish you'd clean up after yourself."

"Baby, we're gonna be gone from here tomorrow. Who cares?"

"*I* do!" She rattled through the cans of food in the cupboards, her fingers thick and awkward with anger and nerves. Since the death of Roy she had not been able to handle close relationships, her capacity for tolerance and sympathy eroded by the bitter grief that was still part of her. It had taken her weeks to commit herself to Abel and she had only done so when she had finally decided he was necessary to the success of her scheme. A crisis in their relationship was something else she had not anticipated, but she knew now that, given the circumstances, it was one of the first things she should have planned for. She grabbed a can of chili con carne, fumbled with it at the can-opener mounted on the wall, swore savagely.

"Baby – " He took the can from her, opened it expertly as he looked at her and shook his head reproachfully. "You wanna watch your language, you know?"

She took the can from him, emptied the contents into a saucepan. She said nothing till she had steadied herself, determined not to let him score any more points off her. "Have you fed the women?"

"No. Let them go hungry."

She found two more cans of chili, opened them herself this time, and added the contents to that already in the saucepan. He watched her, then abruptly he wheeled round and went back into the living-room. She turned down the burner under the coffee as low as possible, began to stir the chili in the saucepan. She felt weak and exhausted and, suddenly for the first time, hopeless. Was it really worthwhile going through with the operation?

When she had driven up the driveway beside the cottage and seen the two women in the glare of the car's headlights, it had been as if the night were gradually climbing to a climax of disaster. The journey back from Manhattan had been a nightmare, even on the almost deserted expressways and roads; and riding with her had been the nagging wonder at who Frank Padua really was and how he had become involved in the kidnapping. She had not planned against the interference of outsiders, but she should have known that nothing in life was ever self-contained. Her four years of isolation since Roy's death had proved that. It had been one long struggle to remain alone: people offering friendship, asking for sympathy, some asserting authority. She had been stupidly naïve to think outsiders would not interfere in such an affair as the kidnapping. The world was full of meddlers, all with their own excuses or motives.

She had switched on the car radio and heard the repeated news that all airports between Washington and Boston had been closed; depressed all of a sudden, she would not have been surprised if a car had appeared out of the driving rain and run into her. But she had reached home safely; only to find the culmination of the night's misadventures right there in the rain-silvered beam of the headlights. She had been fortunate to catch Sylvia Forte before the latter could escape past her, flinging open the door of the car and knocking the Mayor's wife to the ground. Abel, responding to her urgent blowing of the car horn, had come out of the cottage on the run, but too late to catch the Australian woman before she had disappeared into the darkness. When he had returned to the cottage without Lisa Malone she was waiting for him, ready to leave the house and find somewhere else to hide. They had been arguing about where they should go when there had come the hammering at the front door.

She had waited in the living-room, her gun pressed against the side of the shivering and weeping Sylvia, while Abel, gun in hand, had gone along the hallway to the door. If it was the police, if Lisa Malone had by sheer luck found a prowling squad car, she was not sure what she would do. She had thought about murder in cold blood, but now she was so close to it her mind had stopped functioning. The hand that held the gun in Sylvia's side did not belong to her; it was as if her whole right arm had become numb and useless. If the gun went off it would go off of its own accord.

She had almost collapsed with relief when Abel had come back along the hallway carrying the unconscious Lisa. A hissing sigh had escaped her and she had stepped back from Sylvia, half-sitting on the back of the couch to take the weight off her weak empty legs. She had been glad then of Abel's help, leaving him to take the two women into the bedroom, revive Lisa, tie their hands and feet, then board up the window again. If she had needed any proof that she could not have accomplished the kidnapping on her own, he had provided it then.

She could not remember the first time she had seen him, only the first time she had noticed him. He had been in her night class three weeks then, a quiet boy sitting right back at the far corner of the classroom, never asking a question, never putting himself forward to answer one. She had been teaching English, the course aimed at those who had never got above the tenth grade; she knew she was not a good teacher and it had taxed her patience to lower her intelligence to that of the class in front of her. But the school had provided the retreat she wanted. No one was likely to come looking for a *summa cum laude* Barnard graduate in a night class in one of the poorer sections of Kansas City.

Then one night after she had dismissed the class Abel had come shyly up to her desk. "Miss – ?"

"Yes?" She had to struggle to remember his name; none of the students really meant anything to her. "Simmons, isn't it?"

"Yeah. Could I walk you to your car?" She looked at him curiously and he stumbled on, "I heard a coupla guys talking. They gonna wait for you outside."

"Who?"

He shook his head. "Dunno their names. But they been talking dirty about you. I wouldn't want nothing to happen to you, you know?"

She had experienced a little trouble with some of the men in her class, but she had managed them without difficulty; she had wondered for a moment if this was just his awkward way of leading up to a date with her. Her first reaction had been to brush him off, but there had been something in his thin, serious face that had suddenly caught her, a look of concern for her in his pale, cautious eyes that told her that this boy saw her as more than just a pick-up date. And when they got outside the school there were indeed two of the boys from the class waiting there. They had said nothing, just stared sullenly at her and Abel, then hurried off into the night. They had never come to her classes again.

The relationship with Abel had developed slowly, he never pushing himself on her, she giving him only small encouragement. She would occasionally have coffee with him, but she had kept the association on a strictly teacher-student level and he had accepted it. She told him nothing about herself, but she learned that he came from Chicago, that he had run away from home at sixteen, that he had bummed his way through the Midwest and now was working as a laundry deliveryman in Kansas City. He had come to night school because he had some vague ambition to be something more than a working stiff for the rest of his life. But what had intrigued her was that his hatred of the

Establishment (though he did not call it that) and its uses of authority was even stronger than her own.

Then two months ago there had occurred the incident for which she had been waiting four long years, the opportunity to revenge herself on the society that had killed her husband. There had been an added sweet irony that the revenge would be effected through the release of Mark; she had suffered a severe shock when she had seen his photo in the newspapers, because she had had no idea what he had been involved in since she had left home. The plan had come into her mind as a sudden inspiration; she had spent the next few days studying it as thoroughly as any course she had taken at college. Her decision to take Abel in with her had been deliberate; she did not expect him to be surprised by what she suggested and he had not been. She had told him nothing of Roy or Mark: the plan was just to effect the release of five men who believed the same as they did, that all authority was rotten.

But once she had involved him, she had had to commit herself to him. He had at once lost his shyness with her, had told her what she had suspected, that he was in love with her. She had had no man in bed with her since Roy, but she felt she owed Abel something and she had allowed him to make love to her. He was a fumbling, aggressive lover and, to get some satisfaction from the act after so long without it, she had tried to educate him. He had mistaken her self-interest for an expression of love for himself. From then on she had known that when she had to break away from him it would have to be secretly and she would have to head for a destination where he would never find her. She might even have to join Mark in Cuba.

In the living-room Abel had turned on the television set again. Another ancient movie was being shown: Clive Brook and Marlene Dietrich were on a train somewhere in China. But they were ghosts in a world he did not know and was not interested in, and he switched the set off. Then he heard one of the women call weakly from the bedroom.

He was about to ignore the call, then abruptly changed his mind: they were *his* prisoners as much as Carole's. He put on his wig, which he had not worn out into the storm, and donned the dark glasses. He unlocked the bedroom door and went into the room where Lisa and Sylvia, hands and feet bound, lay uncomfortably on their beds.

"Untie us so that we can get out of these wet clothes," Lisa pleaded. "Otherwise we're going to catch our death – "

"Won't make much difference one way or the other. You asked for trouble, you can't complain if you get it."

"What do you want us to do – apologize?" Sylvia lay on her back, her bound hands resting on her stomach.

"Too late for that, Mrs Forte." He smiled at their discomfort.

Sylvia tried to control her shivering, but she was afraid as much as cold and she spoke through trembling lips: "Please let us be comfortable – at least for as long as we've got."

Lisa, still exhausted, felt she was listening to some nightmare dialogue; she struggled as if trying to wake from the dream, but the horror was that she knew she was already awake. She knew she was cut and bruised, but she was so numb with the cold wetness of her clothes that she could feel nothing. She sneezed, and the small ordinary reflex seemed to clear her mind.

"Ask Carole to come in," she said.

"What do you want her for?" Abel stiffened with anger and suspicion.

"She's the boss, isn't she? Perhaps *she'll* let us take our clothes off."

For a moment Lisa thought she had said the wrong thing. Abel took a quick step towards her and she turned her face away from the expected blow. Then he roughly grasped her hands, began to fumble with the cord that bound them.

"You talk too much! You're gonna wind up – " Anger made him cruel and awkward; Lisa had to bite back a cry of pain as he tore at her hands. "Okay, get up!"

She stood up and at once fell forward. He caught her, held

her away from him; then savagely he began to tear at her clothing. But the wool suit and the sweater would not rip; she staggered back and forth as he tried to claw the clothes from her. Then, panting heavily, he threw her back on the bed.

"Take 'em off!"

Lisa, ready to collapse again, shook her head and gasped, "Not with you in here – !"

He glared at her for a moment, the blank dark glasses somehow making his face even more menacing; in her confused and frightened mind she was staring at a death-mask. Then he turned to Sylvia. His head felt ready to burst and he did his best to steady himself. He did not tear at the cords that bound Sylvia; he struggled to keep his fingers methodical as he picked at the knots. He freed her, then stood back.

"Okay, you take your clothes off!"

Sylvia looked at him, then at Lisa, who shook her head violently. Then she stood up, turned her back on Abel and took off her wet jacket. She peeled off her sweater, having difficulty with it as the soaked wool clung to her. She slipped out of her skirt and stood in her brassière and half-slip.

"They're wet too," said Abel. "Take 'em all off."

"Not till you go out of the room. I'm not going to stand naked in front of you."

"Why not? You think I wanna screw you or something? I wouldn't touch you with someone else's – "

"What's going on?" Carole, carrying a tray with food on it, stood in the doorway.

"They wanted to get outa their wet clothes. I'm helping them." Abel sensed at once that Carole was on the side of the other two women. Jesus, the bitches of the world! Why did God invent them? "This one's got some idea I wanna rape her – "

"I didn't say that!" Sylvia could feel her whole body trembling as if it were about to shatter; she knew she was on the verge of hysteria. But she mustn't succumb to it; she searched for some pride to keep her going in front of these strangers. All her adult life had been dedicated to putting up a front: the experience came to her aid now. "I just won't undress in front of strange men, that's all. Neither will Mrs Malone."

Lisa stood up, impressed and encouraged by Sylvia's defiance. She, too, had sensed that Carole would be on their side. Despite the gun she had carried and the kidnapping she had engineered, the girl had betrayed herself as still possessed by middle-class proprieties; Lisa had heard the argument over Abel's language out in the living-room and there had been other hints that Carole did not subscribe to complete permissiveness. Scobie had once told her that habitual behaviour was one of the main things that always trapped a criminal in the end: she took a chance now that Scobie was right.

"I don't think you'd want to do it either," she said to Carole. "It's not that we're afraid Abel will do something to us – " that was a lie: he might not rape them but he would kill them " – it's just – well, modesty, I suppose. Some of us still have that."

Carole said nothing for a moment. She knew the two women were co-opting her against Abel; there was danger if she agreed to let herself be used by them. But she was still angry with Abel; more importantly, she had to remind him that she still was the one running this operation. She put the tray down on the dressing-table, nodded to Abel.

"Leave them to me."

"I'll stay," he said coldly. "Just in case – "

"In case of what? They're not going to try to escape again. Not without their clothes. I'll take them out and hang them on one of the heaters," she said to Lisa and Sylvia. Then she looked back at Abel. "I said leave us, Abel. There's some coffee in the kitchen for you."

He stood absolutely stockstill for a moment, then a faint trembling shook him. His hand went to his belt; but his gun was on the table out in the living-room. He would have killed all three of them there and then if his hand had found the

gun; he was blind with anger and pain. He made a whimper-
ing sound, like that of an animal caught in a trap; then
abruptly he turned and stumbled out of the room, slamming
the door behind him. Carole felt a weakening rush of relief
and she put out a hand against a bedpost to steady herself.

"You're afraid of him too, aren't you?" said Sylvia
quietly. "You have to save yourself as well as us from him."

Chapter Eight

"The Cubans have said they won't take Parker and the others," said Michael Forte. "They won't allow any plane carrying them to land there."

"How do you know?" asked Malone suspiciously: were they playing some callous political trick on him?

"The State Department has been in touch with them through our contact channels – the Swiss spoke to them for us. The Cubans are quite adamant – they don't want Parker and his buddies."

"Why not? Christ, I thought they'd throw out the red carpet for anyone who wanted to blow up this country."

"They didn't give us their reasons, but the Swiss guess they are fed up with being a haven for American malcontents. They've suggested we try somewhere else."

"Where, for instance?" He thought of suggesting Australia, but it would have sounded like a sick joke; Canberra equated even the mildest protestor against the *status quo* with Attila the Hun; five anarchists would be akin to five carriers of bubonic plague. "Russia?"

"The State Department is trying Algeria." Forte could detect the suspicion and frustration in Malone, and he found he could not blame the Australian. "But we have to do that through channels too – we have no diplomatic exchange with them. The Swiss are handling it for us there too. But it will take time – protocol always takes time."

Malone could feel himself seething; but once again he knew he was trapped, that there was nothing he personally could do. Even as a lowly cop he knew the hobbling effects of protocol: it was one of the defences of uncertainty. He had seen it used by inspectors and above when he had been only a detective-sergeant; he could imagine how it was used in the rarefied atmosphere of embassies and foreign ministries. Lisa's and Sylvia Forte's lives would mean little to men in Algiers or wherever who, even if asked to act urgently, would have to observe the rules against the day when more than the lives of a couple of women would be at stake. It's a pity, Malone thought bitterly, ordinary citizens don't rate the status of a hot line.

When he and Jefferson had come across here to City Hall, coming in out of the wind and the rain, they had at once been engulfed by a rip tide of frantically questioning newspapermen and television cameramen. The front hall had been thronged with people, their voices rising to the coffered ceiling of the dome, so that Malone, coming suddenly into it, had the impression of being trapped in a tremendous bowl of shouting. Several people, come down from the Biltmore, still wore their *Forte for Mayor* buttons. The whole scene had a touch of the ballyhoo of election night, except that something more tragic than a mere election defeat was possible.

Uniformed policemen had cleared a way for Malone and Jefferson through the crowd and escorted them down the hall to the Mayor's office. As soon as Malone had entered the room he knew at once there was no good news for him. There was an air of crisis, reflected in the tense manner of all the men gathered there. He recognized most of the faces, but there was one new one: that of Pat Brendan, the District Attorney. He was a short, stocky man with a long Irish upper lip, bright blue eyes and fashionably long sideburns that distracted one's gaze from the thinning hair on the top of his head. He wore a purple shirt and a purple-and-white figured tie and a brown suit that looked as if it had been cut for him by a tailor who had been afraid of running out of cloth. Malone, a quick student of types, guessed that Brendan was a politician who had decided to go for the young vote. At forty-five or thereabouts he had the slightly clownish look of a man who had arrived too late on the scene, the fancy dress guest who had missed last night's ball.

Malone spoke to him now. "You've agreed, then, to let Parker and the others go?"

Brendan looked around at the other men before he replied. "I don't think we'd ever considered the possibility of *not* letting them go – " He saw the look on Malone's face and read it correctly; he might pretend to be a middle-aged swinger, but he was no fool. "Okay, maybe we did think about it. We've had enough pressures on us – " He looked back at Michael Forte. Okay, Mike, he's your pigeon: you tell him.

"We've had advice from all over, Scobie," said Forte. "There have been people calling me up who haven't spoken to me since I moved into this office four years ago. The President, the Attorney-General – they're great believers in law and order down in Washington. Mr Cartwright's chief too – "

Cartwright tried to hide his embarrassment. "I've talked to the Chief, Mr Mayor. He doesn't suggest we should hold out indefinitely. But he points out that the government down in Uruguay called the bluff of the Tupamaros when they kidnapped that British ambassador in Montevideo."

"The governments in Argentina and Turkey didn't manage to call any bluffs," said Malone. "The kidnappers there killed *their* hostages. I don't want that to happen to my wife!"

"We're doing our best to see that doesn't happen," said Cartwright. He had eaten nothing but a couple of hamburgers all day, but he had had innumerable cups of coffee, as he always did when he had to work in long stretches, and his belly felt swollen. He had eased his belt out another hole, but he still felt uncomfortable. "But we're handicapped by this storm – "

"Have you found out anything at all?" Malone said.

"We think we have a trace on one of the kidnappers. A woman phoned in from Jamaica, out on the Island, and gave us a tip. She'd heard the description on TV of the grey delivery truck and she told us about the one she'd seen being driven into the house across the street from her. She said the people who'd taken the house were newcomers, a young couple. We checked – there was nobody in the house, but the truck was in the garage, minus its licence plates. There were some fingerprints on the wheel. They belong to Joseph Abel Swokowski, who was booked two years ago in Louisville, Kentucky, for taking a stolen car across a State line. He slugged the officer who was taking him to court and got away."

"And that's all you have so far?"

Cartwright hesitated, then nodded. What did this Aussie cop expect – miracles? "We'll get Swokowski eventually."

"But not by tomorrow morning?"

Cartwright flushed, then shrugged. "I told you, Inspector – we're doing all we can. But we need one piece of luck – something to turn up – " He sighed, eased his belt away from his middle. "Trouble is, there seems no connection at all between those men in The Tombs and the kidnappers. We don't even have a positive identification on any of those anarchists, except for Fred Parker. Two months and they're still no more than just names to us."

I'm that far ahead of you, Malone thought: Jefferson and I know Parker's real name. But Parker, he was sure, did not know who the kidnappers were.

"I think we're going to have to release those jerks in The Tombs," said Brendan. "As soon as we get the word from the Algerians that they'll take them, I'll go see Judge Kazan. But it bugs me – "

"Not just you, Pat," said Michael Forte.

"What happens if the Algerians won't take them?" said Malone.

"I don't know – I just don't know." Michael Forte closed his eyes for just a moment, as if blinking at a blow. "I have to go on the air in another forty-five minutes. I'm asking them for some definite proof that our wives are still alive. If they produce proof – let our wives speak to us on the phone would be good enough – then we'll release those men at seven tomorrow morning."

"Assuming the Algerians agree, how long will it take to fly them to Algiers? They won't release our wives till those blokes are there."

Forte looked at Manny Pearl, the man with all the facts. "It would probably take seven or eight hours. I've chartered a 707 – it's standing by, ready to go as soon as we give them the word."

"Then it could be tomorrow night before we see our wives?"

"I'm afraid so."

There was a faint rumble deep below the floor. A late train was going uptown, taking home the first of the night-workers, the last of the revellers. Malone had not ridden on the subway at night, but as a plainclothesman he had travelled on late trains out of Sydney to the suburbs, riding shotgun as it were against hooligans and, once, a pervert who had been molesting women. Night riders, he guessed, were the same anywhere.

Silent hunched figures, made pale by the callous lighting above them, their reflections staring at them from the dark-backed windows opposite them: some might look happy, a boy or a girl still excited by the lover they had just left, but most of them had the look of people who had seen their own ghosts at one minute past death. Down there beneath his feet, Malone wondered how much misery was riding uptown, sitting there with their skulls on their hopeless shoulders beneath the advertisements that promised them riches and a better life. But, though he was normally a generous man, he had no pity for them tonight. He was hoarding it for himself, telling himself he needed it. He had reached the last re-sources of a despairing man.

"Where have you been tonight, Inspector?" Sam Forte, in the middle of the worst night of his life, looked as im-peccable as ever. He had had a nap after dinner, then taken a bath, changed his entire wardrobe and come down here

184

to City Hall determined to sit out the hours till Sylvia and the Malone woman were returned safely. Joe Burgmann had been in touch with him before he had contacted Michael, had told him that the swing now appeared to be back to Michael and that if it kept up the election tomorrow would be in the bag. So one issue was safe; now he could concentrate on the safe return of Sylvia. Oh, and the Malone woman. In the meantime Malone himself looked as if he would have to be humoured. If he started talking to the press in his present mood he might alienate the sympathy that was building up for Michael. "I called you, I thought you might have cared for some company while Michael was out, but my grandchildren told me you had gone out with Captain Jefferson."

"Where did you take the Inspector, John?" said Hunger-ford.

Malone and Jefferson looked at each other, then Jefferson, face as bland as the black ball on a pool table, said, "I thought the same as Mr Forte – that Inspector Malone might like some company. We continued our tour that was interrupted this morning, showing him how we operate."

Malone glanced at Michael Forte, saw the quick warning frown and was puzzled for a moment. Then it clicked: Michael did not want Frank Padua mentioned in front of those in this room. "I was just filling in time," he said to Sam Forte. "Trying to keep my mind off what might be happening to my wife and Mrs Forte."

Sam Forte nodded sympathetically, but Hungerford said, "What were you doing over at The Tombs? The Mayor said you called him from there. I hope you haven't been en-couraging the Inspector to do a little private investigating, Captain?" He glanced at Cartwright, then looked back at Jefferson. "There are enough of us in the act now."

Jefferson looked uncomfortable and Malone said, "Blame me, Commissioner, not Captain Jefferson. I persuaded him to let me try and talk to the anarchists, to find out if they knew anything about my wife."

Hungerford jammed a cigarette into his holder, but didn't light it. He gave Jefferson a bad-tempered stare, then he looked back at Malone. "I'm refusing you permission to go near them again, Inspector – that's official."

"They are *my* responsibility, Des." Pat Brendan tightened his gaudy tie, as if trying to strangle his annoyance; but his voice was steady. "However, I agree with you. No more visits to them, Inspector."

"I saw them as a private individual," said Malone, trying hard to keep his own voice steady. "I understand that until those blokes are convicted they are entitled to see anyone they wish. It's part of what Captain Lewton was complaining about this morning when I met him. The rights of prisoners."

"Jesus!" Hungerford's holder snapped in his hands; the cigarette fell to the floor unnoticed. "A cop arguing for *them*! Whose side are you on?"

"I've already answered that several times today," said Malone. "My own and my wife's."

There was a tap on the door and the Mayor's secretary, wan and tired-looking, put her head into the room. "Mr Mayor, the State Department is on the line."

"I'll take it in here." Michael Forte picked up the phone, looked around at the other men as they all leaned forward. Only Sam Forte remained as he was, hands resting comfortably on the arms of his chair. Malone, leaning forward himself, had to admire the old man's calmness. "Yes, this is Mayor Forte. Any news from Algeria?"

The look on his face instantly told the others the news was bad. He listened for a while, once or twice offering a half-argument, but whoever was on the other end of the line gave him no encouragement. At last he hung up, stared at the phone for a moment as if it were some totem that had unexpectedly let him down. Then he looked up and about him.

"The Algerians won't play ball either. The Swiss said they considered the request for an hour, then came out with a flat no. No reasons, just no and that was it."

"But why the hell – ?"

"The Swiss think the Algerians got in touch with the Cubans in that hour and they've both decided it was a good opportunity to embarrass us politically. The State Department agrees the Swiss opinion is probably right. If it had been any other city but New York and if I hadn't been – well, a national figure – " His glance towards his father was so swift that it could have been no more than a tic of the eye. "Anyhow, that's how it is. I'm sorry, Scobie. Your wife is being made to pay for being in America."

"That's no way to talk, Mike," said Burgmann, heaving himself quickly off the couch. "Jesus, if a quote like that got out – "

"Relax," said Malone sourly; he was sick and exhausted. "I'm not going to go quoting the Mayor to the press. I'm sure I'm the only one you're worried about, so put your mind at rest."

Manny Pearl, the pourer of oil on waters that looked like developing into rapids, interrupted. "I think we better start getting ready for your broadcast, Mr Mayor. If you gentlemen would excuse him – ?"

In the next few minutes he gave a demonstration of how to clear a room of people and a volatile atmosphere. Only Malone, on a nod from Michael Forte, and Sam Forte stayed behind, as the others, diplomatically herded by Manny Pearl, filed out the doorway. Manny looked back into the room, winked at Forte, then closed the door.

"He's a genius at it. He once got rid of the Vice-President when he was up here telling me how to run the city." Michael Forte smiled for the first time since Malone had entered the room. "If I'm re-elected tomorrow, maybe I should put him on to slum clearance."

"I thought that was what he was doing then," said Malone; then gestured, "Sorry. I didn't mean that."

"Inspector," said Sam Forte, standing up for the first time and walking slowly about the room; his calmness had been no more than self-control and now his limbs were stiff with the effort, "each of those men has his problems. They are the wages of our system. We like to think it's the best system in the world. It isn't – but as Joe Burgmann said, don't quote me – but I don't know of any other that would work any better in this country. The ideal *might* work, but unfortunately idealism has a natural enemy – human nature."

"Around this time of night," said Michael Forte, "my father tends to get cynical but honest. It's when I love him most."

"In politics this is the only hour for honesty. But something in your face, Inspector, tells me you already know that."

"I've had experience of it," said Malone, but he wasn't going to elaborate on his own cynicism about Australian politics.

Michael Forte had been watching Malone and now he said abruptly, "Where did you *really* go tonight? I mean, before you finished up at The Tombs?"

"Police Headquarters," said Malone, not blinking an eye.

Forte shook his head. "No, I called there after I'd called the house. When I talked to my son I had the feeling he was holding something back from me. Was he?"

"Yes," Malone admitted. "Don't blame him – I told him to keep his mouth shut. I went to see Frank Padua."

"Jesus!" Forte thumped his desk with his fist. "Don't you know when to leave things alone?"

"Ordinarily – yes. But this is different – my wife's in danger and I couldn't care less what happens to you and your bloody city!"

"What's all this about?" Sam Forte said.

His son told him, then looked back at Malone. "And I suppose you got nowhere? I just hope to Christ you didn't let him think *I'd* sent you – "

"He knows who sent me – you don't have to worry. We had a bit of a donnybrook, but it paid off." Malone then narrated the events of the evening. "Jefferson and I have got this small clue about Latrobe. It may mean nothing, but it's as much as anyone else has dug up. We want to go out and check it. Unless you want me to turn it over to the FBI and the Police Department?"

Michael Forte looked at his father, who spread his hands, not wanting to make the decision. You old bastard, Michael suddenly thought: all my life you've been pushing me, but never once have you laid your neck on the line, not even now. He looked back at Malone, suddenly prepared to listen to the Australian. "What do *you* want to do?"

"If I were working on my own, I'd turn it over to them – I wouldn't know my way around. But I think John Jefferson is a bloody good officer – at least he and I get on with each other and he wants to wrap this up almost as much as I do. If it leads to something definite, then it will be a bigger job, too big for us, and we'll turn it over to the Police Department at once. But first I'd like a crack at it with Jefferson. All my working life I've been a cop and this to me is the most important case I've ever had. I don't want to sit on my arse worrying myself stiff while someone else works on it."

2

When Malone had gone Michael Forte looked at his father, then up at the ormolu clock on the mantelpiece. Ten minutes to two: seven hours and ten minutes to the absolute deadline. "It's a crazy time to be making a broadcast. If the kidnappers are as tired as I am, they'll be asleep."

"You're awake because you're worried. They could be worried too. What are you going to say in the broadcast?"

"Whatever I say, it won't be political, so don't be disappointed. I had enough of that, at least for tonight, when I was down at the Biltmore a couple of hours ago."

As he had come down into the hotel lobby, escorted by Manny Pearl and Joe Burgmann and half a dozen of the senior campaign workers, he had been besieged by reporters and spur-of-the-moment well-wishers among the hotel guests. The maelstrom had swung him round and he had found himself looking up at the famous clock.

Beneath it several generations of college lovers had met for dates; his own class at Harvard had regarded it as a stop-watch on romance. The record for getting a girl from under the clock and into a bed in one of the rooms upstairs had been nine minutes; he had never been interested in records and at college had been a shy slow lover. By the time he met Sylvia he was no longer at college, though she was at Barnard. He had met her only once here in the lobby and that had been on an election eve just like tonight, the night before he had been elected Congressman for the first time. He had never asked her if she had ever met anyone else beneath the clock, because she never would have told him if she had. It had been part of an unspoken agreement between them that they had never mentioned past love affairs. Despite their disagreements and rows there had been for him no other women in his life: love began and ended with her. Looking up at the clock tonight he had made a decision.

"If Sylvia is not returned alive tomorrow, I'm resigning as Mayor – whether I'm voted in or not."

"Don't start thinking about that now – that can wait – "

Michael shook his head. "No, I'm telling you *now*. If my political future is just between you and me, then it will be over tomorrow. I don't want any more of it."

The planning of his son's career had not always been smooth going for Sam Forte. He saw the danger signs again and he adopted the same approach as always: you never won arguments with Michael by fiercely disagreeing with him. He had inherited his mother's Calabrian temper when it came to argument; Sam knew it would be his son's major weakness if ever he became President. Sam himself had a temper, but it had long gone cold, the fire of it dampened down by his rigid control. He stood with his back to the fireplace, looked round the room as if he were inspecting it for the first time, then back at Michael.

"And if Sylvia comes back safely – as I'm sure she will – ?"

"What makes you so sure?" But then Michael made a gesture of dismissal. "Never mind – that's just another one of your political statements. You always hedge your bets, don't you? What hedge have you got if I don't go through with what you've spent all these years planning?"

"None at all," said Sam softly. "Neither has Sylvia. We are both depending on you."

Michael looked as if he were about to swear, then thought better of it. He twisted his mouth, the unspoken words bitter in it, and turned his head away. I've won, thought Sam; but managed to feel some pity for his son.

Michael could feel the *petit mal* of boyhood coming back: the old, almost forgotten feeling of detachment gripped him. He was in this room yet not of it; at the edge of his consciousness a white-haired man, faintly familiar, lifted a commanding arm. The floor seemed to move and rumble beneath his feet, yet his feet felt as if they were resting on nothing but air: but his whole life had been built on a foundation just as insubstantial. He did not need to move his head to look around the room; he saw it whole from the outside while still in it. Though he had never listened to it before, he could now hear the ormolu clock ticking: four years ticked away while the minute hand did not move. Voices rang in the room and in his skull, echoes of memories that he could not quite grasp. Suddenly the room was gone: he stood in a grey emptiness, an infinity of nothingness. He heard a moan in his head, the room spun round, then there was a sharp blow on his jaw and a frightening confusion.

He blinked and looked up, lost and dazed. He lay on the floor between his desk and his chair. The white-haired man, whom he now recognized again as his father, was bending over him. He heard a door open and slam, then Manny Pearl was crouched beside him.

"Mike! Mike, are you all right?"

He sat up, felt his jaw. "Did I faint?"

"It was one of those seizures you used to have as a boy." Sam Forte himself looked on the point of collapse; he sat down heavily in the nearest chair. "You made a terrible gurgling noise, then just fell out of your chair."

Michael, assisted by Manny Pearl, got to his feet and moved across to lie down on the couch. "I must have cracked my jaw as I fell." He took the glass of water Pearl offered him, looked up at the little man's strained face. "I'll be all right. It was probably just exhaustion brought it on."

"We had doctors, the best, look at him when he was young," said Sam Forte. "They said there was probably a little damage to the skull when he was being born. Nothing, they said, it happens to lots of babies."

"Maybe we better take you home, Mike, get you to bed."

"I have to make that broadcast – "

"Someone else can do it for you. Pat Brendan or Des Hungerford. Maybe even your father."

Sam Forte shook his head. "Not me. Can I have a glass of that water, Manny?"

"You look almost as bushed as Mike." Manny Pearl poured a glass of water for the old man, looked at him and his son: he could have been another son and a brother, so concerned was he for them. He had dedicated himself to Michael Forte and not just for political reasons. He had a natural warmth of affection, but too much of his life had been spent in an atmosphere where friendship, if it wasn't suspected or spurned, was only an instrument to be used. Then he had met Michael Forte and the Italian rich boy and the Jewish delicatessen owner's son had discovered how much they had in common; a respect and a deep liking for each other had soon made itself felt. Wherever Mike went from now on, to the White House or oblivion, Manny hoped he would take him with him. "Maybe Pat Brendan would be best."

"No." Michael sat up, recovered now. His powers of

recovery had always been exceptional, his stamina that of a football tackle or, as he was, the complete politician. Or almost complete, he thought . . . "I have to do it myself. The kidnappers won't take much notice of anyone else. I've done little enough as it is. I just wish now I'd gone with Malone."

3

"You could lose your job over this," said Malone.

"Maybe," said Jefferson, holding the car steady against the cross-wind as they came up out of the Queens Midtown Tunnel on to the Long Island Expressway. The storm showed no sign of abating; the wind and the rain seemed to have become stronger and heavier. There was little traffic on the expressway and what there was of it was slowed almost to a crawl. "The rumour is that the Commissioner himself could be out of a job after tomorrow's elections. If he gets the axe, he's not gonna be worried about me."

"*You* don't sound worried."

"I am, though. For your wife and Mrs Forte." He glanced sideways at Malone. "It's all of a sudden become as personal for me as it is for you." Then he saw the strain in Malone's face, the pain in the eyes as the Australian looked at him, and he amended what he had said: "Well, not quite. But almost."

Malone knew that he did not have to thank the black man for his commitment; they had reached a stage where words were becoming less and less necessary. When he had come out of the Mayor's office Jefferson had been waiting for him. He had grabbed Malone's arm and hustled him through the crush of inquiring reporters.

"Inspector Malone will be in my office up at Head-quarters," Jefferson had said. "Tell your guys up there they can see him in ten minutes. But he's saying nothing just now."

Once down in Jefferson's car Malone had looked at him. "Is that where we're going – Headquarters?"

"No. I don't think anyone is gonna come out in this rain to tail us up there – they'll just call their own boys who are already there, the regular police beat men. We'll go up to Headquarters eventually, but not just now."

Now, out on Long Island, Malone said, "Where do we go first?"

"We'll try the local precinct house. They'd know where the high school principal lives – I guess they have as much trouble with the kids out here as they do in most places."

They pulled up outside the precinct house, looked out at the swirling rain lit by the green bowl of the light above the door.

"Can you swim underwater?" Jefferson said. "Makes me think we're gonna step out into an aquarium."

They ran through the rain, finished up in a room empty of people but for the duty sergeant dozing at the front desk. He straightened up, stiffening a little as the two wet strangers came bursting in. Jefferson produced his badge and the sergeant, a burly man with a nimbus of red hair round a freckled scalp, nodded and looked with interest at Malone.

"That's why I'm alone here – everybody else is out prowling around looking for your wife, Inspector, and the Mayor's."

"You can see we're really trying," Jefferson said to Malone. "I don't think the kidnappers are out of the New York area, but we sent out the usual 13-state alarm – that links us with all the State and local police right up and down the eastern seaboard."

"But I gotta be frank," said the sergeant, "I don't think they're gonna find much till this storm lets up. The high school principal? Sure, I know him. My kid goes there. His name's Hellibrand. You want me to call him first? He mightn't open his door, you knock on it this time of night."

While the sergeant dialled the high school principal's

number, Malone looked about him. It was just like home: even the pictures on the walls could have been the same, except there were more black portraits here than there had been back in the police station at Randwick, in Sydney, where he had first started on the beat. There were the usual scuffed desk and chairs: nothing from any police supply depot ever seemed to have been new: everything was created as an instant antique. There was a framed picture of the American flag high up on one wall, too high evidently for it ever to have been cleaned: the Union was badly fly-speckled, some of the stars almost obliterated, the stripes fragmented. There were graffiti scribbled on the walls, none obscene enough to warrant scrubbing off; and there was a framed notice that spelled out in large letters: Your Rights. Jefferson nodded at it.

"I know a cop who suddenly went word-blind when they hung that in his precinct house."

"If I meet up with those buggers who are holding my wife, I'm not spelling out their rights for them."

"We won't go that far. We'll hand it over to the Department before then."

The desk sergeant hung up the phone. "Hellibrand will see you at the school. You want someone to go with you? There's a guy out in the squad room."

But Jefferson declined the offer, asked directions to the school, and he and Malone hurried out to the car again. They had trouble finding their way about in the storm, but ten minutes later they were being led into the main building of the Zachary Taylor High School by the principal.

Hellibrand was a plump, curly-haired man in his mid-forties who at another time of day might have been jovial; now he was irritable and curious as to why two policemen, one of them an Australian, should want to look through copies of the school year-book. When Jefferson explained who Malone was, the irritation suddenly went out of Helli-brand's face, to be replaced by genuine sympathy.

"Well, of course. If there's anything I can do – Latrobe?

No, I can't remember anyone of that name – I have a good memory for names. You have to have, if you don't want your school to be just a great big blur of anonymity. How far do you want to look back? Five, six years? There they are. God knows what the kids in them have achieved since. One of them I know, is already a guest of the government. He got life for shooting his father. He wasn't one of the more promising students."

Malone and Jefferson had been flicking through the books. Young faces smiled up at them, re-touched to give them all the same look of bland confidence: in a school year-book, Malone guessed, there was no place for a young person's doubts. Then he stopped, finger pressed down on a face: thin, unsmiling, a white streak in the dark hair. "That's Latrobe."

Hellibrand looked at the caption under the photo. "Mark Birmingham? You mean you think he's one of the men who kidnapped your wife?"

"No, he's in The Tombs on a bomb conspiracy charge. He's an anarchist. But we think he can give us a lead. Where does he come from?"

Hellibrand ran a hand through his hair, shook his head worriedly. "I find it hard to believe – an anarchist! You work your ass off trying to help these kids – you admit to yourself maybe our generation and the one before it fouled up this country for them, but you try to help them – "

"We know, Mr Hellibrand," said Jefferson patiently. "But what about this kid Birmingham?"

"He was always a quiet kid, hard to approach – but his marks were always good, when he left here he could have taken his pick of any college he wanted to go to. His father wanted him to go to Yale, where he'd been, but the kid picked a small college – somewhere in the mid-West, I think. Don't quote me, but I think he was trying to get away from his old man."

"What does that mean?" said Jefferson.

"Nothing." Hellibrand abruptly seemed to realize he had

fallen into the three-o'clock-in-the-morning trap: confiding in total strangers. "Forget I said it, Captain."

"Who is his father?"

"Willard Birmingham – he's a lawyer with one of the big insurance companies."

"Where does he live?"

"Over in Waquoit, near Garden City. I can call him – "

"No, I think it'll be better if we drop in on him un-announced. I'd appreciate it if you didn't try to get in touch with him."

Hellibrand frowned, as if he had been accused of preaching revolution to his students. "Captain, I'd be the last one to want to interfere with the police's duty. It's a sad commentary on the way things are, but teachers *need* the law these days. Why, only last week – "

Malone and Jefferson escaped out to their car, drove off while Hellibrand was still locking up the school again. "I was rude," said Jefferson, "but I'm not interested in his problems. He'll have more next week and the week after that and the week after that – he can wait for my sympathetic ear."

"How far to – Waquoit?"

"We're practically there. I've never been out here, but I've heard about it. It was a development put up after the war – it catered to the middle-class conservatives and it's never changed its character. At least on the surface – "

"What's that mean?"

"Over the past seven or eight years, like a lot of other areas like it, it's had as much trouble with its kids as the ghettos. Drugs, things like that. This kid Mark Birmingham just seems to have gone all the way."

They found the Birmingham house, got out of the car and ran through the rain up on to the front porch. They had to press the bell three times before a light appeared behind the small barred window in the front door and a voice, husky with sleep and apprehension, said something, then repeated it more loudly. "Who's there? What do you want?"

Jefferson had to shout to make himself heard above the noise of the storm. The door was opened a few inches, but still held on a chain, and half a face peered out at them.

"Here's my badge, Mr Birmingham. It's important that we see you. It's about your son Mark."

The chain rattled and the door swung open. Malone and Jefferson shook the water from their coats, then stepped into a warm entrance hall that instantly suggested that this was a comfortable house, a family house where every penny that could be afforded had been spent to make it a home in which the occupants could be cosseted and protected. Yet the farther Malone went into the house the more he felt something, or someone, was missing. The account had been paid but the goods, the ambience, were still waiting to be collected.

Willard Birmingham was a tall, well-built man with a slight stoop; handsome and grey-haired, he would have got second glances from women much younger than himself. He was dressed in pyjamas and a silk dressing-gown and he had the bewildered, dishevelled air of a man who was still not quite certain that he was wide awake. Elizabeth Birmingham, dark-haired, slim, good-looking, dressed in a silk dressing-gown buttoned to her neck, stood at the foot of the stairs that led to the upper floor.

"It's about Mark," Birmingham explained to his wife, and led Malone and Jefferson through an archway into a large living-room. Mrs Birmingham followed them, going to stand beside her husband and take his hand in hers. "Has he asked to see us?"

Jefferson looked at them in surprise. "You know where he is?"

The Birminghams looked at each other, then the husband nodded shamefacedly. "We've known all along. We recognized him the first day his picture appeared in the newspapers, even though he'd grown his hair and dyed the white streak in it."

"We have been trying to make up our minds whether to

go see him," said Mrs Birmingham. "We didn't know whether he would want us to – we haven't seen or heard from him in almost two years – "

"We tried to do our best for him – " There was no whining note in Birmingham's voice; he stated a fact but he was puzzled by it. "We gave him a good home – "

Malone had heard it all before, in another accent; he even felt he had been in this room before. He was taking in his surroundings without moving his head; he had been in a dozen rooms like this on the North Shore back home in Sydney. The paintings on the wall that said the owner wanted them to be of his impressions of the world, not the artist's; the too-impeccable taste of the furnishings that made one look for just one note out of place; the books on the coffee table that would be dusted just as carefully as the furniture. They turn everything into a museum without realizing it, Malone thought, and then they wonder why their kids leave home.

"Why did he leave home?" he asked.

The two people opposite him looked at him again, recognizing for the first time that he had a strange accent, that he was a foreigner. Birmingham's face at once closed up. "Who are you? You're not with the police, are you? Are you a reporter?"

Malone let Jefferson tell them who he was. They looked back at him with sympathetic curiosity, but only for a moment; then they looked puzzled and finally incredulous. "You don't mean Mark had anything to do with the kidnapping?"

"No!" Mrs Birmingham shook her head fiercely; there were already tears in her eyes. "I don't even believe he had anything to do with the bombing! He's a gentle boy – "

Jefferson sighed, looked at Birmingham and waited for him to comfort and quieten his wife. "Your son will get a fair trial and I'm not anticipating what the jury will say – all I *can* say is that he and his friends are gonna have a tough time disproving the evidence."

"It could be a frame-up!" Mrs Birmingham pushed herself away from her husband's arms. Middle-class conservative though she is, Malone thought, she knows all the right accusations against cops when her own son is in trouble. "The police only want a conviction!"

"Not *only*, Mrs Birmingham," said Jefferson patiently; he even managed to sound sympathetic. "We want a conviction, but we want one for the right men. It's not gonna help us if we've just taken in the first anarchists we could lay our hands on and we've left the ones who did the bombing free to plant more bombs. Especially if they kill more cops."

Birmingham soothed his wife again, then nodded at Jefferson. "That's logical, Captain. But how could Mark have had anything to do with the kidnapping if he's been in prison for two months?"

"We don't think he had anything directly to do with it, but we think there could be a connection."

"I'm trying to save the lives of my wife and Mrs Forte," said Malone. He looked at his watch, but it had stopped. It was a cheap one, another manifestation of his reluctance to spend money on small things, and it had to be wound regularly: time had never really been valuable to him, not even as a cop, but now every hour had to be stretched for everything it could afford. He looked around the room for a clock but there was none. He dropped his wrist and went on, "You didn't answer my question. Why did your son leave home?"

Mrs Birmingham glanced at her husband, but he was looking down at his slippered feet. He had taken his arm from round his wife and his hands rested loosely on his thighs; he looked like a man whose strength had suddenly run out, who had finally faced the truth of a fact he had been denying for a long, exhausting time. When he spoke his voice was now just a monotone.

"It's a cliché, but it was the so-called generation gap. Generations? It was more as if we were foreigners to each other – we didn't even speak the same language. We, my wife and I, could have been wrong – "

"No," said his wife. "We weren't wrong!"

He looked up at her, showing the same patience Jefferson had. "Maybe. But we weren't *right*, either. God knows where the answer is – " He looked at the two policemen, but they, with more experience of the problem, had no answer for him. "I had disagreements with my own father when I was young – who doesn't? But we both basically agreed on what way of life was best. He saluted the flag and so did I, without question. But Mark – " He looked at Malone and Jefferson. "Do you have any children?"

"No," said Jefferson.

"My wife and I have only been married eight weeks," said Malone.

"Oh!" Elizabeth Birmingham looked at him, her face all at once clouding with pain. He suddenly realized she was not selfish, that she was capable of feeling sympathy for himself, a stranger. Behind the wall she had built about her, not all the pity she felt was for herself. "I'm sorry, Mr Malone. I hope – "

"So do I," said Malone, softening towards her. "But time is running out. We need your help to get through to your son. He won't talk to us – "

"There's no guarantee he'll talk to us," said Birmingham. "That's why we've hesitated about going to see him." Elizabeth Birmingham seemed to have aged ten years since Malone and Jefferson had come into this room with her and her husband; the night cream glistened on her face, but it would never eradicate the scars that had been inflicted on her in the past ten minutes. "You wonder where you failed. We'd given them everything – "

"Them?" said Malone.

He had been looking around the room again. There was only one photograph in it, a gilt-framed picture standing on a side table: Willard and Elizabeth Birmingham stood on the deck of a boat, arms linked and Birmingham holding aloft some sort of trophy: they were both laughing happily, no relation at all to the two people here in the room this morning. There were no photographs of Mark, their son, or anyone else.

"Them?" Malone repeated. "Do you have any other children?"

Mrs Birmingham pulled her lips together; she had said more than she had intended to. Her husband sat up straight, clenched a fist and tapped it gently on the couch. Suddenly he stood up and went out of the room. Malone half-rose, but Jefferson shook his head. Mrs Birmingham sat quite still, staring at the two policemen; it was evident she knew her husband would be back. He returned in a few moments, carrying a large leather folding frame. In it, facing each other with quiet, knowing smiles, were Mark Birmingham and a beautiful, dark-haired girl.

"That's Mark, taken just before he went to college. And that is Julie, our daughter, taken in her last year at college."

"Where is she now?"

Birmingham hesitated, looked at his wife. Then: "We don't know. We haven't heard from her for almost four years."

"Any reason?"

Birmingham sat down beside his wife again, looked at the two photos in the leather frame, then with an effort folded it shut. "You must wonder what sort of parents we've been – "

Malone could feel the sympathy for them welling up inside him: whatever they had done, they had done it for what they had thought were the best of reasons. But then his own selfishness swept in: his only interest was in getting Lisa back alive and unhurt.

"Mr Birmingham – "

But Birmingham didn't hear him. "Julie wasn't like Mark. She was much more outgoing – she lived our sort of life – " He opened the frame, looked at the photos it held, then shut it again. Malone wondered how many times it had been opened in the past four years. "She was at Barnard, doing so well – "

His voice suddenly broke and he stopped. His wife put her hand on his, then looked at Malone and Jefferson. "She met this boy, this Roy Bates. He was very political – "

"Was he an anarchist?" Jefferson said.

"I wouldn't be surprised – "

Birmingham shook his head. "Be fair, Liz. We don't know. We only met him twice – "

"Three times – counting the wedding. They were married down at City Hall. Julie and I used to talk about what her wedding would be like – I wouldn't have minded how she was married if I'd thought she'd be happy – "

"We had no confidence in the boy right from the start," said Birmingham. "We couldn't see what she saw in him. He let us know right from the start that he had no time for what we stood for."

"Where is he now?"

Birmingham glanced at his wife. Their clasped hands tightened, then Birmingham said, "He's dead. He was killed in a demonstration upstate, at one of the small colleges. He was hit by a policeman and he was dead before they got him to the hospital. There was an inquest and the policeman was exonerated. But Julie – "

"I remember the case," said Jefferson, face expressionless. "Your daughter thought the cop was to blame?"

Birmingham hesitated, then nodded. "She said the policeman went berserk and clubbed her husband to death. We tried to tell her that perhaps the policeman had been provoked – you're just ordinary human beings like the rest of us – "

"Thank you," said Jefferson, but Birmingham was deaf to irony. "Inspector Malone was saying that only tonight. Where did your daughter go after her husband's death?"

"She came home here for a week, then one day she just disappeared. There'd been no argument with us – she just walked out one night when we were out. No goodbye, nothing. Mark had a card from her about six months later, saying she was well and not to worry about her. She had always had a great deal of affection for him, always took his part if we chastised him – "

"What was the postmark on the card – do you remember?"

"New Orleans. But that was three, three and a half years ago."

"Did you ever try to trace her?"

"Of course," said Mrs Birmingham sharply. "We disagreed with her, but we loved her. We wanted her back – "

"You disagreed with your son too. But you've made no attempt to get in touch with him."

"What are you trying to say, Captain?" Birmingham leaned forward, put the leather frame on the coffee table in front of him. He remained leaning forward, staring across at Birmingham. "That we want to disown our children?"

"Do you?" said Jefferson quietly. "Because if you do, that's not gonna help Inspector Malone. And he needs your help – any help we can get – " He looked at his watch. "We don't have much time, Mr Birmingham. *Do* you want to have nothing more to do with your children?"

Both the Birminghams were silent for just that moment too long: they have considered the idea, Malone thought. Then Birmingham vigorously shook his head. "That's ridiculous. If Mark wants us to, we'll help him every way we can. And if it helps Inspector Malone – "

"And your daughter? What about her?"

Birmingham looked puzzled. "We don't know that she needs help. If anything serious had happened to her, an accident or something, surely we'd have heard? People just don't disappear without trace – "

"You'd be surprised," said Jefferson, still amazed after thirty years on the force at the small worlds most people lived in. "Mr Birmingham, two of the phone calls we have had from the kidnappers have come from a woman. It's a long shot – " He glanced at Malone.

"If you're thinking what I'm thinking, it *is* a long shot," said Malone. "But what other odds have we got? Mr Birmingham, there's a chance that that woman could be your daughter."

"How? How the hell do you arrive at an idea like that?"

"Don't ask for logic," Malone said. "This whole bloody business never had any logic to begin with, not for me. The men in The Tombs claim they have no idea who's trying to engineer their release – and we believe them. But someone must have *some* connection with them – this isn't the work of a crank. Your daughter could be getting her revenge on cops, all cops, through her brother – without his knowing it – "

"Julie a kidnapper?" Mrs Birmingham gasped with shock and indignation; we're demolishing her tonight, Malone thought. "What are you trying to do to us? My God, our children aren't monsters – "

"I didn't say they were," said Jefferson. "But if your son was involved in the bombing and your daughter had anything to do with this kidnapping, then they have committed a couple of monstrous crimes. And we want to stop them before they go farther – if your daughter *is* one of the kidnappers. They have already told us that if we do not agree to the ransom demands, Inspector Malone and the Mayor will not see their wives alive again." Jefferson was leaning forward now, speaking brutally. "We know at least one of the phone calls tonight came from Long Island, out at Patchogue. Do you know anyone out that way who might be sheltering your daughter?"

"Patchogue?" Birmingham shook his head.

Then Malone said, "Where was that photo over there taken? The one of you on that boat?"

Birmingham looked across at the photo. A slight frown crossed his face, almost a darkening of the skin as if a shadow had passed across it. He looked back at the two policemen. "Sunday Harbor. We have a summer cottage out there, and a boat."

"That's farther out on the Island," Jefferson told Malone. "Does your daughter know of it, Mr Birmingham?"

"Yes. We bought it years ago, when she was a child. Before Sunday Harbor became as popular as it is now. We always spent our summer vacations out there."

"When were you last there?"

"We closed it up just after Labor Day. We rarely go out there during fall and winter."

Jefferson stood up and Malone followed him, seeing the quickening interest in the other man's face. "We'd like you to take us out there, Mr Birmingham. Would you and your wife get dressed as quickly as possible, please?"

The Birminghams stood up, hands still clasped. They both looked afraid, suddenly aged. This could be the end of their life, Malone thought; and suddenly hoped Julie Birmingham would not be the girl he and Jefferson were looking for. It had happened so often in the past: he had too much pity for the victims, because there was never just one victim of a crime but many. Then he remembered who the principal victims of *this* crime were and the memory of Lisa suddenly blotted out the Birminghams.

They continued to stand without making any effort to go and get dressed and he said harshly, "Would you mind getting a move on? We don't have any time to spare!"

He looked at his watch again, then at Jefferson, who said, "It's half-past three. Get moving, Mr Birmingham, please!"

"You don't have any right – "

"If your daughter is not out at the cottage, if she is not involved in this kidnapping, you can file a complaint with the Commissioner and I'm sure you'll get satisfaction. If she *is* out there, if she is one of the kidnappers, I think she, as well as us, will need your help." Jefferson looked at the two frightened people in front of him; he pitied them, but his face showed nothing of what he felt. "Take your pick."

The Birminghams looked at each other. For Christ's sake, Malone yelled at them silently, get moving! But even as they angered him, he understood their reluctance to move: this house was their cocoon, they could not take the step that might shatter it. Then Willard Birmingham, still holding his wife's hand, led her out of the room and upstairs.

"Do you think Sunday Harbor might be the place?" Malone asked.

"It could be. These summer resorts are pretty deserted this time of year. But we can't go it alone from here on. When I've got the exact address, I'll call Headquarters. We'll take the Birminghams with us, meet the local cops out there – "

Then out in the hall there was the click of a phone being lifted. Jefferson whirled, moving surprisingly quickly for a man of his bulk, and was out in the hall in half a dozen strides. Malone followed him, grabbed the phone on the small table against one wall as Jefferson ran up the stairs.

Chapter Nine

Carole sat in one of the bedroom chairs and watched the two women as they ate the chili con carne. She had freed both of them, had allowed them to strip and now they were wrapped in blankets as, without any attempt at good manners, they wolfed down the food she had brought in. She had made no comment when Sylvia Forte had accused her of being afraid of Abel; but the longer she sat here the more she realized the Mayor's wife was right. She *was* afraid of Abel and she did not know how she was going to handle him. Especially if the storm kept up and things continued to go wrong.

"Will this storm make any difference?" Lisa asked. "I mean to your plans?"

Carole looked at her suspiciously, then decided it was not a trick question. This was supper-time conversation; she was amused that the two women now looked on her as a friend and ally. "Possibly. All the airports have been closed. But don't be hopeful – we're not going to release you till our friends are safe in Cuba."

"And the deadline is still the same?" Lisa dipped some bread in the chili con carne. It was a dish she would normally have turned away from, but tonight she was so hungry she would have eaten anything, even an Australian sausage roll. "Nine o'clock today?"

"Today is right," said Carole, looking at her watch. She found it hard to believe that so much time had passed since she had first met these two women. True, she had found the waiting burdensome, but all the events of yesterday morning were still so sharp in her mind that they seemed to have happened only an hour or two ago. "Mrs Forte's husband doesn't have much time left to agree to our plans."

"How long does it take a plane to fly from New York to Cuba?"

"Four, maybe five hours. Depends how fast they want to fly. I hope for your sakes they fly fast."

"Did you speak to our husbands again?"

"Not to Mrs Forte's. But I spoke to your husband."

"How did he sound?"

Carole smiled, not unkindly. "Worried."

"Poor darling." Lisa looked at the food left on her plate, then put the plate down on the dressing-table. Abel had screwed the legs back on the dressing-table, securing them more firmly with long nails. "Did he have any message for me?"

"No. What message could he have?"

"I don't know." Lisa shrugged helplessly. She looked up at the boarded-up window, then back at Carole. "Are you angry with us for trying to escape?"

"What do you think? You were lucky – " She looked towards the closed bedroom door, then said no more. Abel had turned up the sound on the television set again. She could hear the murmur of voices, the compulsive talkers and exhibitionists who could not resist the invitation to go on a talk show even in the middle of the night.

Sylvia had stopped eating, to pull up the blanket that had slipped from her shoulders. Both women had tried to dry their hair, but it was still damp and hung down lankly: the famous golden-red of her own hair was now almost as dark as (she looked in the dressing-table mirror, then hastily looked away) dried blood. She suddenly put down her plate and put her hand over her mouth.

"Are you going to be sick?" Carole sat up.

Sylvia blinked, opened her eyes wide, then shook her head. She felt the pain in her wrist and for the first time became aware of the stiffness and swelling in it; she must have sprained it when Carole had knocked her over with the car door. She lay back on the bed, drawing the blanket closely around her. Her gaze was unfocused; then she found she was looking at the blank spaces on the walls where the pictures had hung. She tried to remember the pictures that had hung on the walls of her own rooms in the cottage on Fishers Island, but that was too long ago. Even yesterday was difficult to recall now.

"What pictures did you have there?"

Carole looked around the room. She remembered how often she had lain on the bed where Sylvia lay: as a child, as a young girl, even as a widow when she had come here with her parents for two days after Roy's death. The pictures had been ones she had brought home from her one trip abroad. It had been just after she had met Roy and he had persuaded her to accompany him on a charter flight to Russia. They had gone there, ninety young middle-class Americans seeking the truth, as Roy had told her. She had been interested only in him then; and she could remember the young Russians who had tried to make a pass at her and the other girls in the best American style. Roy had taken the pictures, of himself and herself saluting all the Communist ikons, wrapping their arms round a Russian soldier, even toasting a picture of Lenin; and she had brought them back and hung them here in this room, as much to annoy her parents for their opposition to Roy as for any other reason.

When she had come here to the cottage last week she had been surprised to find the pictures still hanging on the walls. Maybe she didn't know her parents quite as well as she thought she had; maybe they had kept this room exactly as it had been, hoping some day she would come back. Suddenly she loved them again and wanted to see them.

"I'd never seen this place till a week ago." She stood up quickly, picked up the pieces of cord hanging on the foot of Lisa's bed. "Give me your hands."

"Do you have to tie us up again? If we promise – ?"

Carole roughly grasped Lisa's hands, began to bind them together. Lisa, noticing the sudden change in the girl's mood, said nothing and did not struggle. Her hands and her ankles were bound; then Carole turned to Sylvia. The latter held up her swollen wrist, but Carole hesitated only a moment.

"I'm sorry. You'll just have to put up with it."

She bound Sylvia as she had done Lisa. Both women lay back on their beds and Carole, relenting for a moment, pulled their blankets up to cover them completely. She grabbed up their clothes, bundling them under her arm, picked up the tray with the plates and went out of the room, closing the door behind her.

The light had been left on and Lisa turned her head and looked at Sylvia. "This is her room, you know."

"What does it matter now?" Sylvia was cold and aching and utterly dispirited. She had been thinking of her children before Abel had come into the room and she had been on the verge of weeping for them, almost resigned never to seeing them again. She had seen the look on Abel's face, first when he had dragged her back into the house and again when he had come into the room some fifteen minutes ago. She knew that her and Lisa's only insurance lay with Carole and she knew that the odds there were terribly against them.

Lisa caught the other woman's despair. "I suppose you're right. All we can do is pray for a miracle."

"Are you religious?"

"Not particularly. Are you?"

"No. But I believe in God."

"I suppose everyone does when something like this happens to them. Or if they don't believe, they *hope* there might be a God." She tried to remember the prayers of her childhood, but they were as dim as the rhymes she had known then. She remembered going to church in Marken with an aunt when she had been there on holiday; she had spent all her time staring at the barque and the herring boat hung from the ceiling and her aunt, a strict Calvinist, had chided her for her lack of attention to God. "I wonder if Scobie is saying his Hail Marys?"

"What?" Sylvia had been lost in her own thoughts,

regretting how little time she had spent with her children over the past four years.

"Nothing. I was thinking of a part-time believer." Lisa turned her head on the pillow and began to weep silently, grieving for the happiness that she was going to miss before it had really begun.

2

"Oh, I agree he may be good Presidential timber, but the termites have got into him."

"I can't *relate* to him, you know? He has so many chips on his shoulders they look like – what d'you call them? – epaulettes."

"Personally, I'd rather eat my own words than someone else's."

All the carefully rehearsed ad-libs came across with their usual hollowness; Carole glanced at the smug faces on the television screen and went on out to the kitchen with the tray and the women's wet clothes. She loathed all the instant pundits one had to listen to these days; wit and wisdom had been diluted to the level of the commercials. She did not know who was the subject of the discussion, but none of those on the screen looked as if he really cared about the truth of his opinions. Talk was the panacea for everything: so long as a subject was discussed, nothing more need be done.

She stopped at the kitchen door, turned back to Abel. "Have they discussed what we've done?"

He stared at her for a moment, then recognized that she was offering him a truce. But he was still cautious; he had lost contact with her and he didn't know if they would ever be as close again. And that frightened him: he had realized he had no future but her. "No, they said nothing. Maybe they been told not to."

"Directives like that have never stopped them before.

Maybe they think everything has been said." She hung out the clothing, some in the kitchen, some in the living-room. He watched her but said nothing and she gave him no encouragement to make a comment. At last she moved across and stood beside him, put her hand on the back of his neck. "I'm sorry, Abel. We shouldn't fight."

He reached up, took her hand and kissed it. "It's okay, baby. We're just getting uptight, that's all. You think everything *has* been said? Or are they holding back, trying some trick on us?"

She reached across, turned down the sound on the television set: the silent faces went on mouthing their skin-deep profundities. She sat down on the floor at his feet, leaned on his knee and looked up at him. They had taken off their wigs and dark glasses: they had nothing to hide from each other. Or so she hoped he would believe.

"We have the final trick in there." She nodded at the bedroom door. "Whatever they try, they're not going to sacrifice them."

"If this storm keeps up, what're we gonna do?" His hand caressed the top of her head; he got immense pleasure just from touching her. "They said on TV it's letting up down south, but they're not sure when it's gonna move away from up here. It could go on for another day. That's gonna be a long time, baby."

"Those men in The Tombs, they're going to be there an even longer time if we don't get them out."

"You think they appreciate what we're doing? I never really been sure how much they mean to you – personally, I mean. You sure you never met any of 'em? One of 'em isn't – wasn't someone you – ?"

"Loved?" She smiled, shook her head. She recognized the jealousy in him and worked quickly to douse it. She lifted herself to her knees, pulled his face down to hers and kissed him. "Honey, I told you – it's nothing but political. It's our *duty* – we believe in the same things those men do."

He kissed her back, convinced again, because he wanted

to be convinced, that she loved him. He was too inexperienced to know that love could be a treacherous echo, that too often it told a man only what he wanted to hear.

"I been listening to the news. We're world-wide – it's all over, everywhere, Europe, Africa, everywhere. We'll get 'em out, baby."

"We've *got* to." She thought of Mark being imprisoned for ever. Had her parents been to see him, to offer him what help they could? Or was he as alone as she had been these past four years? She had never told Abel of her personal interest in The Tombs; that would have meant telling him too much about herself. But Mark had to be rescued . . . "Once this storm lets up everything will be all right."

"Except maybe for this guy – what's his name – ?"

"Frank Padua. I don't know – maybe he's nothing – "

But she looked worried and it was his turn to comfort her. He stroked her neck, felt the satiny skin under his fingers, felt the blood moving into his loins. "Let's go and lay down, baby."

"I won't be able to sleep – "

"Just lay down, that's all." He kept his voice gentle but it was getting huskier; he was still uncertain of her, he did not want to press himself on her. "It may be a long day tomorrow – "

I don't want him making love to me again, she thought. He had all at once become physically repulsive to her; despite her attempts to educate him in bed, he was still as crude as a young animal. She remembered once as a teenager she had gone cycling over towards Bridgehampton. She had been riding down one of the lanes between the potato fields when suddenly a youth had appeared in front of her. She had recognized him for what he was, one of the field workers brought up from the South. He had pulled her from her bicycle and dragged her into some nearby bushes. She had struggled violently and had only been saved when a truck, loaded with other field workers, had come rattling down the lane. Sometimes she thought those two minutes were being repeated when Abel was in bed with her: he raped her but with her consent. All of his brutality came out of him when he thought he was most loving, and it sickened her.

But she needed him, had to bind him to her till at least noon today. She stood up, took his face in her hands again and kissed him. "Gently, honey. No rough stuff."

He stood up, holding her to him. "Have I ever hurt you?"

"No," she lied, "you never have."

They moved towards the main bedroom at the front of the house, forgetting the television set still beaming its silent pictures in the corner of the room. They did not see that the talk show had finished and an announcer, face as serious as that of a priest beside a grave, had come on the screen. He mouthed a silent message at them, but they did not look back. As they went through the doorway the announcer disappeared and Michael Forte, looking equally serious, the principal mourner, came on the screen.

In the bedroom Carole undressed and climbed into bed beside Abel. Then she sat up. "I've left the car out in the driveway."

"Forget it, baby. Nobody's gonna see it tonight. I'll put it in the garage before daylight. C'mon, baby, I'll be gentle like you say."

She had decided she would do the love-making; that way she could control it. He lay back, flattered by her actions. She did love him, he was finally convinced: a girl had to love a man to be the one to start everything. His life once again had a future.

Finally they fell asleep, she turned away from him, he with his arms wrapped round her. When the phone beside the bed rang once, they both came awake instantly. Carole, nearer to the phone, automatically reached for it, then stopped her hand. The phone had gone silent again, but the one buzzing note rang in their ears like an explosion.

3

Lisa, lying awake in the other bedroom, heard the single buzz of the phone out in the living-room. But the phone rang only once and after a few moments' strained listening she convinced herself it had been a trick of hearing, perhaps a noise made by the storm. Then, because her hearing was for the moment so acute, she heard the diminishing note in the fury of the storm. She saw Sylvia lift her head and stare at her.

"Did you hear that?"

"The phone?" Sylvia said.

So she hadn't imagined it. "Yes. But why didn't it ring further? Do you think it was some sort of message for them?"

"Who from? Do you think there is someone else in this with them?"

But they had no answers: they could do nothing but ask pointless questions. But if the storm was petering out . . . "Listen! Is the storm easing off?"

Sylvia struggled up, her head cocked to one side. There *was* a waning of the tumult outside; the rain beat less strongly against the shutters, the wind was dropping. They both knew it would still be a wild night outside, but Hurricane Myrtle was moving away.

"How long do hurricanes take to blow themselves out?"

"It could be a perfectly fine day in four or five hours," Sylvia said. "That is if it doesn't swing around again. Sometimes it goes on raining, but not always."

"Then those men could be on a plane for Cuba by eight or nine o'clock. Perhaps earlier."

"Yes." Sylvia lay back, stared up at the ceiling. The light had been left on and they were glad of it; the darkness was too vast, left them wandering at the mercy of their imagination. "Today's Election Day. I d forgotten about it."

"Do you want to go on being – what do they call you? In Sydney she's the Lady Mayoress."

"In America you're never anything but your husband's wife, whatever he happens to be. I'm the Mayor's wife, nothing more." She was still staring at the ceiling. "I don't know – I mean, if I want to go on being the Mayor's wife. Just being Michael's wife is enough. None of this would have happened – to you or me – if I'd been a nobody. I'm sorry."

"What for?"

"Do you – " She turned her head, looked at this woman who for fifteen or sixteen hours had been closer to her than any other woman since her girlhood, yet whom after today she might never see again. Who, and the thought chilled her, might also die with her. "Do you hate me for what's happened to you?"

"No," said Lisa slowly. "Unlike my husband, I'm a fatalist. This was in my stars – you just happened to be part of the plot."

"Thank you," said Sylvia, but she was incapable of fatalism and she did not know whether to believe Lisa Malone or not.

Chapter Ten

"That was a stupid thing to try," said Jefferson. "Do you want all four of you to finish up in prison?"

"I didn't stop to think." Mrs Birmingham, in a white raincoat and hood, sat slumped in the back seat of the car beside Malone. "It was a mother's instinct, I guess."

Your mother's instinct has been a bit bloody slow up till now, Malone thought. "Your daughter had better be at the cottage," he said. "If she isn't – if she *has* been there and she's skedaddled with my wife and Mrs Forte, I'll see you do finish up in prison."

"I can understand your bitterness, Inspector," said Birmingham, sitting beside Jefferson in the front seat. "We have nothing personal against you or the police – "

"Mr Birmingham," said Malone with none of his usual tolerance, "your tolerance gives me a pain in the arse."

Now the small clues were linking up into a definite trail, no matter how inconclusive it might prove in the end, he had thrown off his exhaustion but at the expense of not being able to control his raw nerves. His self-control was not helped by the fact that he was sustained only by hope; he had placed all his bets on the Birminghams' daughter being one of the kidnappers and Lisa being in the cottage out at Sunday Harbor. He shut his mind against the thought of what his reaction might be if the cottage should prove to be empty. For the first time in his life he was afraid of the black mysteries that lay within himself.

Jefferson, behind the wheel of the car, remarked the change in Malone but made no comment. He saw Willard Birmingham stiffen at the Australian's reply; then the tall man turned up the collar of his raincoat, sank back in the seat and stared out of the car. Jefferson felt only a flicker of sympathy for him, but it was not enough to prompt an apology for Malone's rudeness. He knew where his real sympathy lay.

They were on the Long Island Expressway again, deserted at this hour of the morning but for the occasional patrolling police car looking for vehicles that might have broken down in the storm.

The four of them rode in a prickly silence for several miles. Then Elizabeth Birmingham glanced at the dark, stiff profile beside her. "If our daughter has – has kidnapped your wife and Mrs Forte, then I suppose we're to blame in some way."

"Not necessarily." Malone realized she was trying to offer him some sympathy. He turned towards her, softening his tone. "Don't torture yourself with the idea, Mrs Birmingham. Your daughter, whatever she's done, has chosen her own life."

"I sometimes wonder," said Elizabeth Birmingham, and looked at the silent shape of her husband in front of her. "Though that's the first time I've ever admitted it to anyone."

Her husband looked back at her. "We should've been franker with each other. Because I've often wondered the same thing myself."

Dear Christ, never let Lisa and I have secrets from each other, not if they lead to situations like this.

Then Jefferson said, "Do you know the cops out at Sunday Harbor?"

"Just casually. I've never had any cause to call on them for anything." Birmingham sat up, like a man gradually becoming aware of the fact that he was going into battle.

Jefferson had phoned Police Headquarters and he knew that Ken Lewton and probably someone from the FBI would already be on their way out to the far end of the Island. Headquarters would have contacted the Sunday Harbor police and the Suffolk County Sheriff's Department and asked them to watch the Birmingham cottage but to make no move till Lewton and the FBI men had arrived. Until they did arrive Jefferson knew he would have to be the liaison man and he was always very much aware of his colour and his rank whenever he had to deal with out-of-town cops. There were still a lot of country law enforcement officers who could not understand how a coon had got to be a captain. He did not know how metropolitan the Sunday Harbor cops would be in their thinking.

He noticed the car had seemingly picked up speed of its own accord. "I think the storm's easing up. We could be lucky."

"How?" asked Malone.

"You want that plane to be able to get off, don't you?" Then he screwed up his face, shook his head. He was tired; he would have to watch himself out at Sunday Harbor. He did not want to bitch things up for Malone by making the wrong remarks out there. He glanced at Birmingham. "I'm not gonna explain it to you now, but if your daughter is in this, she could have backed herself into a corner where she can't get out."

"Don't be enigmatic, Captain. Don't you trust me?"

"No," said Jefferson flatly. "But what worries me more is will your daughter trust you when we get you to talk to her?"

Birmingham had no answer to that and he turned his head away, took off his hat and leaned his face against the cold glass of the car window. In the back seat his wife drew her hood about her face and began to weep quietly. Malone sat unmoving beside her, his hands thrust into his raincoat pockets, his eyes gazing unseeingly out at the rain hitting the window like silver splinters. He could feel a sickness growing in him, a fear that he might not be able to face whatever lay ahead of them out at the cottage. For he had convinced himself that Lisa *was* there, that in another hour or so they would have reached the end of the trail. But he had reached a stage where despair was beginning to weigh heavier than hope. He was, against his will, digging a grave, just in case . . .

By the time they reached Sunday Harbor the wind had dropped to no more than a gentle blow with occasional strong gusts, like last salvoes from Hurricane Myrtle. It was still raining, a steady downpour that was the final deluge from clouds that, high up in the darkness, had already begun to move away. Two local police cars and four cars from the Sheriff's Department were parked at the end of the street to which Birmingham had directed Jefferson. They were without lights and Jefferson switched off his own lights as soon as he saw them.

A man in a slicker and rain-hat got out of one of the cars and came running through the rain. Malone opened the back door and the man got in, apologizing for bringing so much water with him.

"I'm Jack Narvo, the Deputy Sheriff of the county." He was a tall thin man but it was impossible for Malone and the others, in the darkness of the car, to see his features clearly; he had a light, friendly voice and a trick of putting his head on one side as if expecting a question after each remark he made. "Which is Captain Jefferson?"

"I am."

The long narrow head went on one side and there was a moment's pause. "Okay, Captain. We have three more cars down at the other end of the street and two cars in the street behind this one, just in case your guess proves correct. One of my men has been down to the house, checked the car in the driveway beside it. It has Missouri plates."

"We don't know anyone from Missouri," said Birmingham.

Jefferson introduced the Birminghams and Malone, and Narvo's head ducked to one side as he acknowledged each of them. "We're pretty sure there's someone in the house, but we don't know how many. The car's been out tonight. The motor's cold, but in this weather it could have cooled off pretty quick. But there are tracks in the gravel of the driveway that haven't been washed out yet."

"Your man seems pretty observant," said Jefferson.

"We try to be." The head went to one side again and the light voice just for a moment lost its friendliness; but it was impossible to tell whether he resented being complimented by a city cop or a black cop. "The Sheriff and the local police chief are away on an administration course – this is usually the quiet time of the year for us. This part of town is unincorporated, so it comes under my jurisdiction."

Oh Christ, thought Malone, here we go again with the bloody jurisdictional protocol again.

"Well, you talk it over with Captain Lewton and the FBI when they get out here," said Jefferson. "Kidnapping is a Federal offence, so I guess the FBI are running things now."

"Who are you then?" Narvo's head looked as if it would fall sideways off his neck.

"Just a friend of Inspector Malone's," said Jefferson. "He needs one, with all the goddam red tape that's been tangling him ever since this business started. That looks like Captain Lewton arriving now. Let's go and introduce him to your jurisdiction, Sheriff."

He and Narvo, the latter stiff and awkward with anger and embarrassment, got out of the car, leaving Malone alone with the Birminghams. The husband reached back over the front seat and took his wife's hand.

"She may not be in there after all, dear. This sort of thing isn't Julie – "

"I know it isn't. But – " Then both of them looked at Malone.

"Look," said Malone quietly, "I've been a cop for quite a long time. One thing that keeps repeating itself in my experience is the number of parents who don't know their children. You don't seem to have known your son too well. What makes you think you knew your daughter?"

"You sound as if you *want* her to be in there!" Mrs Birmingham pushed back the hood of her raincoat, sat forward to be closer to her husband.

"All I want is for my wife – and Mrs Forte – to be in there. At least that will mean I know where they are – up till now

I haven't had any idea where they are or even if they're still alive." Again the Celtic shadow darkened his mind; he shook it off. "I don't care who the kidnappers are – your daughter or Bill Buggerlugs – but if your daughter *is* in there, I'm hoping that you can talk her into letting my wife and Mrs Forte come out safely. What happens after that, I don't care."

The Birminghams looked at each other, then the husband said, "We'll try, Inspector."

Then Jefferson came back, opened the door of the car and leaned in out of the rain. "They're busting into the house opposite yours, Mr Birmingham. They're gonna set that up as the command post. Captain Lewton would like you down there. We can't take the car down, but we should be able to get down there on foot without whoever is in your house seeing us."

Five minutes later the four of them, their lower legs drenched and their shoes covered in mud, were in the large kitchen of the house across the street from the Birminghams'. On the way down Malone had tried to catch a glimpse of the cottage where Lisa might be held, but darkness, the heavy rain and the need to hurry had prevented him from seeing it.

"Oh, what a mess we're making," said Elizabeth Birmingham. "I hope Nell Royce will understand."

"This is Dr Royce's house," said her husband. "I hope you did no damage when you were breaking in."

It was a large house, built ranch style in fieldstone and timber, and the kitchen reminded Malone of illustrations he had seen in the American home magazines Lisa had started buying once they had become engaged. He wondered what sort of money the owners had that they could leave such a house closed up for six months of the year. This was not a holiday place but what he would have thought of as a luxury home. He was beginning to appreciate that his own values were way down the scale from those he had seen in the past few hours.

"We broke the lock on the back door there." Lewton was brusque; he had no patience with a couple who seemed more concerned with their neighbours' property than with who might be in their own house. "Sheriff Narvo has made a note of it and we'll see the damage is repaired. We've also had the phone reconnected – we'll let Dr Royce know about that too."

"Who's in charge?" asked Birmingham.

Lewton looked at Norman Cartwright. He and the FBI man had ridden out together from Manhattan and on the way he had explained to Cartwright the background to Commissioner Hungerford's determination that the Police Department should wrap up this case. Though the case was now a Federal matter, Cartwright had not insisted on asserting his authority; he had explained, though without elaboration, that he did not like to see any man close to retirement being kicked out of his job. For the time being they would be a partnership.

"Is it any concern of yours, Mr Birmingham?"

"Yes! If my daughter is across the street there, I don't want you busting in, maybe harming her. Maybe even – killing her!"

His wife gasped and he put his arms around her. Lewton looked at them both, then he jerked his head and went out of the kitchen towards the front of the house. Several of the men followed him; Jefferson looked at Malone, then they too went towards the front of the house. The light was on in the kitchen, but the rest of the house was in darkness. Malone found himself in a wide hall dimly lit by a guarded flashlight held by a local patrolman who stood with his back to the heavy front door. Lewton and the other men were in the big living-room off to one side of the hall, only their voices telling Malone and Jefferson where they were.

"Inspector Malone," said Lewton, "we have to make up our minds whether to rush that house across the street or just wait till they come out. Assuming, of course, that the people over there are the ones we want. If your wife and

Mrs Forte are across the street, do you want us to run the risk of rushing the place?"

Malone could only dimly see the other men, but he could read their minds. He didn't blame them for what he read there; he had tried the same trick himself in the past. No cop ever wanted to take the whole blame for something that might go wrong.

"No, I don't," he said. "Back home I've been in two cases in the past twelve months where the set-up was something like this. Not a kidnapping, but blokes wanted for armed robbery. At the first place the bloke gave up without a struggle – he had a gun but he didn't even fire a shot from it. The second bloke went berserk – he even killed the dog he had in the house with him. It was panic as much as anything else – but he wounded two of my mates before he finally blew his own brains out. Fifty-fifty, that's my experience of what chances you've got when you rush a place. I want better odds than that for my wife."

Lewton sensed that the men around him agreed with Malone. It relieved him of a decision he would not have cared to make alone. There would have been no future at all for a captain of detectives who gave an order that might have resulted in the death of the Mayor's wife.

"Okay, we'll play it safe. We'll have Birmingham call his house, talk to his daughter if she's there. If it's not her in there and whoever it is refuses to come out, then we'll sit it out till daylight."

"Is the Mayor on his way?" Malone asked.

"Only if we know for certain that his wife is across the street."

"What happens at daylight, if they refuse to come out?"

Lewton was glad of the darkness of the room. "Then I think it'll be time for a collective decision."

2

Lisa, struggling up out of the abyss of exhaustion, heard the phone ringing out in the living-room and in the other bedroom. It went on and on, with that monotonous insistence of the mechanical, and in just a few moments it was rubbing rawly against her nerves: *Answer it, for God's sake answer it!* She looked across at Sylvia, who was also wide awake now.

"Someone must know we're here! God, why don't they answer it?"

"Listen! I think they're arguing – "

Carole, pulling a wrap round her, had come out into the living-room, followed by Abel, who was still naked. The phone went on ringing, urgently and yet patiently, and in the corner of the room the television screen still showed its silent images. Carole reached for the phone, but Abel grabbed her hand.

"Don't touch it, I tell you! It's a trick – "

"What sort of trick? Who knows we're here?"

"It could be your folks – "

That had been one of her few mistakes, to tell him that this cottage was her family's; it would be the one clue he would have to her identity when she finally left him and disappeared again. The information had slipped out when he had asked her why she had chosen Sunday Harbor; even after four years she had not become fully professional at retaining her cover. She was proving every minute, as the phone was underlining now, that she was no more than an amateur in this whole game.

She drew her hand away from the phone, but he still kept his grip on her wrist. "You sure you didn't tell someone tonight we were here?"

"No!" She could see suspicion and anger making him ugly; she sought desperately for a reason why the phone should have rung: "Someone must have seen the car out-side – "

"I'll go put it in the garage." He let go her wrist, massaged it gently with his fingers as the hardness slipped out of his face. "I'm sorry, baby. If some bastard is being curious we gotta get outa here before daylight."

"Where shall we go?"

"Out to the boat – there's nowhere else."

Her parents' boat, anchored at a mooring off the yacht club, had been another reason she had chosen Sunday Harbor. She knew how to handle it and it would have been easy to slip away in it during the time Abel would be away dumping both the car and the women. She would have been almost across to Bridgeport before he could have got back to Sunday Harbor.

The phone stopped ringing. Abel looked at it, then in the sudden silence lifted his head. "The storm – it's going, baby! That's only rain! We're gonna be okay!"

He grabbed her, kissed her, then went quickly back into the front bedroom. Carole remained standing in the living-room, still afraid and now suddenly dispirited. A commercial had come on the television screen, but she stared at it without really seeing it. A woman walked into a bathroom, looked down into a toilet; in the water of the bowl was a motor cruiser, on its deck a handsome man in yachting cap and blazer; silently he offered the woman a package of toilet cleaner, then the cruiser slid away, presumably down the sewage pipes to a larger and less polluted pond. All at once Carole became aware of what she was seeing; suddenly angry with the imbecility of it all, she switched off the television set. The pinpoint of light died away on the darkened screen, the obliterated image of the announcer who was about to introduce the repeat of a special message by Mayor Michael Forte.

Abel came out, dressed now and pulling on a raincoat. "Get some clothes on, honey. Then you better get the dames dressed while I clean up around here."

He went out through the kitchen, opened the back door. It was still dark, but he could tell at once that the rain was coming straight down now, not beating almost horizontally as it had been. He pulled up the collar of his raincoat, closed the back door and ran through the rain and round the corner of the house to the driveway. He was about to pull open the door of the car when the searchlight beam hit him. He staggered back against the wall of the house as if he had been hit a physical blow; he threw up his hands against the blinding glare and turned his face away. A cry of anger and shock escaped him, then he spun round and ran back into the house. He slammed the kitchen door shut, locked it and leaned against it, breathing heavily and trembling like a man who had just, unwittingly, put one foot over a precipice. Then he heard the phone in the living-room start to ring again.

In the kitchen of the house across the street Cartwright held the phone to his ear, then raised a warning hand to the others waiting around him. "This is the FBI. We have you surrounded. If you come out with your hands up, you won't be hurt."

Abel, on the other end of the line, snarled, "Screw you! You bastards get away or something's gonna happen here you won't like!"

Cartwright put his hand over the phone, looked at Lewton. "You better withdraw that squad car with the searchlight, Ken. This guy, whoever he is, sounds nasty."

"Is my daughter there?" said Willard Birmingham. "Ask him if I can speak to her."

Cartwright spoke into the phone again. "Is Julie Birmingham there?"

"Who?" Abel's note of puzzlement was genuine. Who, for Christ's sake, was Julie Birmingham? He had not bothered to look around the cottage since they had been here, but he had found nothing in his casual scrutiny of the rooms that Carole might be anyone but who she said she was. Now he looked at her and all at once knew who she was.

He felt suddenly even more angry; but what was worse, he also felt empty. Christ, why hadn't she trusted him all the way? What other lies had she told him? "You Julie Birmingham? That your real name?"

Carole (Julie: it was a name she had never really discarded in her mind) hesitated, then nodded. "Who is it? Is it my parents?"

Abel stared at her, beginning to hate her. Jesus, how had she conned him, got him into this? He was still getting over the shock of the searchlight blazing at him out there in the driveway and he could feel the nervousness in his hands, the beginning of another headache. He spoke into the phone again. "Who wants to talk to her?"

Across the street Willard Birmingham took the phone in the kitchen while Lewton went through and picked up the extension in the hallway. The curtains in the living-room had been drawn and the lights turned on; advertising where the police were did not matter now, unless the kidnappers were stupid enough to start sniping at the house. If they did that, then Lewton hoped Commissioner Hungerford was out here by that time to make the next decision.

Willard Birmingham said, "I'd like to talk to my daughter – please . . . Julie?" For a moment he looked as if he were about to break down; his face went slack and grey and he looked with pain at his wife. She stood close to him, her ear pressed against the phone as he held it to his own ear. Birmingham recovered and went on, "Julie dear, what's going on? How did you get into this terrible mess? Do you have the Mayor's wife and Mrs Malone with you?"

Julie (Carole: the name no longer meant anything, it was useless to her from now on) did her best to keep her voice steady. "Daddy, I'm sorry about this – I didn't want you and Mother involved – "

Mrs Birmingham choked on a sob and her husband put his free arm around her. "We believe that, Julie – we know you didn't mean to harm us. But we're in it now and all we want to do is help you. You and Mark – "

"I did it for him, you understand that, don't you?" Julie was weeping, unable to hold back the banked-up years of lost love. Her father and mother were wrong, would never change, but they had loved her and she had loved them and that was something she knew now would never change. But she had come to know it too late. "I don't want to harm Mrs Forte and Mrs Malone. All I want is for Mark to go free – get them to agree to that, put Mark and the other men on the plane to Cuba – "

Abel grabbed the phone from her. "We gotta be with them now, you understand? Tell 'em that, Pop – tell 'em we gotta be on that plane for Cuba too! And the dames go with us – we're gonna give 'em back to you when we're safe in Cuba!"

Lewton cut in on the extension. "This is Captain Lewton, of the New York Police Department. We'll have to get back to you – we'll have to check out with the District Attorney that you can go on that plane with those men – "

"You better see we do, man – "

"I'm not arguing with you," said Lewton, trying to keep himself cool as well as the man listening to him. "It's not my decision. I'm sure they'll agree to what you ask, but I have to contact them first. We'll be back to you. If you want to contact us, we're right across the street from you, in Dr Royce's house. The number is – "

"We got nothing more to say to you, man. You call us when you got the word."

Lewton hung up, went back out to the kitchen. As he did so, Cartwright followed him. "I was listening on the bedroom extension, Ken. They don't know anything about the Cubans and the Algerians refusing to let those guys in. They can't have a TV set or a radio."

"There's a TV in our house," said Birmingham. "Or there was when we closed it up."

"The point is they don't seem to have got the Mayor's message," said Special Agent Butlin, leaning forward with the impatience of a man who thought too much discussion had gone on. "I suggest we get on to the TV and radio stations, tell them to cancel the running of those tapes at once – "

"That was the intention," said Cartwright. He pulled his belt in another notch; he felt hungry, empty and lean. "We better do it through your Department, Ken."

Lewton recognized the conflict; some day it would happen to him, he guessed. There was always a touch of the jackal in the young lions; Butlin, he was sure, would have a bit more than the usual. "I'll talk to Headquarters now. How's the weather?"

"The rain's stopped," said Sheriff Narvo and cocked his head. "Look, we got more than enough men outside to handle 'em. It looks like there's no more than two of them, the girl and the guy we saw out by the car. Let's smoke 'em out – we got plenty of gas – "

Lewton looked at Malone. "It's still your call, Inspector. The safety of your wife and Mrs Forte is still our main consideration."

"Let's get 'em out in the open first," said Malone. "For one thing, I'd like to know my wife and Mrs Forte are still alive."

"Of course they are!" Elizabeth Birmingham's voice shook with emotion. "Our daughter is over there – she's not a murderess!"

"It's not your daughter who worries us," said Lewton, the snarl of the man on the phone still echoing in his ear. "It's the guy she's with."

3

Malone and Jefferson stood in the Royce driveway behind some bushes, their backs pressed against the fieldstone of the house as they gazed across the street at the Birmingham cottage. The rain had stopped, the clouds were clearing and daylight crept tentatively up the eastern sky.

"We call this the piccaninny dawn back home," said Malone. "When I was on the beat, it was the time of day when I always felt anything but a piccaninny, more like a bloody old man. Like I feel now."

"It's gonna be a fine day." Then Jefferson realized what he had said. "The weather, anyway."

Malone stared across the street at the white cottage slowly appearing out of the disappearing darkness. "Christ, I *know* Lisa is over there, but I have to keep telling myself it's a fact. How many times have you been in this sort of situation?"

"You mean staking out a house? I've lost count."

"I suppose I could add up the number of times it's happened to me – I'm just beginning to realize that life's much gentler for cops back home. Funny thing is, I can't remember how I felt when it happened before."

"Then, you would have been on the outside looking in. Now – " He glanced at Malone, at the man who had aged so much in so few hours. "One thing's for sure, you wouldn't have been as worried as you are now."

"No, I'm not thinking about the worrying. I'm thinking about the law and order bit. If I could get at them, I think I'd kill that bloke and that girl. I can't see any reason why the world wouldn't be better off without them. A cop's not supposed to think like that."

Jefferson looked across the street. Most of the houses could be seen clearly now, a varied lot that ranged from neat Cape Cod cottages to the large ranch house beside which they stood; this was where the fortunate few came for a few months of the year and an occasional weekend to forget the pressures that ran their lives the rest of the time. He did not blame them for their desire to escape; he, even more than they, knew how interminable was the fight that faced them. Then he remembered the three-room, cold-water flat in which he and his three brothers and sisters had been born and raised, from which the only escape for his mother and father had been death. Some people, including the Birmingham girl across the street, didn't know when they were well off.

Then Lewton came down the drive, keeping close to the side of the house. "The Mayor and the Commissioner are on their way out here by helicopter. We've been told to offer them the deal they want – free passage for all of them to Cuba. I'm afraid we'll have to let your wife and Mrs Forte go with them, Scobie."

Malone looked at him sharply. "Have the Cubans changed their minds?"

"No. The idea is to get those people out of that house. An aircraft is standing by at Kennedy and we'll escort them in there. Once they're out in the open, we can see who we're dealing with and maybe do something – don't ask me what, but *something*. If we come up with nothing, then we'll let them board the plane and it can head for Cuba and we'll just have to plead with the Cubans to play ball for the women's sake."

"In the meantime what happens to my wife and Mrs Forte?"

There was enough daylight for Malone to see the blank look on Lewton's face. "What else can you suggest? Your wife and Mrs Forte are the aces in this hand – and the kidnappers are holding them. Right now our only hope is to go along with them and hope – wait for them to make a mistake."

Malone looked across the street, cursed worriedly, then looked back at Lewton. "If those buggers take my wife on to the plane at the airport, you're going to have to tie me down. Christ, do you think I'm just going to stand there and do nothing while they take my wife off into the wild blue yonder? If the Cubans still won't play ball, what happens then?"

Lewton looked as worried and as pained as Malone. "Scobie, I wish to Christ I knew. But I'm asking you – what else can we do unless those kidnappers make a mistake and we can take advantage of it?"

"What about police marksmen?" asked Jefferson. "Could they pick them off when they come out?"

"There'll be everything waiting for us at Kennedy - police and FBI marksmen, the Emergency Service squad, the lot. But you can't pick a guy off if he has a gun stuck in the side of Mrs Malone or Mrs Forte." He stared across at the cottage. "Our best bet, I thought, was gonna be the girl - I thought with her folks out here, we might have got through to her. But the young punk seems to be running things now - and no amount of talking is ever gonna get through to him."

Then a uniformed patrolman came round the back corner of the house. "They're calling from across the street, Captain."

In the kitchen Cartwright was on the phone. Lewton went past him into the hallway and picked up the phone there. Malone stood irresolute for a moment, then went into the living-room and picked up the phone he saw on a side table. Abel, still nameless to the men listening to him, was doing the talking: "We're gonna get started now, pig. No delays, you unnerstand? You have those guys from The Tombs out at the airport by the time we get there. And no tricks, you unnerstand? We're gonna have a gun in the guts of the women all the way. You give us a nice friendly escort and the women are gonna be all right."

"Can I speak to my wife?" said Malone.

"Who's that?" Abel's voice was sharp, nervously suspicious.

"Malone. I'd like to speak to my wife." Malone could hear Lewton and Cartwright listening in on the other extensions; they said nothing but he could feel their presence in the other rooms; he was butting in on their jurisdiction, but he sensed their understanding. "Let me speak to her, just to assure me she's all right, then we'll agree to everything you ask."

"You ain't in any position not to agree, man." There was a pause, then Malone heard him say faintly, as if his head were turned away from the phone, "Stay outa this, baby.

You leave everything to me from now on. Look, man – "
The voice came back to the phone. "You're gonna see your
wife in about two minutes – you're gonna *see* she's okay.
That all the concession you gonna get. Now let's get
moving – "

"You bastard!" But the phone had gone dead in Malone's
ear. He stared at it, then slammed it down as Lewton and
Cartwright came into the living-room. He said nothing for a
moment, pressing down the fury that shook him, then he
looked at the two men. "You're right. The girl hasn't got a
say in it. He's running the show. If she's everything her
parents say she is, how the hell did she ever pick up with a
bastard like that?"

"We'll ask her that when we take them," said Cartwright,
and tried to sound hopeful. "Well, we better get going. I
don't think he's the sort who's going to be too patient."

Jefferson stood in the living-room archway and Lewton
turned to him. "John, radio the Commissioner and the
Mayor, tell 'em to turn back and meet us at Kennedy. We'll
go in along Sunrise, then on to the Southern State, across on
Laurelton, then on to the Belt Parkway. I've looked up the
map and that should give us the clearest route – at this time
of morning there shouldn't be too much traffic around.
We'll drop Sheriff Narvo and his men off at the county line –
ask the Nassau County fellers to pick us up there and take
over the escort. Our own men can meet us at the Queens line
and take us on to the airport. Tell 'em to get a bull team
out on bikes, clear the traffic ahead as much as they can.
Give strict orders no smart-ass is to try anything on his own –
we'll play the game strictly according to their rules across
the street until we get to the airport. Unless – "

"Unless what?"

Lewton shrugged. "I dunno. Just unless."

Then Sheriff Narvo came into the hallway, flung open
the front door. "He's come out of the house to the car – he's
got one of the women with him!"

The men in the living-room went out of the house in a

rush, unconcerned now with remaining hidden. They stood outside the front door, at the top of the sloping, water-gullied lawn. Across the street Abel had come out of the front door of the cottage, pushing Lisa ahead of him and keeping himself screened by her from the police cars that had now come down the street. The cars were parked in the middle of the roadway, their two-man crews standing behind them, their guns out of their holsters but held out of sight of the armed man they were all watching. Four motor cycle cops were standing behind the line of cars, their motor cycles resting on their stands.

Lewton took a bullhorn from one of the patrolmen standing nearby and handed it to Malone. "It may encourage your wife to know you're here."

Malone gratefully took the bullhorn, aimed it across the street. "Lisa! This is Scobie!"

Lisa missed her step, pulled up and looked wildly around, then over towards Malone. Abel moved in closer behind her, putting his arm around her and shoving the gun hard into her back. But Lisa, eyes straining to see the familiar figure standing in front of the house across the street, felt neither Abel's arm nor his gun.

"Scobie!"

"Are you all right?"

She nodded, her throat closing up; then she managed to shout, "Yes!"

"Mrs Forte – how's she?"

"She's all right!"

It was an inane conversation, Malone's bullhorned bellow booming across the quiet street, and Lisa's thin, exhausted voice shrieking her replies. It was like the conversations that go on between travellers on a ship and their friends waiting to greet them on the wharf. Malone, years ago when he had been attached to the Pillaging Squad on the Sydney wharves, had listened to exchanges just like this. No one had been in danger in those days and he had often laughed at the vacuous dialogues. But no one in the street this morning laughed;

every simple word between the husband and wife had a poignancy for those who were listening. All but Abel.

He shoved Lisa into the front seat of the car, got in beside her. For a moment he was facing away from the street, a good part of his range of view blocked by the cottage. Dave Butlin, down behind one of the police cars, suddenly made a move, his gun held ready. Cartwright grabbed the bullhorn from Malone.

"Stay where you are, Dave! Let them come out!" Cartwright lowered the bullhorn. "I'll have that young smart-ass moved to Nome, Alaska, so help me!"

Butlin looked back at Cartwright, grimaced, then nodded and moved back behind the police car. Cartwright looked at Lewton, who was focusing a pair of binoculars on the cottage across the street.

"Looks like he can't get it to start. If it's been out there all night, it could have water in the plugs."

Abel got out of the car, pushing Lisa ahead of him again. He looked across at the Royce house and shouted, "We want one of the squad cars!"

"He can have mine," said Jefferson, took out his keys and made to move down the path.

"Stay where you are, pig!"

Abel pushed Lisa ahead of him around to the front of the house. The front door opened again and Julie, holding a gun, came out with Sylvia Forte. Elizabeth Birmingham, standing on the sodden lawn beside Malone, waved a weak arm; but Julie, if she saw the greeting, took no notice of it. The four people on the other side of the street, the hostages in front and the kidnappers behind, moved like a small deputation down the driveway and out into the road. As they did so Malone and the others moved down the path of the Royce house.

"Okay, that's far enough." Abel, one hand holding tightly to the collar of Lisa's suit, brought his gun up menacingly. "We want your car, Captain – Lewton, you say your name was? No tricks – which is your car?"

237

Malone, now only forty feet away, stared at Lisa, unable to believe the nightmare of what was happening: the actual fact of seeing her held by the kidnappers was less credible than all the hours he had spent since she had been reported prisoner. The surrounding scene did not help to make anything more real; policeman though he was, this was not the sort of police scene he was used to. This looked much more militaristic: the helmeted men, the sub-machine-guns held by some of them: cops had become warriors. The line of cars suggested armoured vehicles; one of the cars at the end, a late arrival, still had its red light spinning, like the modern equivalent of a battle banner. But this was war, so why should he find it hard to believe?

Lisa stared back at him; then he heard her say hoarsely, "Darling – "

And at that moment Willard Birmingham said, "Julie – "

Malone looked at the other three who had emerged from the house for the first time. Sylvia Forte was even more wan and exhausted-looking than Lisa; he noticed she carried one arm in the front of her jacket, as if she had broken or sprained her wrist. The young man with his long blond hair looked like a thousand other kids he had seen all over the world; it was somehow galling that this bastard, who had caused him so much pain and worry, should look so anonymous. But he would have picked the girl out in any company and he would remember her for ever. She looked as strained and exhausted as the other two women in front of her and she was as beautiful as either of them. There was no look of defiance about her: she looked what she was, an ordinary girl who had suddenly found herself in a situation she could no longer control.

Lewton nodded. "That's my car over there. You're sure you want to go through with this? You let Mrs Forte and Mrs Malone go now and I'll do what I can for you with the D.A."

Julie looked at Abel, but he shook his head fiercely She was not wearing her wig and neither of them wore their dark glasses; no expression on their faces was hidden from each other or from the watchers.

Abel looked back at Lewton. "Nothing doing, pig. You better be sure that plane is waiting for us at Kennedy. Malone, don't you let 'em forget one minute that we got your wife – " He dug Lisa in the back with the gun and she flinched.

"Just don't knock her around or by Christ – "

"Nobody's gonna knock her around, man – but don't you go handing me no threats. You just see those other bastards don't try no tricks. You want your missus back, you see they all behave. Okay, let's go."

"Just a minute," said Lewton. Some civilian cars had come to the end of the streets and a few people stood in a tight, curious group. It was still early and he wondered how they had got here. But sensation, he guessed, had its own smell. He hated to think what the flies would be like when they got to Kennedy. "To see we get a clear run right through to the airport, we'll precede you with two cars and those four motor cycle men – I'll be in one of the cars. The other cars will tail you. At the county lines they'll be changed each time – no tricks," he assured Abel as the latter stiffened with suspicion. "We just want to get you to that plane as quickly and with as little fuss as possible. Your husband will meet us at the airport, Mrs Forte."

"Thank you," said Sylvia Forte huskily.

"Okay," said Abel, "we'll do it your way. But remember – anything happens to us, these two dames go out with us."

A minute later the convoy was ready to move off. Lewton, about to step into another squad car with Malone and Cartwright, stopped and looked back towards the end of the line. The civilian cars had tagged on, led by a station wagon on the roof of which a man was setting up a camera.

"Who are they, for Christ's sake?"

Sheriff Narvo, standing by his own car, looked back. "It's the reporters and TV guys, Captain. They followed you out here from Manhattan."

"Jesus," said Lewton, "they make a circus of everything!"

4

The Police Department helicopter was over Riverhead when the message came for it to turn back to Kennedy Airport.

"Keep going!" shouted Commissioner Hungerford above the clatter of the helicopter's blades, and the pilot nodded. "We'll turn back when we see the convoy."

Michael Forte and Manny Pearl, sitting in the rear seats, looked down on the roiled and muddy waters of Great Peconic Bay; then as they flew on they saw over to their right the flooded potato fields around Bridgehampton. One or two houses had been unroofed and trees lay on their sides, their torn-up roots looking like black claws frozen in a death agony. In the marinas and anchorages around the shore smashed boats were locked together like so much floating junk; out in the middle of the bay a lone yacht, its mast snapped off, drifted like a dead gull. There was no sign of any bird life, but on the roads a few cars were moving, and in the marinas small dark figures clambered over the wreckage like scavenging rats over a rubbish dump. Out to the east the sun, pink and weak, was struggling like a derelict out of a torn blanket of cloud.

"There they are!" Hungerford pointed down.

"It looks like a Presidential motorcade," said Forte. "Do they need all those cars?"

Hungerford was looking at the scene below through binoculars. "I can count only eight police cars. Who the hell are the rest?"

Manny Pearl also had binoculars to his eyes. "The other six are TV and press, I'd say. There's a guy with a TV camera mounted on top of that station wagon."

"They're really moving," said Hungerford. "I hope the son-of-a-bitch falls off. The freedom of the goddam press is the greatest abuse of democracy I know of."

Forte, tired, worried and afraid, still managed a grin. "You sound like the KGB, Des."

"At least those guys can turn a deaf ear to criticism." Then Hungerford glanced at the pilot and shouted, "You heard none of that, you understand!"

The pilot grinned, pointed to the earphones he wore and shook his head. He swung the helicopter about, took it down closer to the convoy of cars as it picked up Sunrise Highway. The long snake of fourteen vehicles slid around two slower-moving cars on the highway, raced on past the flooded and battered countryside. On the roofs of the police cars the spinning red signal lights were as bright as drops of blood in the slanting light coming up from the east.

Forte took the binoculars from Manny Pearl and looked down, trying to pick out which car Sylvia might be travelling in. He tapped the pilot on the shoulder and the latter took the helicopter down lower. Forte saw the third police car in the line waver a little, then caught a quick glance of someone as they looked out of the car and up at him.

Then he saw another face appear at a rear side window, but the angle was too acute, the face too distorted by the window glass, for him to be able to identify it. The pilot swung the helicopter up as it moved on too fast for the cars below, went round in a wide circle and came back. Michael Forte focused the glasses again, kept them aimed on the third car in the convoy, but no faces appeared this time at the car's window. She doesn't know I'm up here, he thought. And felt an insane, suicidal urge to plunge out of the helicopter and down on to the swiftly speeding car below.

In the rear seat of the car Sylvia and Lisa, hands free now, sat side by side, each slumped in her own confused despair. Sylvia held her swollen wrist, but she was hardly aware of the pain of it; she had reached a stage where another bruise or cut or even a broken bone would have been absorbed in the general numbness that contained her. She had looked out at the helicopter when it had clattered overhead, but it had been a reflex action, a response to Abel's reaction to it.

Sitting up front beside Julie, who was driving, he had turned back to them, his gun held on the back of the seat. "They got you watched from all angles, but it ain't gonna help you. That right, baby?"

Julie, driving the car with almost automatic reflexes, like a woman at the end of a hard day's motoring, nodded glumly. The last three-quarters of an hour had seen everything crumble into dust, a bitter dust that she could taste as if fate had force-fed it to her. But the last forty-five minutes, she guessed, had been only the climax; disaster had begun creeping up on her last night. If she had been capable of further tears she would have wept; but they would have been tears of self-pity and she was not capable of that either. Till the storm had struck last night everything had seemed so perfect. Even the kidnapping had seemed perfect: there had not even been the danger associated with other kidnappings, the collection of the ransom: the ransom would just have been taken to a plane and flown out of the country. That would still happen, she guessed, but now everyone, including her father and mother, knew who the kidnappers were. Worst of all, she had become Abel's prisoner, though he might not yet think of her that way.

From the moment he had snatched the phone from her in the cottage she had known she had lost control of the whole operation. It was now just a war between Abel and the police: but he hated her too, the traitor in the ranks.

Abel reached for the microphone of the car radio. "Captain, you hear me? Tell that chopper to get outa here!"

"He's leaving now. It's – " Lewton's voice faded as his car passed under a bridge " – and the Mayor."

At that Sylvia leaned quickly forward, but the helicopter was already swinging up and away, heading back towards Kennedy Airport. Abel switched off the radio and looked back at her.

"He must be pretty worried, eh? Mrs Malone's old man didn't look too good either."

"Leave them alone," said Julie.

He gave her the old look out of the corners of his eyes, the old look that said he trusted no one. "You on their side? I been waiting for you to tell me that."

"I'm on nobody's side," she said dully.

"What about those guys in The Tombs? That brother of yours? Jesus, baby, did you use me! I come all the way from Kansas City for *this*!" For the first time she realized he was afraid; he looked wildly backwards and forward of them. "Nobody, not even my old man, ever conned me like you've done!"

She continued to stare ahead of her, deaf to his abuse as he went on swearing at her. He was one with Carole Cox now, part of the past: she did not have to live with either of them any more. Once in Cuba she would find some way of escaping from him. But she felt sorry for the two women in the back of the car. God knew what was going to happen to them.

She slowed down as the police car up front began to slow. Abel swung round, then relaxed. "Must be a county line. Mustn't forget – what you call it, Teach?"

"Protocol," she said mechanically: they had completed the circle to their first relationship, teacher and student: then she had been as unresponsive to him as she was now.

"She used to teach me English," Abel told the women in the back seat. He turned round, peering out through the rear window as the Suffolk County cars and motor cycle men peeled off and the Nassau County squad took over. "She used to read us poetry. There was one line some of us really dug – or me, anyway. That one by that Limey faggot Oscar Wilde – you remember, baby? *We are all in the gutter, but some of us are looking at the stars*."

He struck a chord in her and she looked at him in surprise: he had never told her anything like this before. "You *liked* the poetry?"

"I thought I did. But it's like everything else – a load of crap!"

"You must have liked it once," said Lisa, as surprised as Julie at the unexpected chink in the boy.

"Maybe. But that was before she turned out to be a bitch like all the rest of you."

The convoy sped on. They were on the Southern State Parkway now and the traffic was thickening. The sirens were wailing and the early morning drivers, pulling their cars over to the slow lanes as the bull team waved them aside, were staring out in puzzlement as the long cavalcade, sirens going, red lights spinning, and the cameraman, crouched perilously on the roof platform of the station wagon at the end of the line, swept by. By the time the convoy had picked up the New York Police Department's escort, had swung over to the Belt Parkway and was approaching the airport, traffic on the parkway had slowed to a crawl. The drivers on the parkway were listening to their radios: the convoy swept by to the sound-track of the commentary on its own progress. Some drivers up ahead, warned of the coming of the convoy, looked out and waved as it went past: as Michael Forte had said, it could have been a Presidential motorcade.

At the airport several mobile control trucks were waiting, the producers telling their cameramen parked around the area what they wanted. "Joe, you concentrate on the Mayor and the other dame's husband, what's his name, Mahoney, Moroney – "

"Malone," said an assistant, eye on the higher job.

"Okay, Malone, Balone. Jesus, what's it matter? Who'll remember tomorrow? Pete, you stick with the kidnappers. Angelo, you stay around the terminal buildings – I'll cut away to you for reaction shots from the crowd when things get slow out on the field – "

"Ah Christ, Merv, don't I ever get to see any action? That riot last week, where was I – ?"

"Angie boy, I'm saving you up for Armageddon. You'll be right up front for that. Walter – where the hell's Walter?"

"He's gone for a crap, Merv. Just in case it's a long day, he said – "

244

In her apartment in the Bronx, slopping around in slippers and dressing-gown, Polly Nussbaum kept glancing at the television set as she prepared her breakfast. *God, the Mayor, do him a favour. Give him back his wife safe and sound. And that Mrs Malone, too. What a world you let us make for ourselves, God. You should be disgusted, I wouldn't blame you.*

In his town house in Manhattan Frank Padua had switched on the television set in his bedroom, watched it as his manservant brought in his breakfast tray. He made no comment, vocal or mental, as he looked at the pictures on the screen. Whatever happened out at Kennedy Airport would make little, if any, difference to his life.

"Tell them to have the car out front in an hour," he told the manservant. "I'm going down to vote. You should vote too, Tony."

"Who would I vote for, Mr Padua? Anyone in particular? Mr Forte, maybe?"

Padua spread his hands. "Anyone you like, Tony. It's a free country."

In Brooklyn Auguste Giuffre came out of early Mass and went into the presbytery next door to the church for his usual morning cup of coffee with Father Lupi. He looked at the television set in the priest's study and shook his head in disapproval. "It's a terrible world, Padre. Too much violence."

"I said Mass this morning for the safe return of those poor women."

"I noticed, Padre. You're a thoughtful man."

"Are you going to vote for the Mayor today?"

"Who else? He's a nice Italian boy."

He looked back at the screen. The long convoy had reached the airport, was moving down the perimeter of the field to the far end on the edge of Jamaica Bay. A big jet stood there and parked some distance from it was a semi-circle of police cars, trucks, buses, three ambulances, two fire engines and a helicopter. He had to admire the efficiency of the City of New York. It was just a pity it was in the wrong hands.

"You look flushed, Don Auguste."

"Just a little fall chill, Padre."

5

The radio in the police car crackled and Lewton said, "Yes? Any trouble?"

"Pig," said Abel, "what're you trying to pull? That goddam army down there – you think we're gonna drive into the middle of that?"

"I had nothing to do with that."

"Okay, you tell 'em they all gotta get the hell outa there – and remember, I can hear every word you say. But first, you pull your car outa this line – you and us are gonna stay right here till every one of them bastards is moved right outa there."

Lewton, riding in the front seat with the driver, switched off for a moment and looked back at Cartwright, in the back seat beside Malone. "This son-of-a-bitch is too smart. Do we agree to what he wants?"

"What else can we do?" Cartwright said.

Lewton spoke into the microphone again. "All cars? Turn round and head back to the other end of the runway."

Then a gruff angry voice came on the air as Lewton flicked the switch over. "This is the Commissioner, Captain. Who gave that order?"

Lewton motioned to the driver to slow down, watched the other cars swing away and go back the way they had come. "With all due respect, Commissioner, I'm afraid our friends are giving the orders. They also want everyone moved away from the plane. We have to stay here till you are all at the other end of the runway. Special Agent Cartwright and I agree that we have no argument, sir." Put that in your cigarette holder and smoke it, Commissioner sir.

Lewton had never been a lover of the FBI but now he was glad Cartwright was here. "Our friend is getting impatient. Will you give the order for the area to be cleared, sir?"

The two cars were stationary now and Malone, looking across at the other car, could see Lisa. He waved to her and she waved back. Christ, he thought, so near and yet so far: clichés were often so brutally truthful. Every minute or so there was a deafening roar, cored with a shrill whine, as a plane came in low above them and touched down on the runway. Over on the parallel runway planes were taking off, climbing steeply and banking sharply, spreading their dark peacock tails of smoke against the now bright sun. The airport might be closed for a hurricane: it did not stop for the affairs of men. Life and death could not be fitted into a traffic schedule.

Three hundred yards down the perimeter the helicopter lifted off from beside the parked 707. Then the police cars and trucks, the green buses, the fire engines and the ambulances pulled away and the long convoy came up the edge of the field. It went past, faces in all the vehicles turned towards the two stationary police cars, and the big aircraft was left alone right out at the far end of the field. Behind it stretched the bay, lit by copper glints as the sun struck on its muddied waters. A ragged arrowhead of birds came in against the sun, splintered into fragments and settled down into the marshes surrounding one of the low islands out in the bay. But for the planes coming in every minute above them, the two police cars and the big jet could have been a thousand miles from civilization.

The radio in front of Lewton crackled on again. "Okay, pig. Let's go."

As the two cars approached the plane Abel suddenly snapped, "Who's that? I said everybody, *everybody*, outa there!"

"It's the Mayor," said Lewton.

Michael Forte had been standing by the foot of the steps

leading up to the aircraft. As the two cars rolled to a stop twenty yards away, he stepped forward, his hands up.

"That's far enough!" Abel yelled, and his gun came out of the window of the car. "What you doing here, man?"

"I came to see that my wife is all right. I'm not armed."

Another plane screamed overhead and Abel waited till it had gone. "Who's in the plane? You know?"

"The five men you asked for and a crew of four to fly the plane."

Abel picked up the microphone. "Okay, Commissioner, you hear me? You in touch with the crew of that plane? Tell 'em I want 'em all outa there, tell 'em to come down to the bottom of the steps. And make it quick, pig!"

In the other car Cartwright looked at Malone and Lewton. "You're right, he *is* smart. But what's with the girl? Out at Sunday Harbor she told her folks she did it for her brother – I got the feeling the whole idea was hers."

"Me too," said Malone, and looked across again at the other car. He could see Julie Birmingham, her arms resting on the wheel, staring straight ahead of her as if she had no interest at all in what was going on, a chauffeuse who only wanted her passengers to get out so that she could drive away from here. "If only we could get to her – "

"How?" said Cartwright. "Let's see what she does now."

The four members of the plane's crew had come down out of the aircraft and stood at the foot of the steps. Julie, holding a gun, got out of the car and leaned for a moment against its door, as if trying to ease the cramp of the long drive from her legs. Then unhurriedly, almost stiff-legged, she walked across to the crew. She passed Michael Forte without a glance and he looked at her with a mixture of pleading and puzzlement. She gestured to each of the crew to come forward in turn, moved round behind him and ran her free hand down over his coveralls.

"Recognize any of those men?" Malone asked.

"Three of them are FBI men," said Cartwright. "The

other guy must be the pilot. Poor bastard – I hope he's being paid a good rate for the job."

"I thought they would have used an Air Force plane," said Malone.

"That would be one aircraft the Cubans would *never* let land. They'd probably shoot it down."

"She's going up into the plane," said Malone, eyes again on Julie Birmingham. "I wonder if she'll pull anything on that bugger while she's up in there?"

"What makes you think she might?" Lewton asked.

Another plane went overhead and Malone had to wait to reply. "I don't know that she will. But she's our only hope. If that plane takes off, Christ knows if we'll ever see any of them alive again."

"If it comes to the crunch, the Cubans will let them land. They'll *have* to."

"I'm not going to bet my wife's life on it," said Malone, and looked across at Michael Forte. "And I think the Mayor feels the same way."

Julie Birmingham appeared again at the door of the plane, stood for just a moment looking out and about her, like some traveller getting her first sight of New York, uncertain now whether she should have made the journey; then she came down the steps, still with the same unhurried, stiff-legged walk and crossed to the other car. A moment later both offside doors swung open and Abel, gun in hand, and Lisa and Sylvia got out. Sylvia looked across at her husband, opened her mouth, but whatever she said was lost in the screaming roar of another plane as it came in to land.

Then abruptly Malone opened his door and got out. Abel swung round, the gun coming up, and Malone, knees buckling after his having been in the car so long, gut tensing for the impact of the bullet, flung up his hands.

"- - - - shoot!" Only his last word came out of the shriek of the receding plane.

"Stay where you are! Captain – you and the other pigs

get outa the car! Come on, move! Take your guns out and throw 'em over here! Come on!" For the first time there was a note of panic in Abel's voice; his head was ready to burst now and suddenly he remembered the attacks he used to have as a kid. Jesus, he mustn't let himself slip out of himself like he used to in those attacks! Nobody had ever told him why they happened to him; maybe they had something to do with the way he was born, when his grandmother, a clumsy old bitch, had been the midwife. But they always finished up the same way, with him out like a light on the ground. "Move, move!"

Lewton, Cartwright and the driver got out of the car, the driver moving round to join the others. The three of them took their guns from their holsters and tossed them towards Abel.

"Pick 'em up, baby."

Julie, face expressionless, picked up the guns, put one in her handbag and handed the other two to Abel. He slid one into each pocket of his jacket, suddenly grinned. His headache was easing, he wasn't going to have one of those goddam attacks. Freedom lay just three or four steps behind him.

Then Malone said, "I'm going with you."

A plane went over and Abel, in the storm of sound, looked in silent amazement at him. The noise faded and he said, "You *what*?"

"I'm going with you. I'm not armed, so you've got nothing to worry about. But if anything happens to my wife, I want to be with her."

"And I want to be with mine," said Michael Forte. "I'm coming too."

"Like shit you are! You must think I'm crazy – "

"Let them come," said Julie.

"Nothing doing! Jesus, what do we want them for?"

"We'll be two more hostages," said Malone, speaking quietly but arguing with more force than he had ever done before. "If you land in Havana with the Mayor of New York, a political figure like Mr Forte, as your hostage, Fidel Castro is going to give you the freedom of Cuba."

"Still nothing doing," snapped Abel. But then another plane roared overhead and in the few seconds of ear-splitting noise the expression on his face changed. All his life he had been a nobody. Jesus Christ, wouldn't it be something to be a *somebody*!

Then in the sudden return of quiet Julie said, "If you don't let them come, Abel, then I don't go."

He turned his head sharply and in that moment Malone moved. He had never moved faster; tired though he was, the old reflexes were still there. Six or seven yards separated him from Abel and he covered the distance in a running, diving tackle. He felt the bullet tear through the shoulder of his raincoat, then he hit Abel around the knees and they both went down as another plane screamed overhead, its huge shape cutting off the sun for just a moment. By the time the sound had coned away to silence, Malone had knocked Abel unconscious.

He was still punching the thin, insensible face under the torn-off wig when Lewton and Cartwright dragged him away.

Chapter Eleven

"Australia sounds a nice peaceful place to me," said Jefferson. "If I wanted to retire there, would they let me in?"

It was an effort for Malone to look squarely into the black, friendly face. "I don't think so, John. But if ever you want a recommendation – "

Jefferson smiled. "I wouldn't embarrass you, Scobie, by trying to come out there."

Malone nodded, already embarrassed. To change the subject he said, "Did they tell you what I was trying to do to that bloke yesterday?" He shook his head, shivered a little despite the warmth of the overheated room where they sat. "I was just like that cop who killed Julie Birmingham's husband."

"If her side of that story was true."

"Who are you trying to protect? Me or that cop?"

"I don't know that other guy, don't even know what his name was. I know you – or I think I do."

"You don't, John. After yesterday, I wouldn't place any bets that I know myself. One of my faults up till now has been that I've always got myself too involved in a case – I found it almost bloody impossible to be objective. But I've never been as bad as I was yesterday – "

"Scobie, those two are locked up and they're gonna go up for a long stretch. You're a bloody hero – " He smiled at the adjective: Americans did not seem able to use the word the same way Australians did. "Nobody's blaming you – "

"I don't care very much whether they are or not. It's what I feel myself. I just don't think I was much of an advertisement for law and order."

They were in one of the VIP lounges at Kennedy. Jefferson had driven the Malones out to the airport, and a

Qantas official had brought them in here to get them away from the attention of reporters and photographers. Lisa had gone to the ladies' room and Malone and Jefferson had been left to say their awkward and regretful farewell to each other.

Yesterday morning now seemed an age away. Malone had only a confused memory of what had happened after Lewton and Cartwright had pulled him off Abel. Julie Birmingham had dropped her gun before anyone had demanded it of her and stood silently and listlessly as one of the FBI men had run forward and grabbed her. Planes had continued to scream in overhead as Cartwright and the other FBI men had run up into the aircraft. There had been the rising whine of sirens as the police convoy came speeding back along the perimeter. Parker and the other four anarchists, all handcuffed to the one long chain, had come out of the aircraft with Cartwright and the FBI men following them. There was a moment of comparative silence between the arriving planes and during it the anarchists passed close to Julie Birmingham.

"Mark!"

Mark Birmingham paused, the chain rattling as the others paused with him. His thin, serious face looked grey, the streak in his hair standing out like a white scar. "It was no use, Julie. But thanks – "

Then the convoy arrived, another plane roared overhead, and everything had become an even more confused memory. Malone and Lisa were put into a car, each holding the other's hand tightly; Michael and Sylvia Forte got into another car. Malone saw Willard and Elizabeth Birmingham standing helplessly by a police car, trying to move forward to their son and daughter but held back by a barrier of four policemen. Commissioner Hungerford was standing in the middle of a circle of senior police officers, like a general surrounded by aides in an out-of-date painting of an out-of-date war, and photographers were scurrying about, aiming their cameras and shooting like harmless guerillas. Then the cars carrying the Malones and the Fortes, escorted by four police cars, were screaming away from the scene. Malone had looked back through the rear window of the car, and at seventy miles an hour the whole nightmarish happening receded and disappeared as if from a television screen that had suddenly gone blank.

The Malones, at the insistence of the Fortes, had stayed at Gracie Mansion. "No," Malone had said at first, "we'd like to be alone, just as I'm sure you would."

"There is no place in New York where you can be alone," Michael Forte had said. "The media boys will plague you. Manny has been taking calls for you – you're wanted on every TV show from Johnny Carson to the Galloping Gourmet. More important, Scobie – Sylvia and I *want* you to stay. If you're leaving tomorrow, as you say, we'd like you to leave with at least one friendly impression of New York."

By evening both Lisa and Sylvia had recovered from their ordeal, if only for the time being. Dinner had been a quiet affair, with only the Malones, the Fortes and their children and old Sam Forte at the table. Sylvia's parents had been at the house all day, but Malone and Lisa had not met them. Instead the Malones had spent the day together in their room, resting, and quietly and gently savouring the fact that they were together again and that the horror of the past twenty-four hours was over. When they had come down for dinner they had re-established their security in each other.

"Voting will finish in another half-hour," said Sam Forte as they were served coffee. "Beautiful coffee, Sylvia. Are you going down to the Biltmore, Michael?"

"Only if we win."

"It will look ungracious if you lose and you don't go down there. But, of course, you'll win."

"Joe Burgmann called an hour ago. He said voting has been very light, the worst turn-out for years."

"I'll feel differently tomorrow, I suppose," said Sylvia, "but the election now seems anti-climatic – I mean, after what Lisa and I have been through."

Pier said, "Inspector, I heard Captain Jefferson say last night you had some photos of Mrs Malone. May I have one? The girls at school are going to be asking me what Mrs Malone is like – "

"I'd like one too," said her brother. "I think you and Mother are gonna be the pin-ups at school. For a while, anyway," he added with the unwitting callousness of his age.

Lisa smiled. "Ahead of Raquel Welch? Of course. Your mother and I may never achieve such a rating again. Unless – " She looked across at Sylvia.

Sylvia shook her head: ambition was dead, or at most stone cold. "That's too far off – another four years at least."

"You mean the White House?" said Roger. "I'll be in college by then and nobody there ever pins up a President or his wife. Geez, I'd be expelled or something."

"I'll wait till you're out of college, then," said Michael Forte, and looked at his own father, "before I make my run."

"In the meantime," Sylvia said to the Malones, "please come back and see us here."

Malone had grinned, shaken his head. "This city is too expensive for a cop on my pay. Especially when it almost cost me my wife, too."

"He's always pinching pennies," said Lisa, but her hand on Malone's told him how priceless he was to her.

Now, at the airport, she was coming towards him and Jefferson. The two men stood up as she and the airline official arrived at the same moment.

"Inspector Malone, it's time to board the aircraft."

Lisa put out her hand to Jefferson. "Goodbye, Captain. I wish you could manage to come out our way some time."

"I may do that," said Jefferson, and glanced at Malone. "Just to see how you run things Down Under."

"How do you think they'll run things here now?" said Malone, and opened the copy of *The New York Times* he carried.

Jefferson shrugged. "Your guess is as good as mine.

Somehow, I got the feeling the Mayor wouldn't have minded if he had lost."

Malone spread out the front page of the newspaper, looked at the two photos side by side. In one Michael and Sylvia Forte stood frozen in the moment they were about to step into the police car on the tarmac yesterday morning; their happiness was poignant, their strained, tearful faces needing no smiles to highlight what they felt. In the other photo taken by flashlight in the lobby of the Biltmore, their smiles were a face wide, Michael with one arm raised in the traditional salute of victory. But, whether it was a trick of the camera or the truth, there was no light at all in his eyes.

"I'm glad the New York voters at least showed they had a heart," said Lisa. "It would have been callous if they had voted for the other man."

"I wonder," said Malone, and led Lisa towards the gate, the plane and home.

256